CRAVING DEMONS

THE SECRETS GODS KEEP: BOOK 1

TESSA COLE

CLARA WILS

Gryphon's Gate Publishing

Craving Demons

Gryphon's Gate Publishing
550 King St. N.
PO Box 42088 Conestoga
Waterloo, ON
N2L 6K5

Print ISBN: 978-1-990587-29-0

ANAIS

I FIDDLED WITH THE BUTTON ON MY SHIRT. I WAS SO GOOD at fiddling with it that I could unbutton and button it back up without thinking about it. It was a habit, but whether good or bad, who could say? Although, at the moment, it *was* helping me get a job.

Somehow, I'd gotten lucky and walked in at exactly the right time. The usual manager — a woman — was out and I was being interviewed by the assistant manager. He was a slick middle-aged man with thick dark hair and dark eyes who wore a three-piece suit, and fiddling with my button had drawn his attention down to the lacy fringe of my cherry-red bra peeking out from my blouse.

I already had the shirt open just a little too low, showing off my fabulous cleavage, and with the blouse a white silk, the red bra beneath showed through. It was all on purpose. Some women may have preferred men to look them in the eyes, but not me.

I liked it when interviewers were men. Let them stare at my tits. My glorious girls were one of the few things I was proud of in my life and I'd prefer men look at them, rather than my eyes.

If, as they said, the eyes were the windows to the soul, then I wasn't really sure what anyone would see in mine, because I felt hollow.

I was a thirty-eight-year-old woman with *absolutely* no clue who she was.

From the outside, I probably looked like I had it all: a beautiful family, a very curvy hourglass figure, and a brownstone in Manhattan.

But I didn't own that house, my uncle did.

And as for my three daughters: the one who I understood, I didn't get along with, and the other two were a mystery to me. And while I might look great, scratch the surface on me and I wasn't sure what anyone would find. I wouldn't call myself shallow... but my sixteen-year-old daughter would — and had — and that probably said it all.

My life was, in fact, a huge mess. That much, I knew for sure.

Other things I knew for sure: First, I had three beautiful daughters... even if they were from three different fathers. Second, my life had rarely, if ever, been stable. Third, I might still be attractive, but after three kids, I made a point to work hard to remain so. And the main thing I knew about myself, the only thing really — and which had caused serious problems my entire life — was that I liked bad boys.

And bad boys liked me.

That meant my relationships — if you could call

them that — never lasted long. Either I got restless and cagey, or the guy found someone else.

Recently, that's what had happened... again.

My last guy, a hot and uber-arrogant, Wall Street playboy, had convinced me to try a threesome with a "woman" who was fifteen years younger than me. He'd watched us tease each other, then banged her and seemed to get off on having me just...watch them. I should have left then, but I'd stayed the night and woken to neither of them in bed. He was doing her in the shower. Not even a "hey would you like to join us?"

So I'd collected my things, left, and swore off men, then and there.

On my way home that day, I'd decided I needed to make my own way in the world. Trouble was, I didn't have much in the way of marketable skills. I hadn't gone to college and had only barely finished high school. I could wait tables and tend bar and... that was it.

The only other area where I was exceedingly experienced was... in bed. But, since I wasn't looking for a career in bed, that meant another serving job for me.

Fortunately, the new high-end club, Elysium, at the top of The Park Lane Hotel at the south end of Central Park needed a server and here I was.

And, from the way the assistant manager was eyeing my... credentials, I was a shoo-in.

"When can you start?" he asked, his gaze moving from my breasts to my resume. It was clear which of the two was more important to him.

"Today. I've got nothing on the go. I'm all yours," I said

with a sweet smile. I wasn't particularly interested in this guy, but it didn't hurt to flirt.

Which was all I could do.

I was off men for a reason. I needed to find out who I was without a man in my life, and I was long past due on that front, being nearly forty and all.

I was also long past due in finding some way to support myself. I didn't want to live off my uncle my entire life. And that meant getting a job, which I was doing.

"Well, Ms. Baker, it seems like everything is in order. I'll need to run this by the manager when she returns, but that's just a formality. Your experience is clear and your look is quite refined. You're hired." The man rose and looked me in the eyes for the third time in a half hour. He smiled. Now that he was standing, I couldn't help but flick my gaze down to his pants, and yup... there it was: the telltale bulge.

"Oh, thank you!" I rose quickly, making sure my boobs bounced for him.

I saw him hesitate for just a moment. Probably wanting to ask me out while remembering he was now my superior and that was against policy or something. I'd seen a lot of looks like that before. Still, he got in one last long look at my tits, then cleared his throat.

"Ah, yes, sorry, I'll introduce you to your shift manager, and we'll get some shifts set up for you. This way please."

He led me out of the office and down the hall. At the end of the hall, we turned, but the door to the corner office was open and I couldn't help myself.

I peeked through and saw the silhouette of a tall, broad-shouldered man, facing away from me and staring out a wall of floor-to-ceiling windows. The view beyond, overlooking Central Park, was spectacular. And the view of that man was spectacular too. He had his suit jacket off and his black shirt was taut across his shoulders and over thick arms. His — probably-very-expensive — pants were tight over a high ass and—

I lost sight of him as we kept walking, and I tried not to be too upset about it. I didn't want another tycoon businessman, especially after the last guy. I didn't want *any* man. Not right now.

But that wouldn't stop me from looking, just a little... maybe.

We passed the service elevator, which I'd used to come up, and the scary-looking bouncer that stood guard there. He was a brute of a man, bald and with a look like he wanted to eat me whole.

I shivered under that gaze, though I couldn't decide whether I was aroused or terrified, probably both.

The assistant manager led me up a set of stairs into the club. He took me to the bar and introduced me to a woman named Maria then gave her the spiel about setting me up for some work and left.

Maria was a short woman, though well-endowed for her size. I looked around at the other bartenders and saw they were all women and all busty. Good to know sexism was still alive and well in the service industry, although I couldn't really complain since I'd been banking on that to get me this job.

Maria gave me a once-over, from face to feet and back.

With her in flats and me being over six feet tall *before* you included my three-inch heels, that put her roughly eye-level with my tits and she had to tilt her head back to look me in the eyes.

"What are you, an Amazon? A Valkyrie?"

I couldn't blame her for thinking I was some freak. I shrugged. "Who knows? I was adopted."

Maria blinked, a bit taken aback by that. It was my go-to conversation stopper when people mentioned any of my odd little quirks.

I didn't know who my parents were, which meant I had no clue why I was so tall or where I got my naturally silver-blonde hair or silver-blue eyes. I also didn't know why I'd never been sick a day in my life or why, after three kids, I still had a perfect — albeit voluptuous — hour-glass figure, with no stretch marks and tits that miraculously remained perky.

As much as I wanted to chalk it up to watching what I ate and working out, I couldn't help wondering if there was more to it, like really good genes or something. Not that I was going to test my theory and stop exercising.

Maria shrugged it off and grimaced, changing the topic. "Let me guess. Markus said your look was classy?"

"Refined."

She laughed. "Ah, yeah, and did he bother to look you in the eye, even once?"

"Three times... over the course of a half hour." Not that I'd minded much.

"Sounds about right," she said, shaking her head. "Ah well, I'll be your direct manager here at Elysium. Let's get you set up with a handbook and a few training shifts."

"I've been a waitress or bartender all my life. I don't really need training."

She laughed. "It's not for that. It's for dealing with our rather... ah... shall we say *elite* clientele."

"Ah." *That* I didn't have so much experience with.

I spent the rest of the afternoon pouring and mixing a few drinks, just to prove I could. Then we set up a few shifts for me over the following days and she showed me what the typical dress code was which was black-tie ball-room-chic.

Maria herself was wearing a purple silk asymmetric gown, which hugged her torso and flared out into flowing skirts. I had a couple dresses that could probably pass, but I'd have to max out one of my credit cards to buy a week's worth of dresses for this job.

But then the pay was good, and Maria assured me the tips were excellent. I'd make back my money soon enough. After that, she told me to read the handbook thoroughly then sent me home.

Having come up the service elevator, I hadn't gotten a good look at the club. So, being curious, I left through the lounge.

I noticed several things very quickly. First, most of the people here were men. I could count the women on one hand. Now, perhaps that was because it was late afternoon, and this wasn't the full evening crowd, but still, I thought that was interesting.

Second, the men all looked dangerous. I couldn't help but think they were all mob bosses or enforcers or high-end hitmen. I might have been wrong, but that's what they looked like. In short, they were all bad boys, exactly what I was trying to avoid.

I bit back a sigh. Somehow, I'd just failed spectacularly at avoiding my kryptonite. This job was going to test my resolve.

And third, every pair of eyes followed me as I made my way across the massive lounge to the foyer with the elevators.

By the time I'd gotten to the elevators, I was just a little warmed through by all that attention. Something about how they'd looked at me made me think I could walk right back in there, pick any one of them, and take him home.

But I wouldn't.

Really.

I needed to figure out who I was, first. Then I could hopefully have a decent and lasting relationship with a good man.

That meant all those bad boys back there with their lusty gazes would have to do without me. And I'd have to do without them.

Yeah, I can do that, I thought to myself as I repeatedly hit the down button, calling the elevator. I needed to leave before one of them came over here and—

The elevator pinged.

Thank God!

But when the doors opened, standing inside was the ultimate bad boy, the most gorgeous brute of a man I'd ever seen.

Six-foot-six of linebacker met gladiator met Mr. Universe. His thick, wavy, black hair was immaculate, with a poised curl over one eye. And those eyes! It would be so easy to drown in those twin pools of midnight blue. The rugged skin of a bronzed god was poured into a very expensive suit, straining against his shoulders and arms. That alone would have been bad enough, but then, as soon as he saw me, his eyes went wide with heat and desire.

Would it be too awkward to wait for another elevator?

I was fairly certain if I got in this one, with this man, we'd be all over each other by the time we hit the ground floor.

Of course, this was the top floor so he *should* be getting out.

He didn't.

Neither of us moved.

The door pinged and began to close, and he moved with lightning speed to stop the closing door and force it back. Then he reached out, caught my arm, pulled me into the elevator with him, and let the door close behind me.

He spun me around and pinned me to the back wall, massive hands on either side of my head as he leaned in close.

"What are you?" he whispered, his rough, deep voice like velvet over gravel.

"Adopted?" I said, trying my usual defense mechanism. But I was melting under his heated stare. I didn't even know this guy, but he radiated power and sex and I desperately wanted him closer.

No. Get a hold of yourself, woman! You're off men. Stop this!

But... I couldn't. He was just too intoxicating. And the way he leaned in close made me think I was just as irresistible to him.

"What are you?" he repeated.

I didn't know what he was asking.

"A bartender?" I tried again.

He shook his head, face turning dark. He was looking for something else, something specific, but I had no clue what.

His voice was low and lethal when he whispered, "What manner of Empyrean are you? And why are you unveiled?"

Empy-what-now?

Unveiled...?

What the actual fuck?

He pressed closer, body crushing against mine, lips dangerously close, eyes burning.

"If you don't veil yourself, I might lose control and take you, right here, right now." His breath was hot on my lips and smelled of cinnamon. "I probably could stop myself, but I'm not sure I want to, given the way your aspect is gushing all over the place. You're practically screaming for sex."

Was I?

I mean, yeah, my blouse was unbuttoned a little lower than most and my pencil skirt was short with a slit all the way up one side, but still...? And what did he mean, veil myself? Like... wear a head scarf or something? This man's bronzed skin did give him an exotic Middle Eastern sort of look, but still, this was New York. I could dress however the fuck I wanted.

I licked my lips, but he was so close my tongue brushed his as well and we both shuddered with that wet contact.

Desperate, my hands rose to his chest, trying to push him away... entirely in vain. He was solid, immovable, and also... I wasn't entirely sure I didn't want this. I did like bad boys after all, half of my fantasies were about taming them and the other half were about letting them be so very, very bad... like this one was now.

One of his massive hands left the wall and slid down my arm, feeling me through the sheer fabric of my shirt. I shivered at his heated touch. When he got to my elbow, he slid off and his hand pressed to the curve of my waist, then down over my hips. He found the hem of my short skirt and the heat of his palm pressed to my thigh. He didn't even need to pull that hard. I moved with him, lifting my leg up his thick thigh to hitch around his waist. Then his hand moved again, moving back up my thigh and hiking up my skirt with it.

Oh... Fuck! If he got to my already wet panties, I'd absolutely melt and there wouldn't be any going back!

Instead, his hand slid to my ass and pressed us closer still. With my leg around him and hips tilted up I could feel the rock-hard salami-sized bulge in his pants, and my inner defenses were quickly fading away.

I pushed myself against him, needing to feel all of that hard body. It was a completely physical, reactive thing, I didn't mean to, but I needed to be closer.

Apparently, some part of my mind was still sane though, and despite my body's actions, I found myself saying, "What if I say, no?"

He drew back a little, looking confused.

"If you don't want this, then veil your damned power!" he hissed.

Again with the veil thing? "What power?"

He looked long and hard into my eyes. "You... don't know, do you?"

"Know what?"

"Fuck, you *really* don't know." He let go. The hand on my ass shifted to push my leg off him as he stepped back.

For a split second, I wanted to follow him, keep myself pressed against him, but sanity was starting to take over again and I backed off, slumping against the wall with a sigh.

Fuck, that had been far too close.

"Know what?" I repeated, a bit more vehemently. All of this was getting very confusing.

"That you're a daemon."

ANAIS

Fuck me, a what now?

A demon?

"I can't tell what type specifically. Your voice isn't engaged with the allure, so I'm guessing you're not a Siren." He became more analytical, and I was growing even more confused.

Siren? What was he talking about?

"It's still daylight, which suggests you're not Lilin, and probably not Qarinin. You're not cold to the touch, so not Yukine."

Now he was just spouting nonsense words.

"Are you hungry?" he asked suddenly.

Why? You want to take me out to dinner? Because... No! And also what the fuck? I mean, yes, you're super-hot, but where did that come from? "Ah... no?"

"So not Eishetine." He looked me up and down again, curious and appraising. "I'd guess Naamahine or Asher-ine... though Rusalken or Mahlatine could be possible."

"What are you talking about?" I asked, trying to figure

out if I could get around him to the door. Had the elevator moved at all? Was I still on the top floor? I'd lost track.

He shook his head. "Whatever you are, your aspect is... powerful. I can't imagine you haven't noticed men falling at your feet all your life."

Men wanting to get me into bed, yes, falling at my feet, no.

"Not really, no."

The door dinged and slid open. I didn't care what floor I was on, I bolted past this crazy man and out onto the ground floor. Thank God!

"Wait, you can't run around like this, you need to..." The man was yelling behind me as I bolted through the lobby and out onto the street.

I hurried along the bustling sidewalk for a while, just needing to get away from that place and that guy. He may have been jaw-droppingly handsome, but he was also completely wack-nuts!

I hailed a cab to take me home and spent the entire ride second guessing this new job.

Would all the guys there be as deranged as that one? I knew the rich were eccentric and all, but... demons... really?

The cab stopped at my brownstone on the West Side. By then, I'd mostly calmed myself and written off the incident as one of those strange moments in life.

Shoving that thought to the back of my mind, I ran up the steps to the door and unlocked it, entering to find Reia, my sixteen-year-old daughter playing chess in the front room with my Uncle Don.

Both of them were... odd. Of my three kids, Reia was the least like me. She was quiet and reserved, analytical and observant and that completely baffled me. Caia, the oldest, had my fire and drive. She, however, had actually put it to good use and was off at university with a double major in business and medicine.

And then there was Eva, my middle child. She looked the most like me and she certainly acted like me: just as rebellious and torturous on me as I'd been on my parents. At eighteen she'd already moved out and was shacked up with her most recent fling.

Then there was Uncle Don. He'd made a killing in finance: hedge-funding or day trading or something. But the last ten years hadn't been kind to him. Now in his sixties, his memory was going. He could still calculate figures like a fiend, but most days couldn't remember where the fridge was. He also had a quirky way of speaking, only half finishing his sentences and while he understood what he was saying, the rest of us were often left in the dark.

Don looked up at me with a brilliant smile. "Oh, hi Ana. How did... you know... with the thing?"

"I got the job," I said, returning the smile.

"Oh, that's..." he said, still beaming, "...something."

"It certainly is," I said. I wandered over to the chess board to observe the game. I knew nothing about chess, but there were more of Don's black pieces than Reia's white pieces. "Who's winning?" I asked.

Reia gave me a look of tired exasperation, saying nothing. I felt like a child, interrupting adults. My daughter had perfect waves of soft brown hair and her father's brilliant blue eyes. I couldn't remember the man's name, but I remembered those eyes. There had been a ruggedly handsome face to go with those stunning blue eyes and a one-night stand that had led to my third child.

"Reia is... ah... she's doing... something," Don said enthusiastically.

"You should really learn the game, *Mom*," Reia said in her usual I-know-more-than-you, tone.

The trouble was she probably did. I'd barely finished high school and I'd missed most of my last year being pregnant and having a kid. I'd gone back later to finish only because Uncle Don had money enough to pay for an in-home nanny for Caia. But after that, I didn't want to depend on his kindness, so I tried to work, which meant I'd never gone to college.

I also hadn't been particularly studious in high school either. I'd been more interested in boys than books, and boys had been very interested in me. It had driven my adopted parents into an early grave. My mom had always had migraines but had never thought to get them checked. She'd died of a brain aneurysm when I was sixteen. Then, a year later, I'd told my father I was pregnant and he'd had a heart attack.

Yeah... I know. How fucked up was that?

Caia, my first, had been an accident. I'd been young and stupid and not on the pill yet. Although even once I was on birth-control, Eva and Reia had still come along.

They say the pill is ninety-nine percent effective. Well, apparently, I'm that *one* in one hundred women for whom it hadn't been so effective... *twice*!

Because of course, the rebellious rogues I liked weren't the type to wear condoms.

Now, after three kids, I insisted and was now a strict adherent to the *no-glove-no-love* policy.

So yeah, perfect little Reia probably did know a lot more than I did. She was stoic and far too wise for her age.

It was unnerving.

"Maybe you can teach me," I suggested, though I heard the hesitation in my voice. I didn't really want to learn, but we didn't have any of the same interests, so perhaps this could be a way to bond.

"Maybe," she conceded, then went back to the game. She moved a piece and said, "Check."

"Oh... that is... something," Don said, nodding.

As a dutiful parent, I should check— "Did you do your homework?"

Reia sighed. "Yes, *Mother*. I did most of it in class and the rest when I got home. I was done an hour ago."

Don moved a piece and Reia quickly moved another. "Check mate!"

"Oh... yes, I see now... That is... something..." Don nodded sagely. "Another game?"

Reia nodded eagerly.

I left them and went to the kitchen, eyeing the box of donuts on the counter. I loved donuts. Donny loved donuts. Reia was vegan and didn't eat any unnatural sugars. If I hadn't spent several hours in labor with her, I'd wonder if she was really my daughter.

I skipped the donuts. If I was going to be fitting into

any nice gowns for this new job, I probably shouldn't indulge.

With a sigh, I grabbed a few of Reia's baby carrots and went back out through the front room to climb the two flights of stairs up to my room. There were two cocktail dresses buried somewhere deep in my closet that I didn't wear often since I wasn't that fancy. But I guess they were about to see the light of day again

Digging them out, I hung one on a hook on the inside of the closet door and slipped into my favorite of the two. It was bright red and backless, with a halter top and a tight smooth skirt over my hips that fell to just below the knee. The neckline in front was a bit high and conservative, not showing any cleavage, but this dress was meant to get guys looking at the long stretch of naked back and the hint of side boob. Yeah, that would work well for this new job.

I slipped out of that and into the other. This one was dark purple, almost black, with an empire waist, spaghetti straps, and a V-neck to show off all my wonderful cleavage. Silken skirts fell to my ankles with a high slit up the left side.

Both of these would do, which meant I'd need at least five more, assuming I was working seven nights a week. But seven dresses would just be the bare minimum, ten would be better, twenty would give me lots of options. I smiled at the thought of a shopping spree.

Curious, I pulled out my phone and checked my banking app. Not quite two hundred dollars in my account. Fuck.

However, I was fairly certain I had enough on one of

my credit cards to buy a new set of nice dresses for this job, and hopefully, I'd get paid before that payment came due. And God, did I need some retail therapy. It might not help me figure out who I was, but it *would* make me feel better.

Maybe I'd see if Reia wanted to come. She'd yet to go to a single school dance, but she was in her junior year and prom was four or five months away and it was never too early to buy a prom dress. I doubted she'd want to go, but I could try. Why was parenting so hard?

I sighed and flopped down on my bed. I wished I still had my adoptive parents around to talk to. I'd not been kind to them. Not that I'd been purposefully hurtful or vicious, but they were plain folk, and I'd been a high-strung, bonfire of a girl. They'd loved me, I knew that, but they'd never understood me.

No one understood me.

Not even me.

I felt a tinge of sadness. I may have been with more men than I could count, but they'd never cared to get to know me. I was fairly certain none of them had truly loved me.

Oh, they'd wanted me, sure enough. But those relationships had all been skin deep, and love was a thing of the soul. I didn't even know if I loved myself. How could I love myself if I didn't even know myself?

Once again, as I often did, I let my mind drift off to fantasies of who my birth parents might have been. My favorite daydream was of a high-class heiress who'd fallen for a rough and ready biker bad boy. They'd had a torrid romance, all fiery young passion, and by the time her parents had discovered it, she'd been pregnant. Her parents had forbidden her from ever seeing the boy again and had given the baby up for adoption in shame.

Okay, the "shame" part wasn't so great, but the rest would explain my rather tempestuous and visceral nature.

I imagined that after those cruel parents had stolen the child — me — away from the girl, she'd been furious and had run away from home to be with her lover and they'd lived happily ever after... but not known where to look for their long-lost child.

I'd tried to get my adoption records unsealed, but apparently my records — and only mine — had been lost. I'd found that quite strange but hadn't pursued it since there wasn't much to pursue.

Except I still felt that if I just knew who my birth parents had been, then I'd know myself. How could I know who I was if I didn't know where I'd come from?

I was a spirited woman and that was pretty much all I could say for sure. Everything else about me — my looks, my loves, my life — felt skin-deep. I'd never been one for a lot of introspection, but perhaps I should start.

Maybe I'd take up yoga.

But — remembering back to my strange encounter with that hottie in the elevator — I knew one thing for sure.

I was *not* a fucking *demon*!

RAMSEY

I walked into Grey's office without knocking. The door had been open anyway. Throwing myself into a comfortable chair, I slung a leg up over the arm and leaned back, relaxed.

Grey didn't even turn from looking out the bank of windows in his office. "Ramsey." His tone was annoyed but otherwise neutral.

"Do you have a new girl working here? Some out-of-control succubus?" I asked, curious.

The encounter with the woman in the elevator still clung to me. She'd been... intoxicating and her aspect had been blazing like a bonfire that had almost shattered my restraint.

Which wasn't good.

I was constantly on the verge of losing control — it was just my chaotic nature — but I'd spent thousands of years ensuring I had a handle on it. I'd lived with this roiling tempest in my soul all my life and knew how to keep a lid on it.

But when I'd seen that woman...

Her look had been unique: silver hair and eyes, definitely unusual for a succubus. Sex daemons varied dramatically, but silver wasn't a common hair color at all. She'd been new and different, and I was still having vivid visions of ways we could have pleasured each other in the confined space of that elevator.

Grey turned, one brow raised. "An out-of-control succubus? Not that I know of." His eyes narrowed for a moment. "Though I do recall feeling something earlier, a pull. I was a little lost in thought at the time. Perhaps she was just a guest."

"She said she's a bartender."

Grey's other brow rose to join the first. "Harmonia had said she might be hiring a few new staff." He shrugged. "Why are you so interested?"

I gave him a you-have-to-ask look. I'd already fucked most of his waitstaff.

"Ah. Of course."

And yet, what I'd felt was more than just a desire to have her. "Also her aspect was like nothing I've ever felt before and it was completely unveiled. She wasn't masking herself at all. Running around like that could be dangerous for her. For all of us."

"True." Grey nodded. "What did she look like?"

"Silver hair and eyes, quite memorable."

"I'll talk to Markus and see if there was anyone in here like that and if we hired them. If so, I'll make sure Harmonia has a chat with her."

I nodded.

"Now," he asked resuming his annoyed tone. "Why are you in my office?"

I gave him my best feral grin. "I've got a joint mission for us."

Grey sighed. "Oh?"

It was clear he didn't like the idea but I didn't blame him. We were very different. Oil and water. As the Lord of Strife, I was all about conflict and maintaining the right amount of natural chaos in the world. Whereas Grey, as the Lord of Conquest, was all rigid order and precision. We rarely saw eye to eye. Still... he hadn't said "no" yet, so I went on.

"There's this bank, The Premier Bank of Commerce or something like that. Anyway, I found out through one of my contacts that they've been funding terrorism overseas. Specifically, a small cabal of their executives is involved in weapons and drug trafficking. We could swoop in, deal with them, and then you can buy the bank while I prosecute them."

Grey nodded. He was nearly on the hook. Luckily, I had one more bit of information that would tip him over the edge. "They also hunt large game in Africa for fun."

"I'm in," he growled instantly.

I flashed my teeth in a large grin. "I thought so."

Grey hated anyone who harmed animals. One of his aspects was The Hunt, but he didn't hunt to kill. He hunted to capture and care for, and he loved animals of all sorts.

I slid my leg off the arm of the chair and stood. "I'll text you the details," I said as I left. I got to the door then turned back. "And if you find out the name of that wild succubus, text me her info. I'd love to tame her."

"I don't think so." Grey shook his head. "I'll let Harmonia handle things. She should be able to restrain the girl's uncontrolled nature."

"You're no fun," I said as I left, hearing his scoff of a laugh behind me.

I left the office floor and took the stairs two at a time returning to the club. I needed a drink.

A stiff drink.

Something hard.

So I could stop thinking about how stiff and hard my cock was.

Gods, that uninhibited daemon from earlier had really set me off. My blood was still boiling, and I couldn't get her out of my mind.

It would have been bad, very *very* bad, if I'd lost control in the elevator. There was a reason I'd learned to keep a lid on my chaos. I hadn't lost control many times in my life, but when I had people had gotten hurt.

As the Lord of Strife, my job was to punish those who spread chaos and caused conflict for no reason. That's why — in this modern age — I'd become a prosecutor. I loved a good courtroom battle. It wasn't quite as good as using my fists to put someone in their place, but it was close, and I could put away those who were chaotic and harmful at the same time.

The only fist-fighting I did was in a ring — or better yet a cage — and only with other Empyreans and monsters. That was my outlet for my chaos, the strife that burned within me. I couldn't allow it to come out any other way. When it did... empires fell.

But just seeing that woman had brought me to the brink, closer than I wanted to admit.

I ambled through the club and sat at the bar. Krystal was working, a fiery little Hestial. She winked at me and gave me a smile that would usually get my blood pumping. She was literally hot and a vixen in bed, but she couldn't hold a candle to that woman from earlier.

Of course, Krystal was controlling her aspect, her fire. The wild power of the woman from the elevator had been like a drug.

I hadn't felt anything like that in a long time. Luckily, it wasn't Krystal who came to serve me. I wasn't sure what I'd say to her if she wanted to go somewhere private. I was almost always in the mood, but today... not so much.

Thankfully, it was Maria who sidled up behind the bar. She was one of the few non-Empyreans who worked at Elysium, mostly because she was just so darned good at her job. She knew about us, of course, and that made things easier, but we didn't reveal our nature to just any human. Most of the time they didn't handle it well. Maria, however, had taken it in stride.

Unlike the woman in the elevator.

Stop thinking about her!

"Fire Whiskey," I said to Maria.

"Single? Double?"

"Bottle."

"Oh... rough day?"

"You could say that." It occurred to me Maria might know that silver-haired woman. She didn't have a daemon-sense, so she wouldn't know what the woman was, but perhaps she'd know her name. "Do you know that silver-haired woman who left a little while ago?"

"The tall one?" She went to the back of the bar and climbed a stepladder to reach the top shelf, looking for a bottle.

"Yeah. What's her name?"

"Anais."

It was a good thing I didn't have my drink yet or I probably would have choked on it or sprayed it all over Maria. It might be a huge coincidence, but the name Anais was derived from Anahita, a Persian goddess of fertility and healing.

"A goddess?" I spat the words.

Maria raised a brow as she stepped down and handed over a bottle of Helfyr Whiskey. The Norse stuff. Good.

"Goddess? Really? Working here as a server?" She shook her head slowly. "You Empyreans are strange folk."

But that couldn't be right. Someone must have just named her after the goddess, or even just named her after the famous writer: Anais Nin. She hadn't known she was a daemon after all, so...

Still, that name was just a little too on point to be a complete coincidence.

I pulled the cork from the top of the bottle and took a long swig, the burning liquid warming me.

"You got the hots for her?" Maria asked, conversationally.

I smiled and breathed a laugh. Trust Maria to poke a daemon lord like that. She really didn't have a clue about our ranks and such, so she was equally as nice or indifferent to all of us. She knew I was a big spender and a lady's man, but probably not much more than that.

"You could say that," I said, then took another long swig. Once that was downed, I sighed, starting to feel a bit more myself again.

"Not that I'm interested," Maria said, clearly leading up to a question, "but it sounds like you're looking to screw another of our servers. I think you've been with almost all of them... but not me. Do you only do Empyreans?" She didn't sound upset, only curious.

I gave another laugh. "Something like that, yeah." She wasn't wrong. One of the other ways I liked to let out my chaos was in bed, letting my passion burn. But normal humans were too fragile for my more forceful attentions. Also... they generally didn't get me excited. Their aspects were barely there.

Still, I liked Maria. She was attractive enough, in a human sort of way.

"It's not that I don't think you're beautiful," I said and winked at her. "But you humans lack a little... something in your auras. You're... bland." She quirked her head at that, raising a brow, and I felt compelled to explain. "Like a curry that looks really delicious but has no heat to it."

"So... I'm a beautiful but bland curry, got it." She shook her head again. "Yup, you Empyreans are strange." Then she left to help another customer.

After a couple more swigs of that Norse Whiskey I was just starting to forget about that woman, Anais, except...

Damn.

Who was she?

Her aspect clearly indicated she was a sex daemon of some sort. It was possible she was a goddess, but... they usually felt different. Love goddesses radiated love, not lust. Although if she was a fertility goddess then... maybe? That might explain why her aspect was so powerful.

Except how could she not know what she was?

She'd said something about being adopted.

Even so, her aspect should have been raging — unveiled as it was — for most of her life, at least since puberty. Other gods and daemons should have noticed her long before I had, but I seemed to have been the first to tell her what she was. It made no sense. Nothing about her made sense, to my mind at least. Everything about her made sense to my body and soul.

If she was going to be working here, I'd have to watch out, at least until Harmonia had gotten her under control. For that matter, every daemon would have to watch out.

That poor woman had a long, hard road ahead of her, fending off daemons left and right.

Though...

I might be able to help her with that.

I smiled to myself as a plan began forming in my head. I'd have to talk to Harmonia before I left.

This could be fun.

GREY

I LET OUT A LONG SIGH AND LEANED BACK IN MY HIGH-backed chair, swiveling to look at my view over the park. I'd been doing a lot of this lately, looking out there instead of concentrating on business.

And I had a lot of businesses to concentrate on. Zagreus Holdings International managed hundreds of businesses from this bar to several banks, shipping companies, real estate, and more. I had more wealth than I knew what to do with, but none of it brought me joy anymore.

I was over five thousand years old, and I'd been hunting and conquering since I was a boy. Except lately I'd been feeling more and more empty.

I'd left Hades when I was still young and begun hunting every known creature on this earth. Some were easy to capture, others much harder, but I'd caught them all at least once. Then, I released them back into the wild. Killing held no thrill for me, only the hunt, the capture.

As centuries passed, I turned to other endeavors,

other ways to hunt. I'd been a merchant since the eighth century, hunting the best deals, the wares which were hardest to acquire. More recently, that meant building and buying businesses. Yet, of all my many holdings, the only ones that brought me joy, were the ones that made no money at all: my animal shelters where I loved to visit the wonderful creatures we cared for.

In truth, most of the day-to-day business of my many companies was run by others. There were only a few I took the lead in, Elysium was one, the shelters were another. Otherwise, I was on the lookout for the next acquisition, or I had been. There were no more companies out there that I wanted.

I closed my laptop and shook my head. I ached for something new, something to fill this void within me.

But I had no clue what that might be.

And before I could go visit my animals, I had to have that talk with Harmonia about this new server we'd hired.

I sighed again. It would have been easier if we hadn't hired her, whoever she was. Markus was one of the few non-Empyreans working here and probably hadn't noticed the woman's out-of-control aspect. If he had, it would have been in subtle ways. I really should have a daemon sit in on interviews in the future.

I rose and made my way to Harmonia's office. She should be back from her outing by now. As the club's manager, she used her aspect of harmony to make everyone feel at ease and at home. Technically, she was my first cousin once removed, but among the gods and daemons, such relationships were rarely noted. Espe-

cially among the Greeks. Those horny gods would literally mate with anything, including siblings, cousins, and
parents, not to mention plants and animals. As it was, I
had three sisters and a brother from three different moth-
ers, but all children of Hades.

I knocked on Harmonia's office door and waited for
her melodic voice.

"Enter," she called out and I opened the door, striding
in... and stopped.

Ramsey was there.

"What are you doing here?" I asked him, my voice
cold. It was my usual tone, especially with him. I liked to
keep my life orderly and with Ramsey around, that rarely
happened.

"I hear we have a new staff member who might need
tending to?" Harmonia answered. "Ramses was just
letting me know a bit about her."

Ah.

"I believe I said *I'd* do that," I said to Ramsey. "Why do
you always cause trouble?"

Ramsey opened his mouth, but again Harmonia
answered, always trying to make peace. "He's not making
trouble at all. In fact, he had an idea you should hear."

I sighed and sat in the other chair in the office. Part of
me wanted to shift it away from Ramsey, but I knew that
small action would only make him smile. He'd think he'd
won. So, I kept the chair where it was, trying to ignore the
other daemon prince.

"Yes, go on," I said to Harmonia, not Ramsey.

Harmonia looked to Ramsey, who answered. "When I
spoke to this woman in the elevator, she didn't seem to

have any clue she was a daemon. So even with Harmonia helping her, it may take a while for her to get herself under control. In the meantime, I didn't think you'd want every daemon in this place fighting to be with her. With an aspect as strong as hers, that's likely what's going to happen."

"And you have a plan to stop them? Kill them all?" I asked evenly. I still didn't quite look at him, looking past his face to the wall beyond. That smug smile of his always annoyed me.

"No, I know how you like peace and order. I was thinking the best way to keep other Empyreans off her was to claim her."

I nodded, this made sense now. "You want to have her all to yourself. And that will keep most other daemons away since you're of a high rank. The bonus being you can seduce her as you like. Is that it?"

He raised his hands. "I don't see any issue with that. If she's game for some fun, then we'll have fun."

I sighed. The man had already slept with most of my staff.

"What if..." Harmonia began and drew our attention back to her, "both of you were to claim her, as it were?"

I raised a brow at that.

Harmonia went on. "Since we don't want to scare away this new staff member by coming on too strong." This with a pointed look at Ramsey. "Perhaps it's better that she not be the focus of only one man. Instead, and *only if she agrees*, we can make it known that because of her presence, you two are both fighting over her. Given your natures, you two feuding over anything isn't...

uncommon. And with two daemon lords already fighting over her, that would surely keep any other interested parties away. Wouldn't you agree?"

I saw Ramsey look at me from my periphery. "You up for a little competition, Zag?" He knew I hated that nickname. "And let's be clear, it was only ever my intention to help this woman, not seduce her. We could make it look like we were fighting over her, but she'd be free to do as she wishes and be with whomsoever she wishes, whether that's you, me, or someone else."

Harmonia's idea did have merit. "Fine, I'll join in with this charade." To Harmonia, I said, "When she's in next, please bring her to see me, so I know who it is I'm fighting over."

"Oh, you won't have any trouble knowing who she is." Ramsey's tone grew heated. "She's very hard to miss with that aspect of hers. If your dick isn't rock hard and your balls aren't aching as soon as you see her, then it's not her."

How vulgar.

I rose. "Is that all?" Then I remembered my reason for coming here. "Harmonia, you'll take this woman under your wing, help her understand who and what she is, and make sure she learns to control herself, yes?"

Harmonia nodded. "Of course. It'll be my pleasure."

Everything was her pleasure. That was Harmonia for you.

"Shall I show you out?" I asked Ramsey. My tone made it very clear I hoped he'd leave. Harmonia was one of the few here with whom he hadn't slept, and I'd prefer if he didn't try now.

"Yeah, sure. Harmonia, it's always an amazing pleasure to see you," Ramsey said, and his words oozed with blatant lust.

She smiled at him. "And you, Master Ramses."

"Ramsey, call me Ramsey."

"As you wish, Master Ramsey. I bid you both a good day."

I followed Ramsey out.

"One of these days I'll win her," he breathed as I closed the door to her office behind me.

"Already forgetting about the silver-haired woman?"

"Hell no!" He gave that sly grin of his. "I see no reason I can't have both."

Of course.

I sighed as I escorted him back to the lounge. He left me there, heading to the bar. I had hoped he'd leave, but alas, that wasn't to be. I needed some fresh air after dealing with that man, so I went out onto the high terrace and leaned on the railing, once again looking out over the park.

I couldn't get too mad at Ramsey. I *had* spent a few centuries where my "conquests" had been women, not animals or businesses. But I'd gotten over my lust by the end of the seventeenth century. Yet Ramsey was a younger daemon, only about three thousand years old, and probably still feeling the pull of his hormones.

I looked out over the city and idly wondered if there was anything in this vast world that could soothe my aching avarice. The hunt and animals had worked for a while. Women had worked for a while. Business had worked for a while. I'd tried my hand at a few other types of acquisitions and conquests, but more and more I was finding nothing worked. I had this growing emptiness inside me that yearned to be filled with the object of my desires.

But I had no clue what it was I desired anymore.

And I needed to find something before this gnawing hollowness consumed me entirely.

FEN

"HEY BOSS, GOT A TOUGH ONE HERE!"

I heard Corey's voice and looked up from the paper-work I'd been going over. The foreman was waving me over, pointing at a concrete wall.

I sighed. My guys wanted another show, but I didn't mind. The beast-wolf within me wanted to destroy something.

I put down the papers and strolled over to Corey and a few others.

My crew was demolishing two floors of a building on East 37th Street. I didn't know what had been here before but knew they'd be putting in some open-concept office space and we were meant to tear it back to just the support pillars.

Usually, that would have been an easy job, but for some reason, the previous owners — or someone long in the past — had added a few concrete walls to the space, thick and well-reinforced. And while my demolition crew were all strong men, they were still only human and a thick concrete wall like that would take them a bit of time to bring down.

But for me...

"What do you think, Fen?" Corey, the foreman, asked motioning to the wall. "They must have had a vault here or something. The door's gone, but the rest is two-foot-thick concrete and steel. You wanna give it a go?"

I did.

I really did.

And I didn't much care that I'd be flaunting my daemon abilities in front of these guys. They loved it. I wasn't sure what it was with strong men admiring even stronger men, but these gruff construction workers loved to see me sweat and break stuff.

"Yeah, sure, I was getting a bit bored anyway," I said and picked up a sledgehammer in each hand.

Someone gasped. Must be a new guy.

My ever-sensitive wolfen ears picked up their whispers:

"Oh yeah, he may not look it, but he's strong as ten men, at least!"

"Watch this, you're in for a treat."

"You can't be serious. Not in one hit."

"Oh yeah, one hit, just watch."

I swung the first hammer, careful not to use too much of my strength and power. I didn't want to bring down this whole building.

I heard the growl-roar of my wolf within me as the hammer struck home and a hole the size of a beachball was blasted all the way through the thick walls. The second hammer struck, and another hole appeared. In less than thirty seconds I had one of the thick walls down and demolished. That was enough for today.

"Holy fuck!" someone breathed.

"Yeah, I know, right?"

"He's not even sweating!"

Amidst the concrete dust settling around me, I threw the hammer in my left hand to Corey. "Think you can get the rest?"

"Sure thing, Boss," he said, chipper and grinning. Corey knew better than to question me or ask me to continue the work. I'd just saved him a lot of work and he was happy for that much. It was one of the reasons I kept him on as my foreman. He knew the limits of what he could ask for *and* what *not* to ask about. "Right men, back to work! Let's see if we can't get the rest of this down before the end of the day!"

I stopped by the rough table of planks and sawhorses that made up my desk and checked my phone. It was two-thirty, and I was famished. As much as I'd eaten a three-course lunch not that long ago, I needed to sate my wolf once again. Just one drawback of having the aspect of devouring.

I called to Corey, "I'll be back in a bit."

"Right Boss, don't worry, we've got this covered."

Good man.

I left, took the elevator down to the first floor of the building, and walked out to the bustling sidewalk for some fresh air which made my wolf perk up. It smelled flesh.

Of course, it thought every one of the passersby were going to be its upcoming delicious meal.

Down boy, I said. The beast growled and settled.

I'd been dealing with my wolf for over a thousand years and knew how to control it. It wasn't Ragnarök just yet. Only then could I set him free to devour the world. For now, however, I'd have to settle for a steak.

Luckily, Wolfgang's Steakhouse was just a couple blocks away on Broadway.

I made my way down the sidewalk, surrounded by humanity. They had no clue we daemons walked so freely among them. And it was better that way. Most people would freak out if they knew.

Suddenly I was stopped by some... force.

I was gripped by the feeling of raw lust and sexual need, which almost overwhelmed me. My mind filled with images of sex, remembering women I'd fucked, and my body responded in kind, my cock instantly rock-hard and raging for a release.

"Blessed Asgard!" I breathed. It took everything I — and my wolf — had to keep myself from coming on the spot. I had to lean on the wall of the building next to me for a long moment, taking deep breaths, while everyone around me went about their business as if nothing was amiss.

"Fuck me," I whispered as the rampaging desire continued to flow through me.

What in Hel was going on?

The only thing I could think of was that some sex daemon's aspect was going wild, out of control.

And that turbulent aspect was coming from inside the store next to me.

I glanced at the sign: Giorgio Fashion. It looked like a high-end boutique.

Desperately curious, though just a bit worried that if I got closer I might truly explode, I entered the store.

A woman hurried up to me and stopped a bit abruptly. "Ah, yes, can I help you, sir?" She seemed confused. A man in construction clothes and a hard hat, covered in concrete dust, probably wasn't their usual clientele.

She wasn't the source of the aspect. That was clear.

"Ah... just looking around?" I said, trying to figure out what in Hel I was doing here. "To pick up something... for my... daughter."

The woman perked up at that. "Oh, yes? A gift? How lovely. We get so few men in here. Do you need any assistance?"

"Ah, no, I'll just look around for a bit, if that's okay? I'll call you if I need you."

"Sure, my name is Denise." She smiled and went away.

It didn't take me long to find the daemon I was looking for. She was the only other person in the small shop... and she was drop-dead gorgeous.

At first, I assumed she was older, given her silvery hair, but when her face turned my way, I could see how youthful and smooth her features were. That made the silver-blond hair all the more striking. Her large eyes were of a similar hue, but with a tinge of blue, and she had a perfect face, with a slightly upturned nose and full blushing lips. The sheath dress that clung to her showed off all her six feet of perfection: full hips and bust and slender waist.

My cock swelled as my wolf growled.

He wanted to mate. Now!

I grunted at the urgency and pain as my need to release reached a painful degree. Desperate, I turned away and leaned against a wall for a moment, breathing through the pain and desire.

I could control myself. I'd been keeping the ravenous beast within me under control for over a millennium. If I could do that, I could get ahold of my body. I could manage to calm my raging hard-on and rampaging heart.

I heard a soft laugh behind me. "You look a little out of place in here." The voice was soft and melodic, and as soon as I heard it, my beast calmed.

That was... new.

I turned around and there she was. She'd drawn closer, her features displaying a bit of shock.

"Oh..." she breathed, blinking at me.

I could almost read her thoughts from those wide silver-blue eyes: he's a lot more handsome than just some gruff, construction worker. Yeah, I was literally a Norse God — or close enough to one — so I got that look a lot.

The look faded after a moment and she smiled. "What're you looking for? Got a side gig doing drag? I don't know if they have anything your size," she teased.

I smiled.

The trouble was what in Hel *was* I doing in this store?

I'd told the clerk I was looking for something for my daughter. That was a lie. I did have a daughter, but she was over seven hundred years old and living in Sweden, working as a model. Still, that story would work for now.

"I'm looking for something for my daughter. How about you?" I asked. I wanted to know everything about this mystery woman. She was intoxicating and over-whelming with her aspect unveiled and blazing, but she'd also somehow managed to tame my wolf with a few words. No woman — mortal or immortal — had ever done that before.

Her smile grew and she seemed to glow with it. "Oh, truly? I'm also looking for some things for my daughter... and myself. I start a new job in a couple of days and need something nice to wear."

The words were out before I could stop them. "You look gorgeous as you are."

She blushed, a rosy hue on those pale cheeks and I nearly came then and there from her otherworldly beauty. But again, I kept myself in check... barely.

"You're too kind, thank you," she said demurely.

"I'm having a horrible time, though," I lied. "I don't know what she'd like. I could use a woman's input." I wanted to stay close to this woman for as long as I could.

"Why isn't she shopping for herself?" the woman asked.

Excellent question. "She... doesn't like shopping. She's shy."

The woman laughed. "Yeah, my daughter doesn't do shopping either. I think she thinks it's beneath her or something." She smiled up at me. "I'm Anais by the way. Most people call me Ana."

"Fen—" I said, stopping myself before I gave my full

name. Most people called me Fen anyway, not that Fenris was particularly awkward, it was just easy to shorten.

"Hello, Fen," she said extending a beautiful, well-sculpted arm and slender, long-fingered hand.

I brushed off my thick, calloused hands on my jeans, probably only making them dirtier, then shook her hand. Her touch was warm and sent a thrill through me, and my wolf let out a sigh of contentment as if someone were petting it.

Yeah, this was definitely new and strange.

"Well, I love to shop, and I'd love to help you find a dress for your daughter. Do you know her size or measurements?"

I made something up.

We began searching through the racks and shelves as Ana went on about dress styles and all sorts of things I didn't care about, but still, I hung on her every word. I'd become a lost puppy, following around the first person who'd shown me any affection. This was extremely strange for me, but I didn't mind at all. I just wanted to be near this woman: Anais.

And so did my wolf.

I ended up buying three dresses, because... I couldn't say no to this woman, and it meant I got to spend more time with her. She bought six outfits that I was certain would be stunning on her, and several sedate and conservative dresses for her daughter.

"Thank you for helping me," I said as we exited the store. But I didn't want to leave her side. "Would you be up for coffee or a meal?"

"Now?" Ana asked, a bit stunned. "It's the middle of the afternoon?"

Right, not everyone was ravenous all the time like I was.

"Just coffee then?"

She smiled at me. "Ah, look Fen, you seem like a nice guy, and you're certainly nice on the eyes, but I'm sort of... off men right now. I hope that's okay?"

"Oh, of course," I said, nodding, my heart aching just a little at those words.

Some part of me wanted to say: *no worries, I could get a sex change if you're into women*, but that seemed like it was going *way* too far. And I didn't think that's what she was saying.

"Well," I said. "It was definitely my pleasure to meet you and I do hope we meet again."

She stood there for a long moment, thinking about something before saying, "Ah... my new job is at this club called Elysium. It's at the top of—"

"I know the place," I said with a grin. It made sense that she'd be working at the main daemon bar in town. I didn't visit the place often, but I'd certainly be going a lot more now. "I might swing by and see you there."

She blushed and grinned and took a deep breath, which made that amazing chest rise prominently.

Holy-fucking-gods! She was too much!

"Maybe I'll see you there," she said. Then she hailed a cab. "Later Fen," she said with that stunning smile and was gone, slipping into the car.

I stood there, a bit dumbfounded, for a long moment. I'd never met a woman like Ana before and knew with certainty that I never would again. I had to be with her, even if only because my wolf loved her! She had tamed the ravenous beast within me, and I needed to know more about this wonderous woman.

But first I needed a release from the aching pain of my raging cock.

Then food.

Then I'd finish work, clean up, and head to Elysium. I didn't know when Ana might be working next, but I'd be there every night from now on until I saw her again.

ANAIS

THAT HAD BEEN A CLOSE ONE.

If I'd spent a second longer with Fen — and that gorgeous, tall, blond, construction worker vibe he had going on — I wouldn't have been able to resist his offer for coffee.

Surprisingly, he wasn't my usual type: he was nice. Though I thought I'd sensed a bit of latent danger lurking beneath that kind smile and those dancing blue eyes. Perhaps it was how pale those pure aqua-blue eyes were. Some might say they were cold or sharp, but I'd found them enticing. And he'd certainly been built, with an easy swagger about him. I could tell he was all muscle beneath that flannel and denim.

And at that thought, my mind began to undress him. It was safe to fantasize as long as I kept it at that. I pictured lean, long muscles on that tall frame with rolling shoulders and a broad chest, then the hills of his eight-pack abs leading down to the rising swell of a thick and meaty cock.

I bet he had tight buns as well and strong legs, but mostly I was stuck on that tower of a cock and how those blue eyes were filled with heat above his kind smile. His hot breath on my ear whispered all manner of kind things about me as he pressed close and slid his hand up between my legs. Deft, thick fingers pushed my damp panties aside and—

Fuck me! Was it hot in this cab?

Lava pooled deep in my core, bubbling and ready to erupt.

Do not masturbate in the cab! I told myself sternly. My hand was low on my abdomen, over my dress and even just pressing there seemed a little too much. *Do not masturbate in the cab. Do not masturbate in the cab. Do not masturbate in the cab.*

I was sure far worse things had been done on this back seat and wasn't so much worried about that as giving the cabby the wrong idea with the show back here.

I should also be reminding myself: *NO MEN!*

I'd broken down a bit at the end there and told Fen where I worked. I had the distinct impression he'd be coming to see me soon, and if he did, I wasn't sure what I'd say to dissuade him.

Except a part of me really didn't want to dissuade him. Not only was he handsome and rugged and kind, but we also had things in common. He also had a shy daughter, and he'd been so sweet to go out and buy her dresses, so out of place in a shop like that. Okay, that was really all we had in common, but it seemed like a lot.

It was taking way too long for the cab to get me home and my fantasies of Fen were not cooling in the least. I recalled touching him and feeling a spark of something, something dangerous and... hungry.

And now I was picturing him looking up at me with those perfect blue eyes as he devoured my pussy, his lips sucking on my sweetness as his tongue flicked my clit or darted into me.

Yeah, I had an active imagination. And by the time I got home, I was raging for a release.

Luckily, I got home before Reia and quickly did a circuit of the house. Don was napping on the couch downstairs, so I went up two flights to my room and my shower and whipped off my clothes to jump under some hot water and imagine Fen a little more while I rubbed myself.

I imagined his ivory tower of a cock — since he was pretty fair-skinned —ravaging my slit as those strong arms pulled me close. His hungry lips on my breast sucked out every last drop of my desire until we both exploded with unimaginable bliss.

I didn't know why it always had to be unimaginable bliss. I could imagine some pretty blissful bliss, and in that moment, I imagined all the bliss as I came in a rush. A very powerful rush.

Even just masturbating, while imagining Fen, was glorious. I should do that more often.

So, once I was out of the shower and dried off, I went online on my little — and very old — laptop to search for *toys*.

There were any number of sex shops I could visit, but I was already home for the day and besides, this just seemed more comfortable. The trouble was, I didn't know what I'd like which resulted in me maxing out my second credit card of the day by buying a — literal — fuck-ton of dildos and vibrators.

Just because I was off men, didn't mean I couldn't get off, and I intended to try everything and see what worked for me. Given the reviews of some of them, I was getting a bit horny just thinking about them.

Them and Fen.

I heard soft steps on the stairs and left my room to see Reia coming up.

"Hi, darling," I said cheerfully. "I have a surprise for you."

She groaned. "*Mom!*" She made it sound like I was about to torture her.

Far from it.

I reached her room first and opened the door. I'd laid out the prom dresses I'd gotten her on her bed. I hadn't been able to decide what she might like so I'd gotten five of them and assurances about the store's return policy.

"Dresses?" Reia said as if they were insects: gross and disgusting. "For what? Why?"

"For prom!"

"That's in March and I wasn't even planning on going."

"Of course you'll go," I said. "Doesn't every girl want to go to prom and be pretty? You're beautiful Reia, and I want you to feel pretty. Don't you like dresses?" Which was a silly question since she'd worn all of maybe five dresses since she'd been old enough to dress herself. Still, I had to try. "At least try them on?" I urged.

"Can you even afford all of this?" Reia asked.

"I'm going to return the ones you don't like, it's fine," I said. I couldn't afford it, not yet, but with the new job, everything would be fine. I'd pay off my cards later.

Reia just stared at me like I had two heads. "You're so irresponsible! I know you can't afford this, so why would you do it? I don't even want to go to prom and you're buying me a wardrobe of dresses. Prom is just another patriarchal scheme to oversexualize young women and show them off to prospective suitors. It's gross, and I won't be a part of it. And I can't believe you'd force me to do it. Just take these back and leave me alone!" Reia had gathered up the dresses as she'd ranted, pushed them into my arms, then shoved me out of her room and slammed the door shut.

I sighed.

Why couldn't I have *one* normal daughter?

Reia was over-serious and smart and just... beyond me in so many ways. Eva was too much like me and lived to cause me heartache. She hadn't gone to prom either. Oh, she'd worn a sexy dress and gone out, but had ditched the dance to make out with a guy who was seven years older than she was. Caia also hadn't gone to prom, she'd been too busy studying and doing all sorts of prep work for her application to Harvard.

Maybe I could go to Reia's prom as a chaperone or something? I'd never gone to either of my own, and I regretted it now. My junior year, I'd been making out with a guy who was far too old for me. Eva's apple didn't fall far from my tree. My senior year... I'd been pregnant.

I took Reia's dresses back to my room and hung them carefully — I'd return them tomorrow — then flounced onto my bed with a heavy sigh. I just wanted a normal life for my girls, but no. They insisted on being abnormal like me.

This was what I got for having tortured my adopted parents so much.

God, I was a mess. I was so clueless about who I was or what I wanted that I'd filled the void with men and was now doing things for my daughters that they didn't want.

I sat on the edge of my bed, head in hands, ready to give up on today entirely when the doorbell rang. I rose and made my way slowly down the two flights as the doorbell kept ringing and ringing and ringing.

Whoever this was, they were impatient and annoying.

Donny was still lying on the couch, fast asleep in the back room, so I answered the door.

Two men waited outside. The first had once been a big bruiser of a man, but he seemed more fat than muscle now — though probably still strong enough under all that padding. The second man was lean and spry with a rat-like face and beady eyes.

"Yeah?" I said, not particularly impressed with these two.

"We're looking for Donny," the large one replied.

There was something in how he said it, something just a bit threatening, which made me suspicious.

"Who are you?" I asked. "What's this about?"

The large one smiled. "I'm Lucky Lu and this here" — he motioned to the other man — "is Sammy Softshoe. We're... collectors of a sort."

"Yeah," Sammy piped up. "We've come to collect."

My raging disinterest was quickly replaced with a curious horror. It was clear these two were gangsters here to shake me down, or more accurately, shake Donny down.

ANAIS

"Ah... Donny's not here right now," I said, my heart racing. "Can I give him a message for you?" Hopefully, that would make them go away.

Lu's lips spread over his pudgy face in a wide, unpleasant smile. "Yeah, you tell Donny that Tommy Two-Toes just got out of Sing Sing and he wants his money."

"Money?" Oh gods, did Donny owe the mob money? I didn't think he'd ever done anything illegal, but then, I didn't really know anything about what he'd done. All I knew was his work involved money and investments and that Donny was filthy rich.

Lu answered. "Yeah, the Boss gave Donny fifty mil before going in. Donny was to keep it safe and help it grow."

"Grow?" God, why was I stuck saying all these inane one-word sentences?

"Yeah," Sammy said, "Boss did some figuring and,

with compound interest or whatever, he thinks his haul should be worth two hundred and fifty mil by now."

Two hundred and fifty million dollars! Holy Mother of Fuck!

What had Uncle Don gotten himself into?

"You tell Donny," Lu went on, "that he's got a week to pay up, or Tommy Two-Toes is gonna come callin' himself. And you don't want that."

I was sure I didn't.

Something told me Tommy Two-Toes wasn't called that because he only had two toes himself, but because of what he did to his victims.

Fuck me. This wasn't going to work. Donny couldn't remember the day of the week, let alone what he might have done with fifty million dollars however long ago.

"When was this, that Donny put this money away for you?" I asked.

"Twenty years ago," Lu answered.

Yeah, there was no way he was going to remember that. I could try to help him remember, but if he didn't, I didn't want to know what these guys would do to him... or me... or Reia!

"Ah... look," I tried to explain. "Donny hasn't been himself these past few years. He forgets things. I don't know if—"

"Well, he better remember this," Lu said, that slimy smile going away and his eyes going dark and hard. "Boss won't be happy if he doesn't get his money."

"Yeah, no money and something terrible might happen to Donny or his lovely young wife."

Wife?

Oh... me! They thought I was...

Ew!

"I'm his niece. He's like sixty. How old do you think I am?"

"Thirty-three?" Sammy guessed.

"Nah, no way, she's too hot, I bet she's still in her twenties." Lu nodded to himself.

Oh, well that was very flattering.

But definitely not the point!

"Look I'll see what I can do, but you may need to tell your boss that his money might not be available," I said, not quite knowing where I was getting the strength to say these things. "And I have the cops on speed dial if he does come for it." I didn't, but I would now. "Sorry, gentleman, and good day!"

I slammed the door shut even as Lu called out, "One week, lady!"

Fuck, fuck, fuck, fuck, fuck, fuck, fuck, fuckitty FUCK!

Where was I going to come up with two hundred and fifty million in one week?

I wasn't.

I locked the door and sprinted to the back room.

"Don!" I shouted, shaking the aged man.

Bushy gray brows rose as his eye snapped open. "Who's the what?" he said, addled.

"Do you know a gangster named Tommy Two-Toes or anything about two hundred and fifty million dollars?" I asked. "Though I suppose it was only fifty million when you had it. This would have been twenty years ago now, and I know you're having trouble remembering things, but this one thing, if you could remember it, would be really good to remember about now, because Tommy has come calling for his money and if we don't give it to him, they're going to do horrible things to your young wife!"

Donny smiled slowly. "Wife?" I blinked at him. Had he only heard that one word? "I didn't think I was...? Do I have a...?"

"No Donny, you're not married. They mean me!"

"You?"

"I'm your niece, Ana, remember?"

"Nice niece. Naughty niece? Knobby-kneed niece. Naturally nice, knobby-kneed niece, not knowing... something...?"

"I don't know where the money is!"

"Money?"

God, I wasn't getting through to him, as I'd suspected I wouldn't.

"Chocolate Cosmos!" Donny announced. "I'm thirsty."

I blinked. "What?" Did he want a drink? A cosmopolitan? But there was no such thing as a chocolate cosmo. There were chocolate martinis but I didn't think Donny drank either cosmos or martinis.

Donny rose and headed toward the basement door. "Time for a bath." There was no bath in the basement. There was a shower stall in the guest room down there, but...

I ran to get him and redirected him up the stairs. Hopefully, he'd find his own bathroom eventually. Then I sat on the couch he'd been sleeping on and put my head in my hands.

I'd thought I had problems before! But now, Reia not

wanting to go to prom seemed rather trivial. I had a mob boss breathing down my neck for money I couldn't get, and I really didn't want to think about what he'd do if he didn't get it.

I could try looking through Uncle Don's computer, but he had so much security on that thing I was certain I wouldn't get far. He forgot everything else, but he remembered the seven passwords to get into his laptop, of course.

The trouble was, Donny did have a ton of money, except *I* couldn't access any of it. It was tied up in special accounts with automated payments and such.

As soon as Don had realized his deteriorating condition, he'd made sure we'd all be set, just in case anything happened to him. The girls all had money for college, and there was an account for the house, which paid taxes and utilities, an account for groceries, and an account for everything we needed. But beyond that... we had to fend for ourselves.

And Donny had left me out of all of that planning. He'd never trusted me with money and frankly, I didn't blame him. I'd never much proven I could handle such things. I had no head for money or long-term planning.

"I'm so screwed," I murmured.

ANAIS

I WAS STILL A MESS WHEN I WENT TO MY FIRST SHIFT AT Elysium the next night. I had six days to come up with a *quarter of a billion* dollars. Yeah, sure, no problem!

The bar manager, a woman named Harmonia, had called me to ask if I could come in early to "go over a few things." I'd said sure and was there promptly at five, even though my shift didn't start until seven.

I wore one of my new dresses, a burgundy number with spaghetti straps that looped over the shoulders, leaving my back bare while the neckline plunged to mid-stomach, showing a good expanse of my prime real estate. It was snug over the hips and eased into waves as it fell to roughly mid-calf. On shorter women, it would have been a floor-length dress, but on me, not so much. To finish the look, I'd worn my hair up in a bit of a messy ponytail with a few loose strands framing my face.

I was shown to Harmonia's office and sat in one of the comfy chairs in front of her desk.

"Tell me, Ms. Baker, did you read the manual Maria

sent you home with?" Her voice was beautiful and melodic.

Aaaand... Fuck!

"Ah... no, I'm sorry, my life has been a bit crazy these last few days and I ah... I missed that. I swear I'll read it before my shift tonight and—"

"No need," Harmonia said. She sighed then, and even that long exhalation sounded beautiful coming from her. She looked at me for a long moment, lips pursed, eyes hard.

Fuck, I really needed this job. Not that it was going to make me two hundred and fifty million in a week. But now, for some reason, I felt like I was about to get fired even before I'd started my first shift!

"How to say this?" Harmonia said softly.

Yup, I was so fired.

"Do you find you have a certain effect... on men?"

Ah... what?

"Sorry?" I asked, a little confused.

"Perhaps you go for women?" Harmonia ventured with a raised brow. "Whatever your type, do you find that they are swarming to be with you?"

"Ah... no?" Though I recalled my last time here and the man from the elevator. "But, the last time I was here, everyone was looking at me like I was fresh meat, and there was a... ah... very intense man in the elevator."

Harmonia quirked a bit of a grin. "You don't say?" By the way she said it, it was clear she knew something. Did they have cameras in the elevators? Did she know? Probably. "Yes, Lord Ramsey did mention running into you."

Had I heard that right? The words were out of my mouth before I could stop them. "He's a fucking lord?"

Harmonia's lips twitched again, but she repressed her smile. "Yes, in a way, though not the English Lord type." She steepled her fingers before her lips for a moment. "He called you something, if I'm not mistaken."

Oh... that!

"Yeah, he said I was a demon. Isn't that just silly?" I laughed.

She didn't laugh.

"It's pronounced daemon," she said. "Like Matt Damon."

"Matt Damon is a demon?" I didn't think I'd heard that right. "If so, then he's got to be one of those sexy demons right?" I joked.

Again, she didn't laugh.

I laughed nervously. "Ah... yeah, so, that is silly, right? Him thinking I'm a demon, or Matt Damon, or whatever?"

Harmonia shook her head. "I don't understand at all. How could you not know? How could your power not have been flooding everyone around you all your life?"

"Power?" I wasn't liking where this was heading.

"Perhaps a demonstration is in order?" she said. It was a question, but not for me I guessed. "You're agitated at the moment, yes? Flustered? Confused?"

Hell yeah, I was! "Well, perhaps just a little, yes. I'm not sure why everyone keeps talking about demons."

Harmonia nodded. "Could you imagine being truly at peace at the moment?"

Absolutely not! I needed to come up with a quarter of

a billion dollars, and everyone around me at work was psycho-religious or something. "Ah... not really, no."

Harmonia nodded. She rose and came around the desk to sit on the front edge, closer to me. She was beautiful, with raven black hair, a perfect Mediterranean complexion, and deep brown eyes. She was a bit leaner than me, more athletic of build, but still had a full bust and ample curve to her hips. She was what I called fit-hot. Whereas I was curvy-hot.

She held out her hand and whispered something that sounded like, "Iremia." I thought I saw her hand shimmer, as if the air around it was suddenly hot and distorted, then...

Then my shoulders eased from being up around my ears and I felt every muscle relax. I smiled just a bit as all my worries drained away, and I felt the deepest, purest peace I'd ever known in my entire life.

"How do you feel now?" she asked.

"Heavenly," I murmured, feeling high as a frickin' kite! With my many bad boy lovers, I'd experimented with weed and a couple other things. But this, right now, was the best high I'd ever had.

"Tell me all the things you're worried about," Harmonia said.

And I did, I spewed it all forth and none of it seemed to faze me at all.

"I feel like you're going to fire me because I wasn't prepared for this job. I promise I'd have read the handbook but well, yesterday mobsters came and said they wanted two hundred and fifty million dollars from my uncle, who might have it, but hell if I know where or how to get at it, and my uncle doesn't remember anymore, and I am so screwed when they come to collect in a week. Also, I have no clue who I am. I don't know who my real parents are, and my adoptive parents died when I was a teenager, and I've spent my life seeking validation from men, but they just want my body, so I'm off men now, but that just means I'm lonely and sexually frustrated. I bought seven hundred dollars' worth of sex toys yesterday. Seven hundred dollars! I know that's too much, but I need a good fucking orgasm. Though, what I really want is a solid piece of man-meat up in my love tunnel. Oh... and I don't understand my daughter and she won't speak to me half the time. Yeah, I think that's most of it."

"Blessed gods," Harmonia breathed. "You poor woman!"

"Yeah, I know, right?"

Still, I didn't feel stressed about any of that at all right now. I felt so wonderfully free and serene.

"Epistréfo," she said and snapped her fingers, and in an instant, the weight of all my worries fell on me like a ton of bricks.

"Fuck!" I groaned. "What was that?"

"That's my power," Harmonia said with a soft smile. "I can bring peace and harmony to any soul, or remove it just as easily."

"Can I have it back?" I practically begged.

"Yes," she said. That was the best news I'd heard all week. "As soon as you understand you have powers too."

Aaaand there it was.

"I have what?" I felt like I knew where this was going. "You're going to tell me I'm a demon too, aren't you?"

"Daemon, not demon."

"Whatever, I'm neither, I'm a nice girl who—"

"Daemons aren't evil, Ana."

"Oh?"

"They're just people with powers."

I got the distinct impression that was a drastic under-statement, but at least it was easy to understand. "And you're saying I have powers? Can I cause people to peace-out like you do? That might help with those gangsters." Fuck! I'd told her about them! I'd told her everything about me! Including the seven hundred dollars' worth of sex toys and a mention of man-meat. Double fuck!

Why had I done that?

Because I'd felt so amazingly carefree.

"No, your powers are of a... different sort."

"Oh?" I didn't really believe any of what she was saying, though I couldn't deny she'd made me feel heav-enly for a moment there. But that must have been hypnosis or some trick.

"Yes, you make people feel good in another way."

And the encounter with the man in the elevator returned to me so I took a guess. "I make people wanna fuck?"

"Pretty much yes."

"Wonderful." I didn't see how — even if that was true — it could help me with Tommy Two-Toes. I rose from my chair. "Ah... look. I thought this would be a good job, but I can see now that ah... I was crazy... and you're crazy. I'm not a sex demon, and I don't know how you made me feel so wonderful, but I should go and—" I turned to leave.

"Iremia," she said.

I nearly fell as, once again, I felt all my worries leave me. I swayed for two steps before leaning heavily on the wall, but my arms were relaxed and weak. I turned, putting my back to the wall, and slid down to a sitting position.

"Wow, girl, you need to bottle this, you'd make a fortune," I whispered.

"I have, and I did."

"Oh, then... yeah."

She came to crouch next to me. "Doesn't this feel real?"

"Yup!" I said, trying not to drool in my dreamy peaceful state.

"So, you can feel my power?"

"Yup!"

"Because I'm a daemon."

"Nope, that's just silly," I said in a singsong way.

She laughed, then sighed. "I can see this is going to take a lot of work."

"Work, yup, that's what I'm here for!" I said, then tried to rise so I could get to work.

Harmonia laughed. "I think it's time for something showier."

I didn't know what that meant, but I was so high I didn't care.

"Wait here, I'll be back," she said and left.

I nodded. I wasn't going anywhere. In my current state, I doubted I could even stand. I just wanted to lie down and...

I woke suddenly when the door closed.

I was drooling on Harmonia's carpet, but I was also still feeling wonderful, so I didn't care too much.

"Ana, meet Krystal, you'll be working with her." I rolled over and looked up. A new woman was here. She was younger, perhaps mid-twenties with a model's figure, straight and thin with long legs and a full bust. Her hair was soft golden brown, and her eyes were a fiery red-yellow. Odd.

"Hi!" I said from the ground. "You look like a model. Do you do modeling? You should."

"I do," Krystal said, just a bit haughty. "You really hit her hard, didn't you," she said to Harmonia.

"Everything I've got. Your turn." Then to me, "Krystal has power over fire." She nodded to Krystal who snapped her fingers and fire leaped to life, floating in the air above me.

At the same time, Harmonia withdrew her powers and everything crashed down onto me once again. I was getting just a little sick from this emotional rollercoaster.

So... I threw up all over that nice carpet... and their shoes.

ANAIS

"Go get Maera." I heard Harmonia say, and a moment later she was kneeling next to me. "Apologies, I know going back and forth with my powers can be disorienting. I was only trying to show you that you're not alone. There are many daemons here on earth and they're not evil, despite what *some people* would have everyone think. So, it's not that big of a deal that you have powers."

Right now, I was more concerned about the puke on my face and on her shoes. They had been nice shoes. I think I just had to accept that this was the week from hell and I was cursed.

"Sorry," I muttered. "About your shoes."

"Maera will get it, don't worry." She sounded calm and that helped to ease my weary mind.

I still didn't know what I thought about demons, or Matt-Damon-demons, or whatever. Though I did have questions. "If you're a demon, why don't you have horns or a tail or anything like that? Why do you look like a normal person?"

"That," Harmonia said with a sigh, sitting back against the wall behind me, "is a bit of a story. Are you up for the history of daemons?"

"Yeah, sure." I didn't really care, but maybe it would make some of what was going on around me make sense.

"I'm guessing you never studied Greek, the language?" Harmonia asked but didn't wait for an answer. Apparently, we both knew I hadn't. "In Greek, daemon simply means a spirit, a celestial being of lesser power than a god. So, to put it simply: there are gods, and there are daemons. That's it."

I opened my mouth but had no idea what to say to that.

"For a long time, all the different gods out there feuded and bickered, even had a few wars," she continued. "Things got really confusing when the Romans decided to rename all the Greek gods. For the most part, the Greek gods just got more worshipers, but there were also some new gods created by that debacle. That's getting a little off-topic though. I only mention it because I used to be the only daemon of harmony, but now I have a strange cousin whose name is Concordia. Anyway, things were fine, and people worshiped us, and then *that* god came along."

I was fairly certain I knew what she was talking about but couldn't help asking. "*That* god?"

But before she could answer, we were interrupted by Krystal returning with another woman. What Harmonia called her?

"Ah, Maera, can you clean this up please and help our friend here?" Harmonia asked.

The other woman knelt next to me and put out a hand toward where I'd been sick.

Ick, I wouldn't want to have the job of dealing with this, but then, this was a bar, I supposed sick did happen and someone had to clean it up.

Water sprayed out from Maera's fingers over the soiled carpet and shoes, and me. I felt a fine mist on my face and hair, cool and refreshing, and the water Maera controlled gently washed the grossness away. Then it seemed to pick itself up — pulling the wetness from the carpet and my face and those shoes — to gather into a floating ball. Everything was clean and dry, and the mess was literally floating away.

"All clean," Maera said. Her voice was breathy and soft.

"Thank you," I said, mesmerized by this strange power, but still very thankful for it. I only wished she could wash out my mouth, but I wasn't going to ask for that.

Maera smiled and rose, taking her floating ball of water and... other stuff... away.

Harmonia had risen and returned with a glass of water. "Here."

I drank, which helped to soothe the burn in my throat. "Thank you."

She helped me up and got me back into a chair while Krystal hung out at the back of the room.

"Where was I?" Harmonia asked as she sat behind her desk once again.

"*That* god," I prompted.

"Oh, yes, right. Well, *He* came along and had a really

good marketing campaign. Part of *His* doctrine was to separate the world into good and evil. *He's* the one who separated the daemon into angels and demons. *His* daemon, they were good — according to *Him* — and called angels. All the other daemons *He* deemed evil and became demons. But in truth, very few of us daemons are truly evil. We're like humans in that respect. Some are goody-two-shoes, some are true motherfuckers, and most are somewhere in between. And we look like you because we always have. It was *His* doctrine that made daemons into devils with pitchforks and red skin, living in hellfire."

"Oh," I said nodding as if all of that had been perfectly logical. In truth, it had at least been easy to follow, but the entire basis behind it: that gods and angels and demons — or whatever — were real was ludicrous. I'd fallen off the good-Catholic-girl train a long time ago, though I wasn't opposed to dressing up as one for a little roleplay.

"And I'm a sex demon?" I asked, then quickly corrected myself seeing her about to do so. "Daemon, I mean. A sex daemon."

Harmonia shrugged. "I can only assume so, given what you're making me feel."

I blinked. "What I'm making *you* feel? Are you into women?"

She gave a breathy laugh. "I'm from the Greek pantheon, we're... flexible. But that's not really the point. It's more like your power makes people feel sexy. It makes them want to have sex... if there happens to be someone around they find appealing."

"And is that why that man in the elevator was all over me?"

Harmonia nodded. "Yes." She then raised a brow. "Although, that was Ramsey, and he's pretty horny to begin with."

"Is he a sex daemon too?" I was curious. "Because I felt like I really needed to... ah..." Yeah, that was too much information.

"No. Ramsey is the Lord of Strife and Conflict. But I'm guessing his natural chaotic nature probably befuddled your power enough that it was working on you as well."

Lord of Strife and Conflict? What the fuck?

"When you say lord...?"

"I mean daemon lord, more like a daemon prince actually."

"Yeah..." I drew out the word.

"You still don't believe any of this? Even after everything you've seen?"

"Ah..." That was the trouble. I know what I'd seen and felt, but a large part of me was still thinking maybe someone had spiked my dinner with 'shrooms and I was tripping balls right now.

Harmonia sighed. "Well, let's hypothetically say that we're all daemons here and that you have power. And let's hypothetically say that your power is just a little out of control at the moment. If that were the case, then I'm here to help you get it under control."

"Ah... thanks? That's very kind of you." *I think.*

"For now, since we're still speaking hypothetically and you're probably not ready to do much yourself, I'm going to use a bit of my power on you. It won't be like before. I'll be targeting just your power to calm it a little. Would you be okay with that?"

"Ah... sure?"

"Good." She rose and came to stand behind me. I turned my head, but she smiled down at me. "Just relax, look straight ahead."

I did as instructed. She put her hands to either side of my head and I felt... nothing. I couldn't tell if she was doing anything at all. But then...

There was no good way to describe it, except to say that the latent *sexiness* in the room seemed to diminish. I felt just a little less flirty, a little less hot and ready. Wearing a dress like this made me feel sensual and sexy and I wanted to show it off a little. I still felt that way, but just... less.

Hmm. Perhaps there was something to what Harmonia was saying?

No...?

No...

Nope, demons were definitely not real.

Harmonia sighed. "That's better. I'm probably going to need to do this again before every shift. At least until you learn to control your sexiness," she said.

"Ah, yeah, sure," I replied.

"Great! Krystal, you can get back to your duties."

"Whatever," I heard the other woman say, clearly not interested in any of this.

Harmonia came around in front of me and held out her hand. "Now, if you'll come with me, the owner of this establishment wants to see you."

I took her hand and got up, even as my mind started freaking out. "The owner? Why?"

"Oh, it's nothing bad. You haven't done anything wrong. He's just worried about you and would like to discuss something." Harmonia was smiling, but it didn't quite reach her eyes. Clearly she was hiding something.

I followed her out of her office to that corner office I'd passed after my interview, where I'd seen that tall statue of a man. The door was closed this time and Harmonia knocked, then waited for the call from inside to enter.

She ushered me in first, but I stopped as soon as I'd stepped through the door.

The office was large and immaculately attired, simple, and clean. It held a large desk with two chairs on this side of it and a high-backed, fancy-looking chair behind it. The exterior two walls held floor to ceiling windows. Shelves lined one inner wall and there was a long couch along the other, next to the door.

And on that couch was Mister line-backer-meets-gladiator-meets-mister-universe.

What had Harmonia called him? Ramsey?

He was reclining, hands behind his head, the position straining his dress shirt over taut, bulging muscles heaped on his arms and chest, not to mention the massive flare of his back, giving him a perfect V-shaped torso. He had one leg on the couch, the other over the back, and those midnight blue eyes were just as heated as they'd been in the elevator, stripping away what little I was wearing as he wet his lips.

Just like before, he was all heat and danger and... wow!

His gaze made me feel exposed and hot as hell all at the same time. A rolling heat rose up deep in my belly and my lady lips were practically salivating.

Then I remembered: he's the one who'd called me a demon.

We could have had glorious elevator sex, but he had to go and ruin it by throwing my life into chaos. That was a mark against him in my book, no matter how sexy he was.

The other man in the room was the one I'd spied in this office the other day. He was standing by the windows again and he must have been even taller than Ramsey, perhaps six-eight?

He had his suit jacket off and the black dress shirt underneath seemed like it was painted onto him. He wasn't quite as burly as Ramsey, but still had strong, broad, squared shoulders and arms heavy with muscle. He was leaner through the torso, still with a massive expanse of chest, but with an even more pronounced V-shape, and he wasn't doing anything to emphasize it like Ramsey was.

And where Ramsey's complexion was deep bronze, this other man — my boss? — had a paler, olive complexion, like Harmonia. The stubble of a dark, well-trimmed beard anchored his face below thick, lustrous blue-black locks. Smokey sable eyes, deep and mysterious, seemed to draw me in while drilling into my soul.

Something about his intense gaze pulled on me and I only just stopped myself from crossing to him and wrapping my body around his.

"Anais?" he said, his voice soft but commanding.

I felt like he wanted to *own* me, in good ways and bad, and I fought against that draw. I didn't like anyone controlling me. I wasn't certain whether we'd end up fucking or fighting, and I didn't think either was a good option for my first day on the job.

"Yes?" I said, not meaning to sound like I was uncertain about my own name.

"I'm Zagreus, you can call me Grey, everyone does." He motioned to one of the chairs in front of his desk. "Please sit."

And sit I did. I felt like I was a dog and he was my master. I had to comply. I wanted to. I wanted to please him even as a part of me grated and resisted, furious at being dominated like this. It was only then that I recalled what Harmonia had said earlier. Everyone here was a demon. And, faced with Grey's unyielding power, I could believe it.

Well fuck!

What had I gotten myself into this time?

ANAIS

Grey sat in the comfy-looking chair behind his desk and looked at me with those dark eyes for a drawn-out moment, tugging on my soul. Then he looked over my shoulder to Harmonia.

"You've suppressed her?"

"Yes."

Suppressed? I didn't particularly like the sound of that.

Then he looked over my other shoulder to Ramsey. "This is the woman?"

"Oh yeah, that's her." His voice wasn't as deep as Grey's but rougher, harder and it sent a thrill through me.

No! No thrills! You're off men! And Ramsey was a jerk for calling you a demon even if it was true. Despite my best efforts to clamp down on my lust, my body still reacted to him in a visceral way. What was it about these men?

Oh right... demons.

I didn't know why, but just being in the room with these two men was making me believe in demons —

sorry *daemons* — more than all of Harmonia's assertions. Although after a moment of thinking, I did know why. It was because of the raw power rolling off both of them.

Grey's gaze returned to Harmonia. "Let her go, I want to feel how wild she is."

He wants to feel how wild I am? A part of me wanted to show him just how *wild* I could be. I'd go over there, straddle that fancy chair of his and let loose. I'd—

Stop it! You're off men, remember? I reminded myself.

But maybe just this one? I tried to bargain with myself. Grey was fucking hot and so very powerful. Could a girl be blamed for breaking a vow or two with him? And then there was Ramsey. *Or maybe just one time with both of them?*

My mind seemed to think that would be acceptable. I didn't want *a man* in my life, but two men for just an hour or two? That couldn't hurt, right? And the thought of Grey pressing close to me in front and Ramsey moving against me from behind got my lower lips so lubed up I was suddenly trying to remember if I had a spare thong in my purse because I was going to need it.

Then Harmonia came up behind me and waved her hands around my head again and—

Heat — stifling sexual energy — erupted into the room.

Grey let out a long low grunt. "Hades!" he breathed. "That's—"

"Didn't I tell you?" This from Ramsey behind me, and his voice sounded a little strained as well. "Makes you want to tear off her dress and do her up against one of those windows."

Now *that* was an image. I'd have my legs wrapped around Grey as he easily lifted me, pressing me to the cold glass as he thrust up into me with grunting need. Then Grey was replaced by Ramsey, but since I didn't want to look at him — remembering he was a jerk — he had me turned around, my face and breasts pressed to the glass with a stunning view of the park as he pounded me from behind.

I was so very glad my dress didn't have much of a front or back. It allowed any possible air in the room to cool me a little, because for a moment, I thought I could feel Grey's and Ramsey's arousal, and it was potent.

I'd gone from having two hot men around me to having two hot-and-horny men around me. And more than just a little part of me wanted to be *had*, naked and screaming, up against one of those windows.

"Okay, turn it off, tone it down!" Grey said through clenched teeth.

He rose, leaning on his desk, looming, and I got the impression he was about to tear off his clothes, leap over that desk, and have his way with me.

Harmonia worked her magic again and the stifling sex heat left the room.

Grey sat back slowly, slightly awkward. I guessed he had something large and uncomfortable in his pants. As for me, new panties were definitely going to be required before my shift.

Curious, I turned my head to look at Ramsey, he was sitting up on the couch now, legs spread wide, proudly showing the hefty bulge in his pants. He wore a feral, dangerous smile and winked at me.

"You're mine," he whispered.

A shiver ran through me. I was fairly certain if he wanted me, I wouldn't be able to stop him. And a part of me didn't *want* to stop him, no matter what he'd called me in the past.

Grey cleared his throat and returned my attention to him.

"Ms. Baker?"

"Miss," I corrected. For some reason I wanted these men to know I wasn't married.

"Ah, yes, well." Grey shook his head and cleared his throat again. "How have daemons not been all over you all your life?"

That was a bit of a personal question, but still, I felt compelled — perhaps by his authoritative nature — to answer. "Well, are there a lot of daemons who are bikers, petty criminals, and failed sports pros who've turned to drinking and such?"

Grey blinked at me.

"Because men like that *have* been all over me ever since my tits came in."

And now Grey was looking at my tits, and this dress had a lot to show. The man — my boss — dragged his gaze up with what seemed like great effort and met my eyes once more.

"Some might be yes, but I'm not talking regular relationships," he said. "I'm talking about men filled with a savage hunger, coming up to you on the street, tearing off your clothes, and rutting like animals."

"Oh... ah... no, none of that."

Grey shook his head. "Which means your aspect must

have only just developed recently? How...? How old are you?" He waved a hand dispelling that question. "No, never mind, you've lived a human lifespan, or you'd have suspected you weren't normal once you were past your first century and still looking the picture of youth." He cocked his head. "But if you've been aging normally, then that would also be curious. You should have slowed or stopped aging once you were in your prime."

"That definitely didn't happen," I said. Yeah, I looked damn good for a thirty-eight-year-old, but that didn't mean I didn't have a few fine lines which had started to come in. Something told me I wouldn't have the beginnings of crow's feet if I were immortal, which is what they seemed to be suggesting.

Also... immortal? Fucking what?

"How old are you?" I asked Grey, probably being way too forward.

He shrugged and answered me easily. "Five thousand, six hundred and seventy-nine."

That couldn't be right. He was just spewing out numbers, making that up. I couldn't help but laugh.

"He is," Harmonia said, behind me. "I'm over five thousand years old as well."

I swiveled in my chair. "You don't look a day over thirty," I quipped. I couldn't really believe any of this. I turned to Ramsey. "Are you five thousand years old as well?"

He frowned, as if that was some sort of insult. "No."

"Oh good, I was beginning to think—"

"I'm three thousand, three hundred and twenty-seven."

I nodded as if that made sense. Then I got indignant, fed up with all these wild tales. "Fine, she can calm me down—" I waved an arm at Harmonia. "—what can you two do? Show me your demonic powers!"

"Daemonic," Harmonia corrected me.

"Whatever!"

Ramsey's grin turned feral. "I can't show you mine, not unless you want me to unleash utter strife and chaos in this office... or if you want me to fight Grey." His grin widened. "I might actually be up for that."

"Not happening," Grey muttered behind me.

I turn to him. "And you?"

"My power is The Hunt: conquest and acquisition." He quirked a grin that got my blood pumping. I had a hunch what was coming next. "And the only thing in this office that isn't already mine is you. Would you like me to *conquer* you, Miss Baker?" Those dark eyes pulled me in.

Hell yes! I clamped my mouth shut, only just managing to avoid saying so. Still, I felt a raw, ragged heat bloom all over me.

Grey continued. "I think human resources would have something to say about that."

"Given she just turned red enough to match her dress, I think she might just want to be conquered," Ramsey said behind me.

God but I *was* super-heated. I looked down and indeed my skin was flushed a deep red. Fucking traitorous skin.

"If it's consensual, HR doesn't have to get involved," Ramsey said, then he laughed. "If it's an orgy, then get HR involved, the more the merrier."

I rose. Enough of this, I was leaving. "I need... I need to..." I stammered.

"Sit." Grey's tone was firm and, like the puppy I was, I sat again instantly. Fucking traitorous body.

I couldn't look at Grey or Ramsey, so I looked out the window at that stunning view of the park.

"We haven't even gotten to the reason I asked you here," Grey said with a huff. "We want to protect you."

I inched my head toward him enough to give him some side-eye. "Protect me? I don't need—"

"Yes, you do, Miss Baker. Remember what I said about daemons on the street, with the tearing-off of clothes and the rutting. It's a miracle you've lasted this long. If you don't want that, then you need our help."

"I'm listening," I said, still not sure about any of this.

"Ramsey and I are both respected and feared by other daemons."

That reminded me of something. Harmonia had said Ramsey was a lord. "Are you a daemon lord too?" I asked Grey.

"Yes. More a prince, actually."

Right... yes, that had been mentioned as well. "So your father's a king? King of what?"

"Hades. My father is Hades, the King of Hades. Yes, that's confusing, I know."

I may not have known much Greek mythology, but I knew that name. Well, fuck me with a gilded dildo.

"Oh." And what had started all of this? Yes, right. "And you want to protect me?"

"Yes. My rank, along with Ramsey's is enough that if we claim you as ours, then other daemons should stay away from you, even if your power is driving them crazy. Fear of us is a pretty primal thing as well."

"You're that powerful?" I looked at Grey with slightly more front-eye and less side-eye.

He grinned. "Yes."

"Oh." I sensed power from him, but if he was actually like princely powerful...? "And you'll... claim me?" I asked. "What does that involve?" I was very curious about this claiming process and if there was a physical element to it.

"Ramsey and I will both claim you," Grey said, serious. "We'll say we've both claimed you and are fighting for you. If there's anything more dangerous than one daemon prince, it's two. As for what that entails... nothing really. It's all just words. As soon as the word gets around that you're being fought over by two daemon lords everyone else will stay far away from you."

"Oh." I tried not to let there be too much disappointment in my voice.

"Well, actually," Ramsey said, and I flinched. He sounded like he was right behind me.

I spun around and there he was, tall and looming and dangerous, next to my chair. I hadn't heard him move at all. A man that big moving so quietly? That was frightening indeed. Although the reason my heart was pounding wasn't all fear.

"I think we'd need to be seen with her to really get the message out. So, perhaps we can go on a few dates with her." That dangerous smile of his spread on his face as his voice lowered to a conspiratorial whisper. "And if anything should happen on a date, well, then that's what happens on dates, now isn't it?"

Heat pounded through me, and I was sure I was blushing to match my dress once again, though it was the wet heat pooling in my core which made me press my legs together tightly. Yeah, this current thong was toast.

Fuck me.

"Is that an invitation?" Ramsey breathed, leaning down over the back of my chair with that feral grin.

I gasped. "Can you read minds?"

"No, you said that out loud. Not very loud, but we all heard it," Harmonia said.

"Fuck me."

"Yeah, like that," Ramsey said. "And I repeat, is that an invitation? You don't start your shift until seven, right? We've got most of an hour to—"

"Sit, Ramsey, no fucking allowed," Grey commanded, power rolling off him.

"If she wants to fu—"

"Sit!" I felt that command in my gut and would have sat if I hadn't already been sitting.

Ramsey spun on Grey. "You don't control me, despite your petty need to control everything. I'm chaos, remember? I love a good fight, so don't tempt me!"

Huh, I hadn't noticed that until now, but these two really didn't like each other.

Ramsey turned to me. "He really likes telling people to sit. Like we're all dogs. But I won't treat you like a dog." He grinned. "Well, I won't speak to you like a dog, but if you ever want to fuck like a dog, then—"

"Ramsey, I swear—" Grey was up and around his

desk in a flash and the two of them were suddenly in a toe-to-toe, heated-stare, chest-pushing competition.

At first, I thought Grey would win, he was taller and so commanding. Yet Ramsey was massive and stood his ground. And — if I believed any of what they'd been saying — Ramsey's power was conflict, so he must have been loving this.

"Put your dicks away, boys," Harmonia said and moved to get between them. That was the last place I'd want to be while these two men were fighting, but also exactly where I wanted to be if they weren't. The image of both of them roughly hate-fucking me, one in front, one behind... oh wow.

Then Harmonia touched them and those heatwaves emanated off her. Both guys instantly relaxed and backed off a step.

Whoa, that woman had some balls — and some true and honest powers — to get between those two alphas and make them back down like that.

She turned to Ramsey. "If you wouldn't mind returning to the couch?" There was an odd quality to her voice. He nodded and walked backward, not taking his eyes off Grey, before sitting.

"And you," Harmonia said to Grey. "Sit." She pointed to his chair.

He grimaced and turned, returning to where he'd been.

"I really am sorry for these two," Harmonia said to me. She sighed heavily, closing her eyes and pinching the bridge of her nose.

When she spoke next, I knew it wasn't just for me, but all of us.

"Here are the rules." Her tone was hard. "Yes, you both will need to be seen out and about with Ana here. You'll be complete gentlemen and there will be no talk of fucking or fingering or licking or kissing or anything unless *she* brings it up first. Got that?"

And now I was thinking about strong fingers stroking my clit while hot, wet lips plucked at my nipples with playful kisses, followed by some tongue-lashing.

Yup, I'd definitely need new panties before my shift, I was fairly certain my thong had been consumed by my hungry pussy. I pressed my legs together even harder — until they were shaking — to make sure I wasn't making any more of a mess.

"You're no fun," Ramsey mumbled.

"That wasn't a yes." Harmonia rounded on him.

"Fine, yes. I'll let her bring it up, and I'm sure she'll want to bring it up." I was certain I knew what he wanted me to "bring up," and it wasn't a sex talk.

"Agreed," Grey said stoically.

"Good, now I'll let you call or talk to her on shift, but if you'll excuse us now, I really need to get her ready for that first shift." She indicated we should leave, and I was quickly out the door behind her.

"They're... something else," I said, not really knowing what I'd meant to say.

"Yeah." She seemed a bit more relaxed now that we were away from those clashing alpha egos. "Grey isn't bad. He's actually a huge softy once you get to know him, but Ramsey brings out the worst in him."

I nodded. I'd seen that firsthand.

"Ramsey is pretty much what you see: a horny and cocky ass, who is hot enough and persuasive enough to get what he wants when it comes to most things, especially women. Don't let him persuade you." Harmonia shrugged. "Unless you really want to be persuaded."

Curious, I asked. "Have you been *persuaded*?"

Harmonia sighed. "I've resisted... so far. But enough of my staff have been *persuaded* that I have a good idea what he'd be like."

"And?"

"From what I've heard, he doesn't disappoint, but he also doesn't stick around. If you want love or a lasting relationship, stay away from him. If you want a mind-blowing one-night stand, then by all means, be *persuaded*." She stopped to look me in the eyes. "But I'd caution against it. As long as you say no, you have all the power over him. He'll hate it but he'll be at your mercy."

Huh, interesting advice.

That reminded me though... I'd been roped into having those two men take me out. Not that I minded, but given how potent they were, I wasn't sure how well I'd resist any advances they might make. So much for *No Men*.

Oh and... "I think my purse is in your office still, mind if I grab it?" I asked. It was time for some new undies.

"Sure," Harmonia said. "And when you get back, let's have a chat about these mobsters that want money from you."

Oh... right... she knew about that.

Fuck.

ANAIS

"And you're sure they're just humans?" Harmonia asked about the gangsters.

"They didn't react to me like you daemons do." I was — slowly — getting a handle on this new terminology and also the fact that *I* wasn't human. That was still messed up, but then so was I. "So, I assume that means human?"

She nodded. "And they want two hundred and fifty million?" she said it like it was nothing. "In a week?"

"Yup. Six days now."

Harmonia blew out a breath. "Let me see what I can do. There may be other ways around this. Try not to worry about it too much for now. We daemons help each other."

I blinked. "You'd do that? Help me with this?"

"Of course. Your life is very unharmonious at the moment and I'm compelled to fix that." She smiled.

I threw my arms around her in an embrace. "Oh, thank you! You don't know what that means to me!"

"I... I think I do. Now, let's get out there and start your shift, shall we?" She escorted me out to the bar and oversaw the first portion of my shift.

Luckily, once I was working, I began to feel normal. The bar was just like any other bar, except the patrons — who looked normal — were apparently all daemons.

That would explain why the last time I was here — walking through the lounge — I'd thought they were all gangsters and hitmen. They gave off an aura of power and a don't-mess-with-me-ness. But when they came to the bar to ask for drinks, most of them seemed normal, even... nice.

I'd almost forgotten about Grey and Ramsey — okay, yeah, I wasn't soon going to forget either of those gorgeous men — when they both stormed into the lounge. Instantly, the entire place was filled with the tension and animosity they exuded.

"Now what?" I whispered.

Harmonia gave a soft breathy laugh. "Now we watch the show."

The show? Oh! They hadn't publicly "claimed" me yet. This should be interesting.

"Oh, one thing," Harmonia said, turning to me. "The guys might get a little rough around you. Don't worry, it's all a part of the show."

"Around me or with me?" There was a big difference.

"Mostly around, maybe with. But it shouldn't be anything serious. They just need to show everyone that they're claiming you." She backed off as Ramsey threw himself over the bar after the initial part of a yelling match with Grey that I'd missed while talking with Harmonia.

Ramsey stalked up to me and grabbed my arm... sort of. He had big meaty hands and could easily wrap one of them around my upper arm, but despite the heated lust-rage in his eyes, and the trembling strength coursing through his body, he didn't actually squeeze my arm. The hand around my arm was clenched and shaking as it lifted my arm a little but it was all a show.

I'd been in a few theatre productions in high school. I was a horrible actor but had been very pretty and that had been enough. I'd learned a little bit about stage fighting, where you supposedly grab someone, all tense and looking harsh, but really, they're in control and you're not hurting them at all. That's what this was like.

"She's mine!" Ramsey spat out over his shoulder at Grey.

He stepped in close and pulled me into a fierce embrace. This too was for show, his arms were surprisingly gentle around me for all his massive size and strength. But the hard-as-rock, salami-sized erection pressing against my belly? That was very real.

He whispered to me, his hot breath on my ear, "You *are* mine. I *will* have you." That wasn't for show, and it sent a thrill through me, heat bubbling to life in my core once again. "I'll prove I'm the one. Just say the word and I'll make you come over and over."

Holy fuck. I shuddered at the thought of him possessing me, kissing and licking, fingering and fucking, as I had orgasm after orgasm. And as much as I wanted to think of him as a jerk, all I saw now was a bad boy and that just meant I wanted him more.

Aaaand there went my second pair of panties.

Suddenly, Ramsey was torn away. I was released and staggered back, as Grey, with a single punch, drove Ramsey to the ground.

Holy Mother of Fuck! I hadn't thought Ramsey would go down that easy. But then he winked at me as he looked up from the floor. Ah, this was part of the show. They both had to claim me after all.

Grey moved in on me, hands to either side of me, leaning on the back bar, pinning me in place, looming close, radiating heat and desire.

"She's mine!" he hissed over his shoulder, though it was loud enough for everyone in the room to hear it. "And I'll bring the full wrath of Hades down on anyone who tries to touch her!"

Oh... wow... the full wrath of...

And when he turned back to me those dark eyes felt like they were sucking my soul right out of my body and I nearly went limp.

He caught me as I swooned — yeah, I fucking swooned — and held me close bringing his hard lips to my neck. His kiss was possessive, demanding, his teeth raking over flesh before he pulled away.

My body thrummed with want, nipples spiking as I felt Grey's hard chest through his shirt and the sheer fabric of my dress. I must have been beet red because I was so fucking hot, I couldn't catch my breath. Sweat was pooling in all the worst places. Hopefully, I hadn't ruined this dress, but if I had, it might just have been worth it.

He nipped at my ear, and I moaned — I actually moaned — far too loudly.

"Too much," he whispered into my ear.

Hell yes! Or should that be Hades yes?

"Sorry, we'll be done soon, then I'll fire the HR department before they find out."

I almost laughed at that but stopped myself. Now wasn't the time.

And just like that, he released me and deftly sent me into the waiting arms of Harmonia as he spun on Ramsey, who'd just gotten up. "Just try to take her from me!"

"You bet your ass I will," Ramsey spat the words and I saw just a hint of I'm-going-to-enjoy-this mirth in his eyes before—

The punch he landed in Grey's gut made the man double over with a loud "oof!" Then, as if Grey weighed nothing at all, he picked up the taller man and threw him a good fifty feet, right down the middle aisle of the lounge, somehow not damaging a single table.

Then Ramsey vaulted over the bar again. Grey got up before Ramsey reached him and the two fake-duked it out. Or at least, I think it was fake. It looked real. They fought their way across the lounge to the lobby area with the elevators.

"And stay out!" I heard Grey shout. Then he stalked back in and I could see that it hadn't all been fake, there was a bruise on his cheek.

Fuck me.

I expected him to shout something like "She's mine!" to everyone here, but instead he just stalked back to me and leaned heavily on the bar. "Your shift is over. You're coming with me. Now!"

I didn't need to fake my shocked surprise. "Ah…"

"Get your things. We're going out." There was no room for debate.

"O-okay," I stammered and fled to the back room to grab my things. Harmonia met me there.

"This was part of the plan," she reassured me. "Don't worry, we'll cover your shift tonight, go."

"Do you know where he's taking me?"

"Nope, but remember my rules, no funny stuff unless you instigate it."

I nodded.

I'd only actually worked for maybe an hour and now I was done. If this was what all my shifts were going to be like, I could live with that. I grabbed my things and rushed out to meet a huffing and hard-eyed Grey, who actually scooped me into his arms and carried me to the elevators.

Once we were alone in the elevator, he sighed and put me down.

"How was that?" he asked.

"Intense."

"Good." He laughed and actually smiled. "That was a ton of fun. Especially the punching Ramsey part."

"Ah, yeah… sure," I murmured, just a little scared of the large man next to me. Also, had only 'punching Ramsey' been fun? What about that intimate moment with me? Well, I shouldn't be upset, this was supposed to be a charade after all.

Still…

He reached over and placed his hand on my exposed back and suddenly I was stiff but melting all at the same time.

"Don't worry, I'd never hurt you." His voice was soft and soothing. His hand stroked up my back to my neck, his thumb shifted up behind my ear. I shivered and leaned into it and, yup, my traitorous voice moaned again.

Oddly, his hand jerked back at that.

Oh… right, Harmonia's rules.

"Sorry," he said stiffly, and all the lightness and fun were gone.

Well, fuck.

FEN

It had been a long day at the demo site, but the job was done. The crew could take a couple days to recoup, then we had a complete building demo starting early next week. I'd rushed home, showered, shaved, and dressed, then hurried to Elysium.

As I arrived at the high-rise hotel, I found Ramsey exiting one of the elevators. He looked like he'd been in a fight with a few new bruises on his face, and even though I knew he was the Lord of Strife, this was odd for him. Usually, he kept his fighting to underground Empyrean fight clubs.

"What happened to you?" I asked. Then knowing he wasn't one to lose a fight added, "And how dead is the other guy?"

Ramsey looked up at me and smiled. "What? This? It's nothing. It was a bit of an act."

An act? Ramsey, the Lord of Strife was play-fighting? That was odd. I didn't know what to say to that, so just stepped past him to hit the up-elevator button.

"Don't see you here often? What's up?" he asked me. "And actually, now that you're here, I've got a job for you, if you're interested."

"A job?" That was curious indeed. Most of Ramsey's "jobs" were illicit missions to punish the rich and powerful who were causing undue strife in the world. Then I added, "I'm here to see a woman. She works here. I've only met her once, but I think I'm in love."

Ramsey squinted with suspicion. "Which woman?"

The elevator dinged, and the door opened. Inside was Grey... with Ana.

"Ana?" I said, excited to see her, not sure why Grey might be with her. I hoped they were just coming down together, nothing more.

"Fuck," Ramsey hissed behind me.

"Fen?" Ana smiled at me.

There was something different about her. Well, there was the gorgeous burgundy dress she was wearing, which hugged her full curves and gave an excellent view of her cleavage.

I felt my cock stir and start to rise... but that's when I realized what was truly different. Her aspect wasn't overwhelming me, making me rage with desire.

And seeing her, for the first time without all of that, I knew she was the one for me. Her aspect may have drawn me in last time, but without it, I could see her true beauty. All I wanted was to hold her close and kiss every inch of that tall, statuesque body of hers.

"You know him?" Grey muttered.

And instantly I sensed the tension solidifying around

me. Something was up. Unseen, but very palpable friction snapped between the two other men.

"What is it?" I asked.

Grey looked to Ana, then back to me. "You want us to keep him away?"

Away? Why?

"No!" Ana said quickly. "I know Fen, and we hit it off. You don't need to do your little act for him."

Act? Also... she thought we hit it off too? That was the best news I'd heard in centuries.

"I was on my way to see you," I said with a grin. "You look amazing, by the way."

Those pale cheeks of hers colored with a rosy blush. "Thank you."

"She's off limits," Ramsey grunted behind me.

Ana shot him a look filled with daggers. "That's not for you to decide. Why can't he join our little game?"

Game? What was going on here?

Grey and Ramsey glared at each other for a long moment. I wasn't surprised, they'd never gotten along. What did surprise me was that they seemed to be working together on something for Ana.

Grey shrugged. "He's powerful enough, another prince like us. It couldn't hurt."

Ramsey muttered something I couldn't hear but ended with "Fine."

"What am I a part of now?" I asked, still curious about this strange encounter.

Grey looked around, but there were no other daemons about. "We're protecting Ana. Her aspect can get a little out of control. Right now, Harmonia is helping to keep her in check, but that won't last. So Ramsey and I are pretending to fight over her, hoping that will keep any other daemons away." He cocked his head. "Speaking of which, if you met her before, why were you not affected by her out-of-control aspect?"

I smiled and winked at Ana. "Oh, I was. I felt it even before I saw her and had to investigate. It wasn't easy to endure, but when you've been suppressing a beast like mine for over a thousand years, you learn a thing or two about self-control."

Grey nodded. "Ah."

"Beast?" Ana asked, looking just a little worried. "You're one of them? One of... us? A daemon?" She seemed surprised. Though the way she said *us* made me think she hadn't known she was a daemon until just recently.

I shrugged and nodded. "Perhaps a proper introduction is in order. "I'm Fenris, Lord of Destruction."

Her eyes widened. "Destruction?"

Yeah, it was a bit of a heavy title.

"I promise I don't bite... much, and I'll only eat you if you ask nicely," I said, voice low and husky, eyes taking her all in.

"Oh... oh!" she said and that blush on her cheeks bloomed again, and this time it sank all the way down that low V-neck of her dress.

"Exactly." I looked at Grey and Ramsey. "I'd been hoping to speak to Ana tonight, would it be possi—"

"No," Grey cut me off. "She was seen leaving with me and I need to be seen with her tonight. If you have each other's numbers, you can meet up some other time." I felt the push of his command. Grey was far older than me, which usually equated to more powerful, though I was no slouch myself.

"Do I get a say in this?" Ana asked.

"No," Grey said, just as hard.

"Well fine then." Ana definitely didn't like being told what to do, that was clear. She turned to me. "Give me your phone."

I pulled it out and had it unlocked in an instant, then handed it over. She put in her number and handed it back. "Call me, whenever you like." She smiled at me then glared at Grey.

Good.

I took my phone and sighed as Grey escorted Ana away, out of the building.

"You too, huh?"

I turned, remembering Ramsey was still there. His words sank in a moment later: *you too*?

But then I saw how his gaze was following the couple — no, not the couple, but Ana — as they left.

Ah.

So, I had competition, did I?

I laughed. "May the better man win. Unless you want to fight over her?"

Ramsey glared at me. I knew what he was thinking. He could probably take me in a fight. He was almost two thousand years older than I was, after all, but then everybody was just a little wary of my beast.

No one really wanted to piss off a world-ending daemon. The few times Ramsey and I had fought at one of the Empyrean fight clubs, it had always ended in a draw. He was better than me but always stopped the fight when — inevitably — my beast threatened to come out.

He sighed. "That's for later. For now, about that job I mentioned."

And just like that all the tension seemed to drain out of him and he was all smiles and slaps on the back. "I need someone with access to explosives and experience using them. And you're just the man."

It couldn't hurt to listen.

We left together since I no longer had a reason to go up to Elysium and he'd been on his way out to begin with.

But my mind wasn't thinking about his job. I only had thoughts for Ana, and deep within me, my wolf growled its bestial need.

Something told me, if I couldn't have her, my beast wouldn't be happy. And if that happened... the world might just be in for a premature Ragnarök.

GREY

I took Ana to another club, one daemons were known to frequent, since we needed to be seen together. We chose a booth that was visible to most of the club — instead of the darker, more private booths in the back — and I offered her a drink. She chose ginger ale. Apparently, she didn't drink a lot.

Her temperance was just one of a growing list of things I found fascinating about her. The top of that list was her sheer power. When Harmonia had removed her suppression, I'd nearly been overwhelmed by Ana's aspect.

The fact that she could overpower me was significant. Even suppressed, Ana had been nearly irresistible. From that first moment, when she'd walked into my office, I'd felt odd... different, and more than just physically attracted to her. I *needed* to be near her and a part of me hadn't been "playing a game" when I'd fought Ramsey to claim her.

It was shocking. I'd never felt anything like this for

any woman before, and while I'd been told, many times, that my aspect drew people in, pulled by the black hole of avarice within me, this was my first time being on the other side.

I'd never felt that kind of pull from anyone and I didn't know why I was feeling it now from Ana.

It piqued my curiosity, driving me to find out everything I could about this gorgeous, captivating woman. But, at the moment, she wasn't the topic of conversation.

"Tell me more about daemons," she asked.

"Anything specific you want to know?"

"Assume I'm completely oblivious," she said with a grimace. She put down her drink and leaned forward, elbows on the table, head in her hands. "I'm still just a little... I can't decide whether you're all mad, or the rest of the world is."

Ah.

She glanced up, an exasperated look in her shimmering silver-blue eyes. "What *are* daemons?" *And how could I be one?* I hadn't outright heard her thoughts, but it was easy enough to figure out that was what she was really asking about.

"It may sound odd to say it, but we're not the all-powerful beings we may seem to be," I replied. "You've probably heard a lot of mythology about how this god or that one created the world. Well, that's a load of complete crap."

She blinked. "Oh?"

I nodded with — what I hoped was — a soft smile. I honestly wasn't used to being soft... or smiling. I was used to boardrooms and hard faces, mergers and lay-offs, and deals so large most people couldn't comprehend them. I wasn't used to this one-on-one sensitive time. Well, not with people anyway. I'd always been better with animals. But for some reason, I wanted to be soft with her, *needed* to be soft with her.

"Yeah," I continued, trying to not let my thoughts wander to the strange feeling growing inside me or be distracted by the realization that the feeling wasn't just lust for a stunning woman. "Gods and daemons didn't create the world, they didn't create humanity, none of that. We didn't create squat. The truth is that humanity has always been the creator. We exist because humanity created *us*."

She frowned and I could see she wasn't fully comprehending this... or perhaps she was trying to figure out how and when humanity had created her.

"Early humans were very superstitious. They revered the sun in the sky, the fire that burned their forests, the power of a lion, and the mystery of the dark. So they created gods and spirits to help them make sense of things. And when enough of them put enough energy into their beliefs, those beliefs manifested and became real. After that, many of the gods and daemons took on lives of their own. Some, like me, are second-generation. We weren't brought into existence by humanity, but the normal way, by two parents who happened to be gods."

She nodded slowly. "You said Hades was your father?"

I nodded. "And Persephone is my mother. They were created by the ancient Greeks as part of their mythos and once they existed, they found love and desire like normal people and had kids."

"You say that, and it sounds so... normal," she said shaking her head. "But then you talk about gods and... I can't imagine what that must be like, to be a god, to have that power."

I nodded. "For some of us, like you, it can be hard to feel your own power."

"Actually, I did feel it."

That was curious. "Oh?" I prompted.

"Well, I didn't really notice it before I met all of you, but when Harmonia took it away, I noticed a lack of—" she grimaced "—sexiness? And when she brought it back in your office, I felt it then. But before that, I guess I was just used to it?"

And that was something I was desperately curious about. "But you hadn't had anyone react to it before?"

She shook her head. "No, not until Ramsey cornered me in that elevator. That was the first time anyone had ever mentioned anything."

The mystery of why her powers hadn't manifested until recently was another thing I found curious. Perhaps the strange feeling inside me was the hunt for answers, the need to solve the riddle that was Ana. How could she have gone through her whole life without triggering everyone around her to heights of lust and desire? I didn't ask since it was clear she didn't know, but perhaps there were other ways to find that information.

"What do you know of your parents?" I asked.

She deflated at that. "My birth parents? Nothing. I was adopted as a baby and raised by the Bakers. They died when I was a teenager."

I could see the guilt and sorrow on her features and

her pain made something twist in my gut. A new emotion? A craving? I mentally shook my head and refocused on what Ana was saying.

"I drove them into an early grave," she said. "I wasn't the easiest girl to deal with. I mean, I guess I've always been a bit... lusty. I also wasn't interested in school but put a bad boy in front of me and I was paying attention." Her gaze dropped and she started drawing circles on the tabletop, trailing her finger through the condensation that had slid down her glass and beaded on the surface.

The urge to get closer to her swelled even though Harmonia had suppressed her power.

"I wanted them to *want* me. I don't know why. Some didn't and just wanted a one-night stand. Some did and I —" She huffed out a heavy sigh. "I got bored with them once things cooled. So, I started looking for the next hot and passionate thing." She dragged her silvery gaze back up to mine. "Maybe I've always had this power?"

"No," I told her. "If you did, those boys wouldn't have been able to leave you. They would have taken one look at you and *needed* to be with you. Always."

Which was — much to my confusion — how I felt about her.

"Though to be fair," I said, doubling down on my determination to ignore those feelings. "Humans are affected differently by our powers. It depends on whether they believe in us or not. They don't need to know the person before them is a god, but if they happen to believe in that god, they'll be more swayed than if they didn't happen to believe. And for most humans these days, belief isn't as big a deal for them."

She nodded but I could see that she didn't really fully understand it yet.

And not knowing her birth parents didn't help. She hadn't grown up knowing about daemons and her power which meant it was going to take a while for all of this to sink in.

Worse yet, she could be anyone's offspring. Aphrodite certainly had enough demi-daemons running around the world that could be one or both of her parents, but there were also other gods and goddesses of love and sex and fertility and beauty. There was also no way of telling if only one of her parents was a daemon or both.

Regardless, most daemons, whether they were male or female, rarely gave up their kids for adoption. Mostly because humans raising a daemon would be in for one Hades of a hard time once that young daemon came into their power. Although as much as it sounded like Ana's adoptive parents hadn't fared well with her, it didn't sound like she'd truly manifested her powers. Which was something that was curious about her.

Perhaps she'd been controlling her powers until recently?

Except that didn't make sense. How could she control them if she didn't know she had them? Most daemons had to work hard to control their aspects.

"Has anything changed in your life recently?" I asked.

She grimaced. "The only thing that's really changed is my decision to go off men and find out who I am on my own."

"Off men?" I found myself smiling at that, liking the thought more than I probably should.

"Yeah, you can see how well that's working out for me."

"Indeed." I couldn't help myself. "And... what about me?"

"You?" She blinked. Apparently, she hadn't considered me at all from that look which made that strange sensation in my stomach twist tighter.

"If I was a potential suitor, assuming you weren't off men, what would you think of me?" I shouldn't have asked, but a part of me was so drawn to her I had to know.

She cocked her head. "You're my boss, so I'd probably try *not* to think of you. But you're also... ah... well..." A heavy blush colored her cheeks and seemed to be spreading to her entire face. I didn't know what that meant. Was she flustered because she *did* like me or because she didn't and didn't know how to say it?

"Don't worry about it, just an idle question. Perhaps some of your aspect is still affecting me." It was, I could feel it, even suppressed. She was still ever-so-slightly too alluring to anyone who laid eyes on her, and I could feel the tickle of desire stirring within me. A desire, not necessarily for her, but to be with... someone. That was her power. She instilled lust and the need for sex into people. It just so happened she was gorgeous and would probably end up being the target of anyone who was affected.

"Oh... yeah? Ah, okay."

I switched the topic back to her. "Nothing else changed in your life before this happened?"

"I got the job at your place," she said with a shrug. "I can't think of anything else more significant than that."

That wouldn't have done it.

Very odd indeed.

She took another sip of her drink, then smiled at me. And in that moment, just seeing her smile, I felt... content.

I blinked.

Content?

Contentment and I didn't go together.

That's it! I hadn't realized exactly how she was affecting me, why I'd wanted to be near her — and not just because I desired her — but now I knew.

When I was with her, I didn't feel empty.

The void inside me was gone and something about her fulfilled me in a way no business deal, no hunt, no other person ever had, and I wanted more. I wanted to feel that way forever. She *had* to be mine.

I leaned across the table and took one of her hands in both of mine, unable to stop myself now that I'd realized the truth.

"Ana," I breathed, and she was suddenly looking at me just a little skeptically. I couldn't blame her, but still, I had to tell her. The words burned in my throat, desperate to break free and be spoken.

"I know you're off men, and I know that us being together is only supposed to be a game, a charade," I said. "But I need to tell you that when I'm with you, I feel... whole. It's like you're the missing piece that I've been looking for all my life. I know that's probably a lot to take in, but I had to say it. I had to let you know how I felt. This isn't your power, this is just... you."

She stared at me, wide-eyed for a long moment before breathing out an, "Oh."

"You don't need to do or say anything. I'm not expecting anything from you. I'll play this game with Ramsey and Fen and keep you safe, keep others away from you. But know that if you ever did start to feel anything for me, I'd be there. I'd be with you in a heart-beat. Anything you ask, that's in my power to give, I'll give it."

I clenched my jaw, trying to stop myself because what I was saying didn't make sense.

I didn't know her and had to assume it was her power influencing me, and yet I couldn't explain why being with her, just sitting here talking to her, made me feel complete. Or why this new and strange feeling bubbled within me determined to break free and make me... happy? Was that what I was feeling?

She swallowed hard, her entire body — all that I could see — had turned a deep red to match her dress. I knew I'd put her on the spot but the illogical part of me that had taken over didn't care. She had to know that I needed her and that I'd do anything to have her.

"I realize you don't know me at all. But... if you'd like to get to know me... I could..." Gods, I was suddenly excited and flustered. I'd *never* felt anything like this before and I sure as Hades had never been flustered. "Would you like to see one of my animal shelters?" I blurted out with a hopeful grin.

"Shelters?"

I nodded. "I have many businesses, but the ones that are closest to my heart are those that help animals. My aspect is The Hunt, except I don't hunt to kill. I hunt to tend to and care for. I love animals, and I've put my life into helping them. Would you like to visit a shelter with me?"

And now I was babbling.

Me babbling!

If Ramsey heard about this, I was never living it down... and I still didn't care. How could I care about what Ramsey thought when the aching void inside me was gone?

"Ah... sure?"

She was definitely not sure, but still, I beamed at her like a Hades damned lunatic.

"Thank you." I released her hand, fighting to regain some self-control. "Now, I see that I've overwhelmed you. I should probably take you home?"

"Ah... yeah, thanks," she replied, her tone, her eyes, her whole expression confused and uncertain.

Fuck. Stop being an idiot and play it cool.

I'd been too honest, said *way* too much, and was going to push her away. What the Hades was wrong with me?

Still, she'd accepted a trip to one of my shelters, so I'd have another chance to woo her.

Woo her?

Yes. That's exactly what I wanted to do. I'd show her that once she was done being "off men," I was the one for her. I had to be.

I'd never acted this way around any woman — any person — before, and in truth, I had no clue about relationships. Oh, I'd been with women, many of them, but they'd all been conquests. When it came to truly caring for someone, I had no clue what to do... and I had to get a hold of myself before I completely fucked it up.

Still, she sat quietly next to me as my chauffeur drove us to her residence. She seemed to be thinking about something and when we stopped, she didn't get out right away. Instead, she turned to me, giving me a long hard look.

"Did you mean what you said?" she asked, a curious note in her voice.

I'd said a lot of things — a lot of stupid, terrifyingly true things — and I had the feeling she was referencing only one small part of it. But still, I said, "Yes, all of it."

"You'd do anything for me?"

"Yes."

"Just like that."

"Yes."

"Like, you'd give me two hundred and fifty million dollars if I needed it?"

I blinked. That was an oddly specific — and very large — amount.

"It would take me a few days to liquidize some holdings, but I could get that sum," I said. "What do you need it for?"

"Ah... n-nothing... I was just..." she replied. "Would you really do that? For me?"

I shrugged, fighting the urge to nod and grin like an idiot because there was a possibility that I could give something to her. "Yeah. It's not an insignificant amount, but I'm worth far more than that."

"But you hardly know me."

I raised a hand, tentatively, knowing I'd already seriously overstepped this evening. I moved it slowly to her face and when she didn't flinch away, softly cupped her cheek and chin.

That thing inside me, the strange emotions—joy and fulfillment—sang with pleasure at the contact.

"You're right," I told her. "But sometimes the heart knows well before the mind does. My heart is telling me I can trust you." I stroked a wayward lock of that silvery-blond hair back over her ear. "I'd also like to spend more time with you. Real time. Not just time to keep the façade going."

Her breath picked up, her pupils dilating with desire.

"I'd like that too," she said softly, offering me a warm smile. "I think you're going to need to fire your HR team after this."

"Technically it's Harmonia who runs the club, even though I own it," I said with a chuckle. "Hiring and firing are her decisions, so I think we're safe."

She licked her lips and the movement of her tongue across those full, plump lips made my heart twinge and my body shiver.

"I... look forward to it," she said and our gazes locked for a long moment.

I wasn't sure what she wanted. Did she want me to trample over her no man vow and take control or not? I certainly knew *I* wanted to kiss those soft lips. But with Harmonia's rules firmly in place, I wouldn't. I'd wait. Besides, she wasn't just some conquest. She was something more. And I sure as Hades wasn't going to fuck it up by behaving like a caveman. It was bad enough I'd just spilled my heart to her.

"Thank you," she said. Then she slipped out of the car in a rush and hurried up the steps to the door of her brownstone.

With a groan, I dropped my head on the back of the seat. I desperately needed to hold someone or, since she was gone and currently off bounds, something. It would be a far cry from Ana, but I knew my pup, Kerberos, would be happy to see me.

"Home," I said to the chauffeur, that thing in my stomach rising into my chest and starting to ache.

Is this what love feels like?

ANAIS

I was too flustered to sleep and couldn't stop tossing and turning in bed.

Grey had asked me out for real, and what he'd said... well, he'd said everything short of, "I love you, Ana." He'd seemed so desperately curious when he'd asked: *If I was a potential suitor, assuming you weren't off men, what would you think of me?*

It was clear he'd been serious, especially given everything he'd said to me, and I'd been a flustered mess with no clue how to respond.

God, he hadn't even batted an eye when I'd asked for a quarter of a billion dollars.

It would take me a few days to liquidize some holdings. A few days! Like he just had to search under the couch cushions or something.

I bit back a hysterical laugh. People like me did *not* know people like him.

I was supposed to be off men then along comes this

gorgeous — and very powerful — man who was practically throwing himself at me.

The entire time I was with him, my heart had been a rampaging mess of flirty highs and what-the-fuck red flags, and my pussy hadn't been able to decide whether it was a bank vault or a slip-and-slide.

Also, demons!

Daemons, I could practically hear Harmonia's voice correcting me.

They were daemons.

And I was one of them.

I still didn't really believe that, couldn't believe it. Far too much had happened in the last couple of days for me to process any of it. Like my handsome-as-fuck boss wanting to do *anything* for me.

My thoughts whirled around and around, jumping from Grey to daemons to everything else and back again.

Was this a fairytale?

I mean, he wasn't a bad boy at all, he was all gentlemanly and refined. Even a little old-fashioned. He definitely wasn't my usual type, but he was still tall and dark and drop-dead gorgeous and apparently so fucking rich that he could easily scrape together two hundred and fifty million dollars.

What was a girl supposed to do with a man like that?

Marry him. Snap him up, put a ring on it, and live a life without any cares in the world! my flirtatious and carefree mind said.

But we're off men, remember? That was my we-need-to-figure-out-who-we-were mind.

Screw that. Why do we need to know who we are when we've got a man who's richer than God and takes care of us?

That's a fair point.

See?

Yeah, but... I really mean it this time. I need to get away from men and spend time with myself and figure out what I really want.

Whatever it is, he can buy it for us. He's probably also amazing in bed.

What? Where did that come from? How could you know that?

We're a sex demon thingy remember? I know. Also given how tall he is, his cock has to be at least eight inches and thick too.

Now you're just fantasizing.

Yes.

Yes, I was.

Suddenly I was really hungry for cucumbers.

With a groan, I removed my hand from where it had been idly stroking myself over my panties, but couldn't get my mind out of the gutter and my thoughts jumped to Fen. He was kind and just as tall, maybe taller, and bigger in all the right places.

Don't forget Ramsey, the way he held me when they were fighting over me, you can't fake that.

Yes, you can. Many men have.

But he wasn't. I'm sure.

Ramsey was an ass and a lech, but gods, he was handsome and big and...

Stop it!

I was off men!

And even if I wasn't, Ramsey was the last man I wanted. He was a jerk who just wanted to get in my panties. Except, even as I thought that, I knew he was actually first on my list because he was the true bad boy of the bunch.

I rolled my eyes at myself.

I didn't want any more bad boys. Really. Honestly.

Yeah, you do.

No, I don't! I mean I want him, yes, but I don't want a relationship with him! I had to be firm with myself. I had to keep seeing him as a jerk and a lech who only wanted my body and nothing more and be firm with myself. *No more bad boys!*

I got up, turned on my bedside light, and sat on the edge of the bed for a long moment, trying to figure out whether I needed a cold shower or a bucket of ice cream and Chris Hemsworth movies, or—

To suck on a cucumber?

Shut up.

"Fuck me." I sank forward, head in hands. My life was a mess and even though it was the one thing I wasn't supposed to be doing, I was thinking of men.

Though to be fair, Ramsey, Fen, and Grey were not really men. They were daemons. Sexy-as-fuck daemons.

I sighed heavily.

Cold shower it was.

RAMSEY

THE NEXT DAY I WAS JUST ABOUT TO GET OUT OF MY CAR when my phone chirped, making me pause and check the screen.

Grey.

I really didn't want to talk to him right now, but he'd been looking into the bank cabal I'd tasked us with taking down and he might have found something.

Sighing, I tapped the screen, putting him on speaker. "Ramsey here, go."

"Thought you'd want to know, Premier Bank is owned by a daemon." Grey's voice was just a little tinny. It made him sound small. I liked it better this way. Still, this news wasn't good.

"Who?"

"Mammon. And I think there's another daemon working with him, but I'll need to do more digging."

"Fuck." Mammon was a prince like us, but — as much as I hated to admit it — far more powerful. The only thing keeping him from being a god by our definitions was his lack of aspects. Gods had more than two, but Mammon still only had wealth and greed. His strength came from his age. He was over ten thousand years old, and he knew every trick in the book. Hell, he'd practically *written* the book.

"Indeed. That may change our plans a little. We'll have to be careful," Grey said stoically.

I rolled my eyes at him even though he couldn't see me. He was *always* careful. "Keep digging and see if you can find who the other daemon is."

"Will do," he said then he hung up.

I brushed a hand through my hair and sighed. That wasn't what I'd wanted to hear today. Hopefully, my next stop would be a bit more inviting.

Swinging the scissor door of my Lamborghini up, I slid out and made my way up the steps to Ana's house where I knocked on the heavy wooden door and waited.

There was no way I was going to take my time with Ana, and I didn't give a fuck about Harmonia's rules. It was clear Fen was hot for her, and Grey had been just a little too anxious to get her to himself last night. No way was I going to play it safe.

The door opened and an aging, grey-haired man peeked out. "Yes?"

"Is Ana home? I'd like to speak to her."

"Ana? Oh yes, yes. My niece, nice girl." The man blinked up at me with a grin.

"Can I speak to her?"

"Speak to who?"

"Ana."

"My niece? Yes, she's a nice girl."

"I know that, and I'd like to speak to Ana, your niece who's a nice girl." Well actually, nothing about her was girlish. She was all woman.

"About what?"

"What?

"What?"

"I…" I had no idea how to respond.

"Oh hello, who are you now?"

Had this man just forgotten everything up until now? The way he was blinking at me, his expression confused, suggested he had.

Fuck me.

"I'm Ramsey, and I'd like to speak to Ana, your niece, about a date."

"A date? Any date in particular? I like October fifteenth, when it's just starting to cool down a bit and the leaves are beginning to change. Such a beautiful time of the year."

Oh. My. Gods.

I was stuck in an episode of the Twilight Zone where I just kept repeating myself over and over again and was forever stuck on Ana's front step.

"Please." I was on the verge of begging, and I'd never begged for anything from anyone, but my only other option was to throttle this infuriating little man, and given he was Ana's uncle, I didn't think that would endear me to her. "Can I speak to Ana."

"Ana, oh yes, my niece—"

"Nice girl," I said in unison with him, then sighed. "Can I come in?" I asked, defeated, trying a different tactic.

"Oh, yes, sure," he said, shuffling back and opening the door wider.

I stepped into a well-appointed front room decorated in warm browns, light and dark, with a rich blue accent. A low round coffee table sat in the center on a plush blue and beige rug surrounded by furniture that was stylish but still comfortable. On top of it sat a wooden chess set, decorated with ornamental swirls carved around the edges of the board, the pieces set ready and waiting for the next game. Someone with taste had decorated here. The only thing out of place was a beat-up old recliner in one corner, which looked extremely comfortable, if not that stylish.

I felt Ana coming long before I saw her, her aspect flooding around me, caressing my senses and rousing a hungry passion within me.

Harmonia's work from the previous night was wearing off, and as soon as it hit me, I felt my cock go rock-solid. Thank the gods, I was in a suit and the jacket fell low enough to cover any obvious bulge.

"Uncle, who was at the door?" Ana asked from up the stairs before gliding lightly down several steps and coming into view. "You?"

At the same time, a young woman, probably still a teenager, came out from a back room and staggered to a stop. "Holy fuck-balls, you're huge!"

"Reia?" Ana said. She came the rest of the way down the stairs and leaned over the banister at the bottom to look back. "This is Ramsey, he's here for me."

The young woman — Reia — sighed heavily, as if this was a common and overrated occurrence.

"Oh." She gave me a once over, then shrugged and left, leaving me stunned. I didn't think any woman had ever dismissed me so thoroughly.

"Oh, Ana. This is... a man... who is here... for something," the old man said, just as kooky as ever.

"He's here for me," Ana repeated.

"Oh, yes?" The old man turned to me. "Nice to meet you." He held out a hand to shake, but I was still stunned and didn't take it immediately, which meant that by the time I reached out the man dropped his arm and walked away as if I wasn't there at all.

"Your uncle is..." I didn't want to insult him or her.

"Yeah, I know. Sorry about that. I hope he didn't give you too much grief," she said coming down the final few steps to lean on the wall, arms crossed under her breasts, which only served to pull her T-shirt tight over those glorious orbs and show them off even more.

Gods, she was sexy.

I knew part of that was her aspect, but I was certain even without all the lust and desire raging around me, I'd find her hot.

Today she had her hair up in a rough ponytail and even without makeup on she was beautiful. She wore tight jeans, riding low on her full hips, and a T-shirt that didn't quite reach low enough, revealing a sliver of her toned belly. And there, on her pale skin, peeking through between the bits of clothes, was a tattoo: a rose. It was just the top, the rest hiding under her jeans.

Fuck, that was hot. The tattoo, the sliver of skin. All of it.

Now if only I could appreciate her beauty without

this raging hard-on that made me want to tear off her clothes and do her up against that wall.

"What do you want?" she asked, sounding vaguely annoyed.

Aaaand that was the problem with her power.

As much as it made me fucking hot for her, it didn't make her hot for me, so I was just an annoyance.

I had a lot of ground to cover if I wanted to win her over and pry her away from Grey and Fen. Fen had charisma and the ladies loved him. Grey was a moron when it came to women, but he had that tall, dark, and brooding vibe that made women fall for him, even while he remained oblivious. As for me? I was just a brute.

"I'm here to set up our date."

"Date?" she said, a cute little line forming between her brows. Then she sighed and rolled her eyes. "Right, we need to be seen together." As if that was going to be a chore.

Fuck me. I tried not to let my pent-up frustration — from dealing with her uncle, and from the sex I wasn't going to be getting even though my body was demanding it — affect me, and could only pray my smile came across as genuine.

"Yeah. I figured we could have a nice dinner, then, just to be sure we're seen by other Empyreans, there's a place we can go. But I'd like to keep it a surprise." I hoped she liked surprises.

"Dinner sounds good," she said. "As for surprises, it better be a good one."

And suddenly I was doubting that she'd like my sort of surprise. I'd hoped to take her to one of the underground Empyrean fights, which was one of the few outlets for my strife.

"And what's an Em-peer-ee-an?" She was sounding out the word. "Is that like a daemon?"

I nodded. "Yeah, since daemon sounds so much like demon and that has a negative connotation these days, some of the younger generation decided to give us a new name. It's a term which encompasses gods and daemons alike."

"Ah." She still seemed a bit standoffish about anything to do with daemons, as if she were afraid of what she was. But I could understand that. A lot of humans didn't react well to knowing we were out there. It had to be even more difficult learning she was one of us.

"Is that it?" she asked. "If so, just text me when and where for dinner and I'll be there."

"I'll pick you up," I said.

"Do you have a chauffeur like Grey?" she asked with one raised brow.

"No, I drive my own car." I liked to be in control, feeling the power of the engine and knowing I commanded over three thousand pounds of racing metal.

"I bet it's some muscled-up Ferrari that you can't even really drive in the city."

Fuck. I bit back a groan. She could see right through me. "It's a Lamborghini."

She nodded as if that confirmed all her worst suspicions of me.

Double fuck.

She sighed. "Fine, should I dress up?" she said eyeing my suit.

Perhaps I could win this one. "No, casual is fine, I wear this for work, but I'm a simple guy most of the time."

"Simple... yeah," she scoffed.

I'd walked into that one.

Well, that had been an utter failure, time to make a calculated retreat — as Grey would put it — and plan for the next encounter. I was about to grab the doorknob to leave when a knock sounded on the door.

"Out of the way," she said brushing past me. I stepped back, out of view, as she opened the door. But instantly I felt something was wrong. She'd gone from lax and mildly perturbed to stiff and on guard.

"Hey there, lady," came a true New York drawl from the other side of the door. "We just dropped by to remind you and your uncle of what you owe us. Two hundred and fifty mil. You better have it all ready for us in five days or else we might break a few of old Donny's fingers."

Another voice piped up, higher pitched but with the same drawl. "Yeah, and we'd hate to do anything to that pretty face of yours."

Fuck this.

I made to move around the door and give these fuckers a piece of my fist, but Ana wildly waved her one hand, hidden behind the door, gesturing me to stop as if she knew I'd be on a rampage, even though she wasn't looking at me.

I got up close behind her, wanting her to know I was there, supporting her, ready to do anything — and I meant anything — to protect her.

I reached out and put a reassuring hand on her back,

feeling the heat radiating from her body. With her aspect storming around me, it was all I could do to keep from grabbing her hips and grinding my hard cock between those high, round ass cheeks. Still, I kept close.

"I know," Ana said, voice strained. "Just leave me alone, and I'll do what I can."

Who were these guys? And why were they extorting her for way too much money?

"Maybe we'll just steal us that pretty Lambo as a down payment," the high-pitched one said.

"That's mine," I said, ignoring Ana's wave-off and rounding the door to come into view.

And gods, how I loved the look of bullies when they saw me. There was a big bruiser, mostly run to fat now, and a skinny dude. Both of their eyes went wide at the sight of me.

Ana sighed heavily.

"Allow me to take care of this, darling," I said, faking that our relationship was much more advanced than it was.

She put a hand on my chest to stop me before turning back to the men at her door. "Sorry guys, can you give me and my... *darling*... a moment?" She shut the door and rounded on me. "What the fuck do you think you're doing?" she hissed, clearly furious.

"Helping you."

"No, you're not. Because now that they've seen you, the next time they come it won't be just the two of them. They'll bring a small army. And you're not going to be here when that happens, given I don't really want or need you around."

Ouch. Even us brutes had feelings. But she had a point. "They were going to steal my car! And if they're extorting you, I can have them arrested and prosecute them. Did I mention I'm a state prosecutor?"

She blinked at me. She hadn't been expecting that. Most people didn't. They thought of me as just a lump of muscle, nothing more.

"You can't arrest them, because—" She snapped her mouth shut, clearly realizing she'd said too much.

"Ah." I nodded. "So, you and your uncle are in deep with these guys, aren't you?"

"Not me!" she hissed. "And I have no clue what Donny did. It was twenty years ago and given who these guys work for, he may not have had much choice. He hid some money for someone named Tommy Two-Toes, and now Tommy wants it back. But Donny doesn't remember anything these days. You met him. Do you think he could remember where he hid fifty million dollars?"

"I thought they said two hundred and fifty million?"

"They expect interest."

"Oh."

"I heard my name," Donny said walking in from the back room. "Do you need... something?" he asked.

"Yes, Donny where did you hide Tommy Two-Toes' fifty million dollars?" she asked directly.

He blinked at her for a long moment. "Who wants chocolate cosmos?" he asked.

"What?" I asked.

"Yeah," Ana whispered to me. "Exactly."

I'd heard of Tommy. He'd once been a mob enforcer but was now a lieutenant. This wasn't a good situation.

"Let me help you," I insisted.

She grimaced. "Unless that car of yours is worth a quarter of a billion dollars and you feel like selling it, I don't see how you can help."

Yeah, I was well off, but not *that* well off. Grey was the one worth billions. Maybe, if I sold everything I owned, I might be able to pull together a quarter of a billion dollars.

Ana nodded at my silence. "Yeah, I thought so, now stay back." She returned to the door and opened it. I stayed out of sight as she finished talking to the two guys.

"Hey, sorry about that, ignore that guy. He's my second cousin once removed on my birth mother's side. He's got more muscle than brains, and he's not sticking around. Don't worry. I'll have your money in five days, I promise."

"You'd better, lady," the one said then their footsteps clomped away.

Ana closed the door and leaned on it heavily. "Fuck me," she whispered.

"Your uncle can't remember where the money is?" I asked, an idea forming in my head.

"He can't remember where his bathroom is half the time. He keeps wandering into mine."

I didn't need to know that. But still— "What if I knew someone who could help him remember, someone who's good at reaching into foggy minds and finding the truth?"

Ana's eyes widened. "Who?"

"We daemons have a wide variety of powers. I know a woman. Her name is Freyja. She's actually Fen's grandmother... sort of. She's a seeress and has a way of looking into people's minds. She might be able to pull out the information you need."

"Really?" Ana was clearly interested now. "Fuck yeah! When can we set that up? You heard those guys. I have five days!"

"Perhaps tomorrow or the day after. I'll give her a call."

"That would be amazing!" Ana said and took a step forward as if she was going to hug me.

My cock surged with hope, but then she stopped herself, seemingly remembering who I was. Still, she smiled up at me and there was definitely something in that smile that hadn't been there before.

"If you do this for me, if you can figure this out... then maybe I'll have a surprise for you, on our date."

By all the gods of the Nile!

"I'll set it up right away!" I smiled at her and headed for the door.

This time, as I open the door, I interrupted a delivery-man. He saw me, eyes going wide, then tripped over the top step and fell, throwing the box he'd been carrying.

It flew into the air and I tried to catch it, but my chaos chose that moment to rear its ugly head. One of my hands got to the box before the other and with my super-human strength, I succeeded in batting it into Ana's front room and punching a hole in the side of the box. It landed hard and burst open spilling dozens of dildos and vibrators.

"Fuck me," Ana groaned behind me.

"It looks like you had plans to do just that." The words flew out of my mouth before I could stop them.

Her face turned bright red, the blush racing down her neck and disappearing beneath her T-shirt and her expression went from pure embarrassment to shock to fury.

"That's none of your business."

Crap. In an instant, I'd lost all the brownie points I'd just earned.

She grabbed the door and pointed to the street. "Out. Now!"

For a second my stupid mind wanted to say something, tell her it was nothing to be embarrassed about, even if I could do a much better job at satisfying her than those toys.

Then I regained my sanity, clamped my mouth shut, and left.

Ana slammed the door behind me, leaving me on the front step with the image of her pleasuring herself using multiple toys at once.

In the vision, she was screaming, naked body writhing in ecstasy and—

Oh fuck. It was too much. With her power still surging around me — she must have been right on the other side of the door — my cock couldn't take any more. I came hard, ruining a pair of eight-hundred-dollar pants.

"Fuck me," I echoed Ana's words from a moment ago.

"Not fuckin' likely!" I heard from the other side of the door. The comeback and the ridiculousness of the moment made me throw my head back and laugh.

Because if I didn't laugh, I was going to kill someone just to release all my pent-up emotions.

ANAIS

I waited until I heard Ramsey's heavy steps move away before sliding down the back of the door to sit, head in hands, glaring at the offending pile of sex toys. I was shaking, experiencing *all* the emotions, terrified of those gangsters, mortified that Ramsey had seen my newly acquired toys, and curious and anxious, trying not to get my hopes up about this Freyja person. Also, I was exhausted and frazzled after a rough night of not-sleep.

What was a woman to do?

First, *this* woman had to clean up her own mess. One thing at a time, right?

I pushed all the various pleasuring implements back into the broken box and carried them upstairs. Then, just because I was feeling sucky, I opened them all, realizing after the fact that I'd need a fuck-ton of batteries for most of them. I'd have to run out today and pick some up because I desperately needed some self-loving.

I could try some of the dildos I'd purchased, but frankly, they just intimidated me. While purchasing them online, I'd assumed bigger was better, but looking at them now, I wasn't so sure. I'd need to be really well lubed for half of them, the other half were strange shapes or glass. I'd even purchased a couple specifically for anal play but wasn't up for that at the moment. No, I'd work up to the dildos, but that meant batteries for the rest.

With that mission firmly in mind, I slipped out to the corner store and bought way too many batteries, all the while trying not to think about anything. I didn't want to think about how amazingly good Ramsey looked in that suit. I didn't want to think about Tommy Two-Toes or Donny or this seer person. I didn't want to think about *guys* at all. Men in my life were just trouble right now.

As for the women in my life, Reia was still a mystery. Harmonia, though a bit intense, was actually really nice, and a great boss. She was more like a long-lost sister than a boss, actually. She seemed to really want to help me.

Aaaand clearly I was failing at my not thinking.

"I wonder what the surprise is," I whispered to myself as I gathered another handful of batteries.

What would someone like Ramsey surprise me with? He'd said not to dress up, which meant a casual date, which seemed relaxing. I was a bit thankful that he wasn't expecting much in that department. Still, surprises could be good or bad and something told me Ramsey's would be unlike anything I was expecting, and probably bad.

I also couldn't stop the hope springing to life inside me. If this Freyja person could help Donny remember, I'd be forever grateful.

The trouble was, I'd also have to be grateful to Ramsey, who was supposed to be in the no-fuck-zone.

Maybe I could spin my gratitude in such a way as to torture him even more. Perhaps a sexy striptease for him, getting him all worked up, but then only allowing him to use his fingers on me, leaving his poor hard cock out in the cold. Something told me he wouldn't say no to any chance to see me naked. Yeah, that could work.

I got home, spent a half-hour unpackaging batteries and reading instructions, then locked my door and tried out a few of my purchases. There was a little one that mimicked oral sex, providing suction to a small area, and though it wasn't really the same as having a guy go down there, it was... very stimulating.

Another looked like a cactus, but without the prickles. It took a little bit to get it into the right spot, but once it was... Holy Orgasms! It was screamingly good, stimulating my clit, G-spot, and ass all at once! I tried a few others and even a couple of the dildos now that I was well worked up.

I couldn't decide if this was better or worse than having a man. Yes, I could focus on exactly what I wanted and needed, but there wasn't the warmth of a body pressed to mine, no whispered words of adoration.

Still, it was a pleasant afternoon, until Reia banged on my door and told me to tone it down... I may have been shouting and screaming a bit too much. Not what a teen daughter wanted to hear from her mother, I was sure.

It was only after I'd cleaned up that it occurred to me that my sex aura — or whatever my power was — might be affecting those around me.

I went to check.

Reia's door was closed. I knocked. "Sorry about... earlier. Are you okay?" I asked.

"Go away!" came the heated reply.

I listened a bit more intently and heard some heavy, huffing breaths. That could have been nothing, or I could be making my staunch and austere daughter horny.

Swell. The mom of the year award was certainly coming my way.

For a moment, I thought about offering her some of my way-too-many sex toys. If she was going to be horny, she might as well have something to help her get off. But I quickly dismissed that idea. I was fairly certain the last thing she wanted was sex toys from her mother.

I didn't really want to check in to see if Donny was also feeling turned on, but I did. Slipping into his room, I heard soft grunts coming from his ensuite. That was enough. No part of me wanted to know what my sixty-year-old uncle was doing that caused grunting in the bathroom.

I went down to the basement of the house to hopefully put more distance between myself and my house-mates, slumped on a couch, and put on whatever happened to be on TV, not really watching it.

It was clear I was affecting those around me. And that, for whatever reason, seemed to solidify for me that I was indeed something different, a daemon, or whatever.

It still seemed ridiculous, but I was apparently running out of denial.

I sighed. If this was all true then I really should learn to control it. I'd go in early to work tonight and talk to Harmonia again.

When the doorbell rang, I froze up with trepidation for a long moment. It was only after a follow-up knock, that I rose and went to the door.

Through the spy hole, I saw a bored-looking man in a courier's uniform so I opened the door.

The guy took one look at me, his eyes widening.

"Whoa," he breathed. "You're—" He swallowed hard and cleared his throat, regaining some composure. "You're Anais Baker, yes?"

"Yes."

He handed over a small envelope. "This is for you. And could you please sign here that you received it?"

He held up a tablet with a big box for a signature. I flicked my finger over it, and he was satisfied with that.

"Have a good day, miss." He smiled at me and tried to walk backward down the stairs leading up to my door, but missed the last step and tumbled into the sidewalk. Still grinning stupidly at me, he picked himself up and made his way over to a moped.

I sighed and closed the door.

The only mark on the envelope was an old-fashioned wax seal with a stylized "f" pressed into it. I slid my finger under the seal to loosen it, then opened the envelope and drew out a thick card.

You are cordially invited to lunch with:
Chef Fenris Lokisen
at
The Aesir Restaurant and Bistro
11:30 October 8th

Please arrive by the side door in the alley off East 74th Street

Fen was inviting me to lunch... and he was a chef?

He hadn't mentioned that. He'd looked like a sexy construction worker when we'd first met, but perhaps the man had many talents.

The eighth was tomorrow.

A thrill of anticipation rushed through me making my heart flutter and my body shiver with warmth.

I was going to see Fen again.

Yeah, vibrators could do a lot, but they couldn't quite mimic this feeling of joy.

And even though I had most of a day to get myself in order, I rushed up to my room to pick out something to wear. The invitation hadn't said anything about formal attire, so I looked up the restaurant online and found a small section where it suggested guests wear jackets and formal wear. Good. A part of me wanted to dress up for Fen... specifically in something that would be easy to get out of.

I thought we were off men? the horny part of my mind mocked.

Okay, so maybe I'll make a few exceptions. It may take me a while to find out who I am. I can't go without sex that whole time, now can I? Nothing serious just... maybe have a fling or two. I'm mostly off men, with a few... get-off men.

Horny me just gloated at that.

I didn't care.

Fen was hot without being intimidating and

dangerous like Grey and Ramsey. Also, he wasn't a bad boy — I didn't think — so he'd be okay to play around with a little.

At least that's what I told myself.

Once I'd picked something out, I realized I was running late if I wanted to get to work early. I dressed, snagged a couple slices of bread and an apple from the fridge, then caught a cab to work, all the while reveling in this light and flirty feeling fluttering inside me, a welcome relief from the terror and confused lust, which seemed to have been my norm the past couple days.

If Ramsey could get this seer person to help Donny tomorrow then between that and lunch with Fen, tomorrow was going to be a very good day.

ANAIS

"Okay, Harmonia, work your magic," I said sauntering into her office. I was so excited about tomorrow that being a daemon didn't bother me at all right now.

She looked up from the papers on her desk and smiled. "I felt you coming. I think you're getting stronger." She rose and came around her desk to me. "Oh yes, definitely stronger. Wow," she breathed, flushed and shaky.

"Then you'd better turn it off, or I think I'm going to feel you coming in a moment," I joked, and she gave a breath of a laugh before putting her hands to either side of my head and doing her heatwave-magic thing.

After a moment, she sighed, and I felt just a little less sexy. "That's better."

"Good, now teach me how to control this sex aura of mine." I was adamant. I could do this. A few hours and I'd have it mastered. Sure, I'd never been good at learning and studies, but this was all about sex and I'd always been good at that.

She laughed again. "You seem brighter and cheerier today. Have you accepted your daemonic side?"

"Yup!" In this moment I felt confident enough to say so.

"I don't know how much I can teach you in a few hours, it usually takes months of working with a young daemon as they slowly come into their power to help them control it."

"Well, I'm not young, so this should be easier." I didn't really know the logic behind that statement, but it made sense to me.

She blinked. "You really are different today? What's changed."

"Do you know a man — actually, I guess he's a daemon — named Fen?"

Harmonia nodded, smiling. I think she sensed my attraction to him. "Yes. He does have that Norse blond-and-blue thing going for him, very attractive."

"Yeah, and apparently, he's a chef?" Perhaps she could provide some clarity on that point.

"Yes, he works in demolitions during the day and runs a restaurant at night. It plays to his two aspects of destruction and devouring."

Devouring? That was... I didn't know what to make of that.

"Well, he invited me to lunch tomorrow, and I'm excited to go, but I don't want my power to make him feel awkward. So let's master this thing!"

"Ah, I see." She directed me to a chair. "Have a seat and let's see what we can do."

She sat on the edge of her desk. Her black hair was up

in a bun, and she was wearing a white blouse and black pencil skirt to mid-calf.

"Let's start with this," she said. "Where do you feel your power when it's on?"

"Feel it?" I blinked. "I don't really feel it at all."

Her brow furrowed at that as she scowled for a moment. "Nothing at all?"

"Nope. Well, I felt it just now when you calmed it. I felt just a little less sexy, but before that, I hadn't really noticed it."

"Oh... wow... okay." She blew out a breath. "Well let's try this. I'm going to remove the calming block I've put in place and when I do, see if you can feel where in your body your power is strongest. For me, it's always here," she said putting a hand over her heart, mid-chest. "I've heard that Grey feels his in his head, behind his eyes and through his senses. Krystal feels her fire in her abdomen, higher when she's angry, lower when she's... ah... aroused. Make sense?"

I nodded as she moved around behind me. "Okay, I'll remove the block in just a moment. Close your eyes and just feel with your body, see what you notice."

I focused on my body as my powers returned, a heat seeping into me, infusing my skin and tingling over every part of me, but then... it sunk and pooled low in my belly. I moved a hand over the spot, low on my abdomen, pressing down into my lap a little. I supposed that shouldn't have surprised me too much. But then... I felt something else, something... more.

"I can feel it in my ah... lady parts," I said just a bit awkwardly. "But also... I feel something, not quite as strong, near my heart." I raised my hand, fingers coming to my sternum between my breasts.

"I see, and—"

But I wasn't done. "I also... I think I feel it everywhere, it's like my skin tingles with it." I sat with that for a moment and Harmonia was silent, letting me take it in. I nodded. "Yeah, it's sort of everywhere, but on the outside, like a shivery-warm blanket all around me and... and I think I feel it a bit more over my palms and in my fingers." Those areas seemed extra sensitive.

Harmonia waited a moment, but that was it. She put my block back in place and I tried to feel my power still.

I felt something, not as strong, but only at my core and on my hands and fingers. Odd.

"Well," Harmonia said, moving around from behind me to sit on the desk again. "I... I don't know what to say to that." She pursed her lips for a moment.

"What is it?" I asked. Clearly, she'd had a thought she wasn't sure she wanted to share.

"Well, I think... and it's only a theory mind you, I can't be sure, but..." She hesitated again.

"What?" I was drop-dead curious now.

"I think, given the multiple locations you mentioned that one of two things is possible."

"Oh?" I prompted.

"Yes, either your power is more than just sex, but maybe something around how sex makes you feel in your heart and the sensations on the skin?" She didn't seem certain of that. She sighed. "Or... you are more powerful than the average daemon." She wet her lips and nodded. "That seems the more likely possibility to me. I think what you were feeling were multiple powers — multiple aspects — but if that's the case, then you're on a level with Grey and Ramsey and other daemon lords. You... you may even surpass them."

Stronger than them? Really? "What would that make me?" I asked softly.

"A goddess."

Fuck me.

I thought I'd said that internally until Harmonia responded with, "Yeah, I know."

I'd only just accepted I was a daemon, but a goddess?

"Can we ah... Can we just assume that's not the case for the moment? I was just barely coming to terms with not being human. I'm not ready for godhood yet."

Harmonia laughed. "Yeah, sure. And it doesn't really matter in terms of taking control of your power." She knelt next to my chair and took my hand. "Don't worry Ana, we'll figure this out." She smiled and her deep brown eyes danced with light. "Now, let's start with the basics, breathing."

We spent some time practicing several "control" techniques. The first was breathing, which felt like a Lamaze class, only I was focusing on the place in my body where I felt my power, not the pain of childbirth. Slow breaths, holding and focusing, then releasing "the power" as I exhaled and calmed it.

Then we did a bit of meditation and even some yoga-like poses, which I could do if I was on my own. They'd be a bit too odd to do in public. Mostly this was to focus my mental control and claim my power.

Power.

I kept calling it that, but the others called it an aspect, something I should probably start doing.

Aspect.

Aspect.

And all too quickly it was time for my shift. I asked Harmonia to loosen her *suppression* a little so I could practice my control as I worked. But given how many men came to me that evening with bulges in their pants, I didn't think I was controlling things well.

Still, these men weren't trying to tear my clothes off, so that was something. But whether that was from fear of Grey and Ramsey or Harmonia's remaining blockage, I didn't know.

At ten thirty, Grey strode into the lounge and all the flirty hard-ons around my station suddenly fled.

Apparently, the "claiming" thing was really working.

"How are you doing tonight?" he asked, his voice low as he leaned against the bar, those sable-black eyes sucking me in once again.

"Good, thanks," I said, feeling just a little breathless around his intensity.

"Why don't you take a break?" he said. "So, we can be seen."

God, the way he said that made it sound so very dangerous and sexy, like we were about to perform some sex act live on stage for a bunch of voyeurs.

"Ah, yeah sure." I looked over to Maria, the shift manager, and she nodded to me. Then I slipped out from behind the bar.

Grey was there, a heavy, possessive arm draped across my shoulders. I'd worn a dark blue bodycon dress, off the shoulders and tight to my curves with a sweetheart neck-line and mid-thigh skirt.

His fingers skimmed up off my sleeve to the exposed skin of my shoulder and drew a shiver. But his hand didn't stop at my shoulder, it slid to the back of my neck, and he did that thing again, stroking his thumb up behind my ear.

Thankfully I didn't moan this time, well, not out loud anyway. Instead, my body just got very warm and parts of me got very wet.

He offered me a chair at a table near the window overlooking the park and the lit-up city, the lights bright in the evening's darkness. Then, instead of taking the chair opposite me, he shifted it around so it was next to me, close, very close, so I was between him and the window.

"There," he breathed, words just for me. "Now I have you all to myself."

I shivered, the sensation rolling down my spine and adding to the liquid heat pooling in my core.

Boy was I glad I'd learned from yesterday and brought several changes of panties just in case. If Grey kept talking to me in that low and heated tone, while stroking my ear, I was going to need them.

ANAIS

WE SAT IN SILENCE FOR A WHILE, HIM BEING ALL TALL, dark, and possessive, and me being all melty and gooey and flushed.

"If you don't mind me asking…" he said, his hand on my back lifting away so just a single finger could trace the neckline of my dress. More shivers of anticipation swept through me, and my heat ratcheted up a notch to boiling. "What was all that last night about two hundred and fifty million? Was that a joke?"

And in an instant, the bubbling lava in my core turned to a hard rock in my gut.

He must have sensed my stiffness.

"Sorry," he said almost instantly. "I didn't mean to pry." He sighed. "It was just an oddly large and specific amount."

"Could we talk about something else?" I asked, mouth dry as a desert. "And can I get a drink?"

He nodded and signaled a server, ordering two ginger ales.

I smiled. He'd remembered what I liked to drink and that I didn't do anything alcoholic when I was out at a club.

"What would you like to talk about?" he asked, his voice still hushed, just for me. The way he had his hand on my back while leaning on the table with his other arm, facing me and leaning in, made it feel like he was the only thing in my world and I was pretty sure that was intentional.

I wracked my brain for a conversation topic before remembering he liked animals. "Do you have any pets?"

He smiled, and instantly the dark and dangerous Grey was gone, replaced by a warm and tender-hearted Grey. Wow, what a shift.

"Yeah. I think of all the animals in my shelters as mine, until they find a good home. But I have a dog, as well. His name is Kerberos." The name sounded odd, like care-bear-oos. And I couldn't help but smile at the inno-cent-sounding name.

"What type of dog is he?" I asked, hoping to keep light-and-heartfelt Grey around.

"A hellhound. Well, technically *The Hellhound*. He used to guard the gates of Hades until I left and he came with me. He always liked me better than Dad."

What the fuck? Apparently, it just wasn't possible to have a normal conversation with these guys without seers and hellhounds coming up.

The server arrived and gave us our drinks.

"Ah... yeah..." I tried not to be too put off by his beloved pet being a hellhound. And now I was desper-ately searching for another topic.

Thankfully, he saved me.

"What about you?" he asked. "Do you have any pets?" Those dark eyes of his sparkled with faint shimmers of light in the void.

I frowned and sighed. "No, we used to have a cat. My eldest daughter named him Ramses the Great, but I called him Ra-Ra."

Grey choked on his ginger ale, eyes bulging a little. It sort of looked like he was trying not to laugh but failing miserably.

"What?" I asked.

"You don't know Ramsey's full name, do you?" he laughed.

"I just thought it was Ramsey."

"No... It's Ramses the Great. He's the son of Set and was a pharaoh of Egypt long ago."

"So, my cat...?"

"Was named after Ramsey, yes." Grey breathed another laugh. "He'll *love* that."

Given how Grey said it— "I take it Ramsey doesn't like cats? I thought Egyptians worshiped them or something?"

Grey shook his head. "No, not quite. They were revered, but not worshiped. It was thought they were Holy vessels for the gods, which means to Ramsey, every cat is just his relatives checking in on him."

I laughed. "Oh... that's unfortunate."

"Indeed," Grey said and laughed a bit more before giving a long sigh. He returned his hand to my back — which he'd withdrawn when choking — and began tracing lines over my shoulders, back, and neck.

I shivered at his touch once again, especially when it brushed up into my hairline. I hadn't had time to do anything fancy with my hair, so it was just up in a ponytail.

His seeking fingers paused after a moment and he whispered, "Is this too much? Should I have asked permission to touch you? Do you consider that a part of Harmonia's rules?"

"No, touching is good," I purred, wanting more than just the light and flirty brush of his fingers.

"And... kissing?" He leaned in close, our faces too close to see clearly, our hot breath mingling between us. He shifted to one side just a bit, his lips brushing my cheek as he asked, "Would you allow me to kiss you?"

Hell yes!

"Yes," I breathed, the horny side of me shocked I'd agreed so easily.

But Grey was just so hot and near, and I was desperate for contact. I'd spent all afternoon fucking myself but hadn't felt the press of a kiss in what felt like ages.

A warm, soft, chaste kiss brushed my cheek, and I closed my eyes, savoring the feel of his lips on my skin. Heat pulsed within me, tingling over every inch of my skin, then seeping down to pool in my core once again, quickly bubbling to a boil.

And when he kissed his way over my cheek to my lips, tasting and tentative, I moaned softly against him, my entire body blossoming with heated need. I felt it like I'd felt my aspect earlier with Harmonia. It tingled warm on my skin and pounded in time with my heart and it made all my lady bits loose and lubed.

I gave myself over to him, as one kiss turned to many and we plucked and played. Then, his tongue brushed across my lower lip, as if asking permission to enter.

Come on in!

I opened to him and felt the warmth of his tongue on mine, seeking and deep. I moaned, louder this time as we merged, our kiss becoming a long and lingering hot-as-hell affair.

His hand on my back came up to the back of my head, threading into my hair to press me closer, and my hands also went exploring.

One came up to brush into his thick dark hair and keep him close, the other began on his shoulder, then slid over his suit, feeling the hard planes of his shoulders and chest beneath.

I turned. He shifted. Our legs intertwined as we faced each other, both on the edges of our seats. And yeah, one of my knees pressed into his groin, feeling the pulsing heat of his erection trying to break free from his expensive pants.

I wanted more than a kiss but didn't know if I should say anything. Given Harmonia's rules, asking for more felt like opening Pandora's Box. So, I dove headlong into this kiss, head tilting, mouth gaping and sucking, licking and claiming his lips and tongue.

After what seemed like an eternity of kissing bliss, he pulled back. I kept sucking on his bottom lip for a moment as he drew away, before finally, reluctantly, letting it go.

"Would you like to go back to my office?" he breathed, and every part of me was screaming *hell yeah!*

But before we did, there should probably be rules. I didn't want to lose the steamy lust resonating between us, so I used a soft and sultry voice.

"And what are you going to do to me in your office?" I asked, inviting him to tell me every sexy detail.

"What do you want me to do?" he countered. "It's up to you, after all." His gaze was deep and soul-sucking once again. I truly could lose myself in those dark eyes.

So, what did I want?

Everything! Horny me was adamant. *Get him to whip out that side of beef in his pants and fuck our brains out! Oh, but not before he goes down on us. Don't you want to see those dark eyes looking up at you as he sucks on our clit?*

I did, but the other part of me, the side that was off men, didn't want to give too much away on the first date. There had to be a happy compromise.

And there was.

He'd already proven he was good with his fingers after all.

"I want you to kiss me like you're claiming me, then I want to feel your hands everywhere. And I mean *everywhere*. But just your hands. We'll save more for later."

"Agreed," he said, hot and close. Then he rose and swept me into his arms, all in one motion. I yelped with shock and glee before he stopped my mouth with another kiss, even as he carried me out of the lounge and back to his office.

ANAIS

Grey had his lips hard on mine even as he kicked the door closed and set me on his long couch.

I lay with my head on a pillow as our lips crashed together and the full force of his desire slammed into me. God, he was a good kisser, sucking and licking and claiming me, just as I'd asked. He knelt next to the couch, his one hand combing up through my hair. His other hand, which had been under my knees when carrying me, slid up my thigh and over the curves of my hip and waist before seizing a breast.

I gasped into his mouth, his large hand enveloping my ample softness in a hard massage, kneading and pressing. My nipple went rock hard and strained against the fabric of my dress. I moaned and writhed on the couch as he continued his rough manhandling.

Except this wasn't what I'd asked for.

With a groan, I pushed his face away from mine long enough to give him a heated stare and say, "Everywhere!"

God, I hoped he got the point.

He did.

His hand left my breast and slid down over my stomach to my thighs, pressing hard until he came to the hem of my dress. He caught the hem and slowly pushed it up, as his hand slid back up my thigh.

Too slow! Touch me now! My pussy ached, already wet and pulsing with heat. Yet his hand seemed to take forever to push my dress to my hips. Then, he left off with his hard pressing and with a single finger, traced lightly over my thong.

I squirmed and moaned in breathless suspense as that finger drew patterns over my panties before finally slipping down between my legs.

I opened to him, pushing my legs out to give him room to work. His finger traced my pussy over my thong and if my panties hadn't been wet before, they were certainly soaked by the time he was done. God, at the rate I was going through underwear since I'd met these hot-as-hell daemons, I wasn't sure if I'd have enough to get through a week!

Screw panties. Go commando! my horny self shouted.

I wasn't sure I was ready for that... but maybe?

Except then there wouldn't be anything to keep me contained at all.

Perhaps sensing how desperately I wanted to feel his hands on me, Grey looped his finger into my panties, brushing my folds and setting them on fire, then yanked the flimsy fabric down to my knees.

Slowly, torturously slowly, he slid his hand up the inside of my thigh back to my aching core.

My breath was ragged, my need screaming for his

touch, and I squirmed, trying to get him to move faster. But that only made him smile against my lips and slow down.

"Please, Grey," I gasped, my whole world focused down to the fingertips of his one hand and how far away they were from where I wanted them. "Please."

I needed to come, every cell in my body screamed for a release. I trembled, unable to fully catch my breath, the anticipation ramping me higher and higher.

God, how could a man get me so worked up just by running his fingers up my thigh?

But I knew how. Grey was intense and gorgeous, and I couldn't deny his pull on me.

Finally, he reached my folds, sending the shivering promise of an amazing climax rushing over me. With a mewl, I rolled my hips, desperate for more. I was so close, perched on a precipice, aching with the need for completion, for the bone-melting bliss building inside me.

"Not yet," he murmured, as he pulled back from our crushing kiss.

I tried to rise and follow him, not wanting the kiss to end, but his hand in my hair kept me where I was.

"I want to watch you come," he said, a raging fire burning in the depths of his dark eyes.

Oh. Wow.

Well, if the voyeur wanted a show who was I to deny him?

Slowly, I slid my hands over my chest and pulled down the top of my dress, freeing my girls and savoring the hitch in his breath when they fell free. In return, he trailed his fingers through my folds before brushing them over my clit, teasing me.

My eyes rolled back in pleasure and I bucked against his hand even as I rolled my nipples between my thumbs and forefingers. Except I was pretty sure I got more out of it than him, because playing with my tits when he was teasing my clit only increased the building need inside me until it was on the verge of shattering.

He worked me up, higher and higher, his thumb against my clit rubbing rough then soft then rough again while he teased my entrance with his fingers. They dipped and retreated, one at a time, then two, inching deeper and deeper inside me but not enough to fully satisfy me.

Fuck, was this one of his powers?

I didn't know how it related to the hunt. Perhaps it was the hunt to wring the most perfect orgasm from my body. Hell, if I could think straight maybe I'd be able to figure it out.

Then, suddenly, he froze.

No. No no no no.

I grabbed the front of his suit, my eyes flying open, ready to yell at him, and instead fell, breathless and yearning into the deep darkness of his eyes. It was like time was frozen or drawn out, the tension, the need for release, still growing and growing inside me, waiting for him to finally release it.

God, I was so turned on, all he had to do was twitch the right way and I'd come.

The moment stretched out between us and his gaze

raked over my tits and down to where his hand disappeared beneath my skirt then back up to my eyes.

The hunger there had deepened and his breath was quickly picking up.

"You're so beautiful," he said, his voice low and thick with desire.

His words sent a shiver rolling over me, and my hips twitch, the moment wrenching him back into action.

He plunged two fingers inside me, working me up until I was gasping and moaning and shaking, desperate for a release, for that final push, for God! Please!

Then he rubbed down hard on my clit and everything shattered. The world exploded into blinding white light, spinning me around and around and around. My pussy clamp down on his fingers, trying to milk them like a cock, even as he continued to pump them inside me, drawing out the blazing, brilliant bliss.

Oh, yes. Oh God, yes! This was exactly what I needed and so much more.

"Fuck," he grunted as I slowly returned to myself.

Without a doubt, I'd left a puddle on this nice leather couch, but I didn't care. Nor did I care that I was a sweaty, half-dressed mess of a post-orgasmic woman, because when I opened my eyes and looked up at him, all I could see was a bonfire of desire in his dark gaze.

He wanted more. And horny me wanted to give it to him.

But stupid, responsible me was stronger and a good fingering was all I'd permit. At least for myself.

"You want to come?" I purred, squirming on the couch and shaking my tits a little for him.

"Tell me how." His words were clipped. I knew he was desperate for me.

"Got a condom?" I asked, knowing I was sending the wrong message since we weren't going to have intercourse. But given that I didn't have anything else to wear except extra panties, I didn't want to leave work covered in cum.

He raised a brow, but didn't otherwise question my request, and went to his desk, returning with an extra-large Trojan. Yeah, of course, it would be extra-large.

I shifted so I was sitting on the edge of the couch, not bothering to do anything to cover myself. My tits were still on display, pushed up by the taut top of the dress and I kicked off my panties — they weren't much use to me now anyway — and sat with my legs wide, so he could see my pleasured pussy.

"Here," I said, taking the condom from him and tearing open the foil as he began to undo his pants. "Stop," I purred. "I want to do that. I want to feel you."

His gaze came up to mine and I smiled as I reached out to run a hand over his pants, caressing over the bulge of his cock and savoring his shudder of pleasure.

With a groan, he drew his hands back and I undid the button and the zipper of his expensive pants revealing a pair of silk boxers and — God I hope my eyes didn't bulge too much — his massive cock straining to get out.

Slowly, trying to tease him like he'd teased me, I slid his pants down to his knees then pulled the front away from his boxers before shifting them down and licked my lips at the thick length of man-meat that throbbed before me.

Boy was I going to enjoy that... when I was no longer off men, of course. And right now I was still off men. Really.

I rolled the condom over his cock, savoring how hard he was for me, and glanced up at him. His jaw twitched and his eyes were hooded, barely open as he let out a ragged breath.

Yeah, this is payback.

I pulled him close, my hands going around to grasp his tight ass, forcing him to step in between my legs and placing his cock right where I wanted it. Leaning forward, I let out a hot breath over his tip and began stroking him, my mouth watering and my desire starting to pick up again. But sucking him off wasn't what I wanted. I wanted to watch him come, wanted to see him fall apart in my hands, like he'd done with me.

"I know you want to come," I whispered and leaned back, wanting him to see all of me, my exposed tits and my legs spread wide as he gazed down. "Close your eyes and imagine letting loose without this condom on, covering me with your cum."

"Fuck," he grunted.

He was already so close, I could feel it in the trembling of his body, the twitching strain of his flared and heated erection, so, I was surprised when he didn't come right away. Instead, miraculously, he held on, his cock swelling larger still, throbbing in time with the rapid beating of his heart, getting closer and closer to the edge.

I slipped a hand down to cup his heavy balls, feeling their weight and massaging them while my other hand ran to the tip of his cock and squeezed hard before continuing to pump his length in savage strokes.

"Fuck!" he growled. "Fuck fuck fuck fuck."

His hips bucked and every muscle in his body tensed. With a long, loud groan and the most amazing, fierce, and strained expression, his cock pulsed, and hot cum shot into the condom, making the end bulge.

Holy fuck!

And it just kept coming, each spasm pouring more and more into the condom. His balls contracted and tightened as he emptied himself. I knew condoms could hold a lot, but I was beginning to worry he'd overflow this one.

But eventually, his breathing began to slow and his cock started to soften and the condom held it all in.

Wow... just wow.

With a grunt, he took control of himself, grabbing the condom and retreating to his desk to toss it into his garbage with a wet and heavy thud. I did *not* envy the janitor who was going to find that.

"You can't tell me that wasn't fucking hot," I said. I got up and slowly shifted myself back into my dress, but didn't bother with my panties. I'd go commando until I could get to my purse and grab a new pair.

"*You're* fucking hot," he groaned. Then he quirked his head to the side, brow furrowing just a little. "That tattoo you have. Is that a Celtic Rose?"

My tattoo? Oh!

I slid a hand over my dress to the spot low on my abdomen. No one had been meant to see that. I'd gotten it after I'd decided to go off men, so I hadn't had it very long. It was a stylized rose-in-bloom made of criss-crossing red lines, like a Celtic knot. The flower sat over my uterus with a winding stem — in the same Celtic style — delving down toward my lady parts.

I'd had that rose symbol in my head for some time and had thought it would be a great symbol of my metaphorical rebirth. There was no way I was getting my virginity back, but this was a symbolic *refreshing* of my sexuality. The hope had been that — where it was placed, and with me being off men until I knew myself and could find the *right* man — the first man who saw it would be my true love. I still hadn't *found* myself yet, so Grey seeing it was... very premature for my plans.

I didn't know what to say, so I simply said, "Yeah. It's a Celtic Rose."

"It's beautiful and perfect for you," he said, cleaning himself off and putting his pants back on. He couldn't stop staring at me. He spoke in a breathy way, as if in awe. "I've been with various daemons before who had the aspect of sex, love, fertility, or beauty, but none of them compare to you."

Holy fuck, really? That had to be pillow talk. Every man said that to every woman after sex, didn't they?

Still, I felt just a little thrilled by his words. "Yeah, I'm one of a kind," I said with mock arrogance.

"You're exceptional, unparalleled, perfect."

Oh, wow.

And it wasn't just the words. At some point or another, I was sure I'd been called all those things before. No, it was how he said them, so earnest and sincere.

He came to me and clasped my hands in his. "I know

this was supposed to be a game, a show," he murmured, "but I don't see it that way. I've already told you how I feel. Though maybe it's hard for you to understand. Hades! I'm not sure *I* fully understand."

"Oh?" I asked, curious, prompting him to go on. Mostly, I wanted to hear him say more about how wonderful I was.

"My aspect is The Hunt: acquisition and conquest. And mostly what that's meant for me recently is that no matter what I acquire or *whom* I might conquer, it's never enough. I'm left with this hollowness inside me that eats at me, asking for more and more. I've felt less and less—" He gave a harsh laugh. "Less human, less myself, less whole, less of everything as that void swelled inside me. But now with you..." He lifted his gaze and I was falling into his dark depths again. "Ana, you fill that void. Not just part of it, but all of it. You are literally everything I need. I don't know if I can be without you. If I was, I might go mad."

Fuuuuuuuuuuuuuuuck.

No man had ever said anything like *that* to me before.

And I had no clue how to react or what to say.

He grimaced. "Yeah, I know, that's probably more than you wanted to know. I don't know how you'd even respond to that. I understand. You don't need to say anything, I just wanted you to know how much I need you, not just sexually — though that was *amazing* — but all of you, Ana. I'd happily give up all my billions just to be close to you."

And again. *Fuuuuuuuuuuuuuuck.*

I blinked, dumbfounded. "Oh."

He smiled. "Don't worry. You don't have to say anything. Just know that I'm not going anywhere."

I smiled at that. It was truly heartwarming to hear. And for the first time in my entire life, I felt truly seen and appreciated, respected, and actually *loved* by a man. My heart didn't know what to do with it, swelling and pounding and making my eyes well with moisture. A tear broke free and rolled down my cheek, but I quickly wiped it away and pursed my lips to keep from joy-sobbing on him.

"Thank you," I said, my voice choked with appreciation.

He smiled. "Anything for you, Ana. Always remember that. I'll do anything for you."

I didn't have words, so I leaned forward and wrapped my arms around his neck pulling him close, hugging him tight, showing him how he made me feel. And when his arms enfolded me, I felt only warmth and devotion from him.

ANAIS

I FINISHED OUT MY SHIFT FEELING LIKE I WAS GLOWING AND floating on a cloud.

Even after I got home, I was still a little buzzed from that amazing moment with Grey. Grinning like an idiot, I went up to my room and had a long, luxurious shower where I fantasized about Grey's powerful cock slamming into me. The image warmed me more than the shower and made a giddy feeling rise up inside me.

When I finally let the fantasy slip away and opened my eyes, my gaze dipped to the rose tattoo on my abdomen. It was supposed to represent a new me and no one, not even Grey, should have seen it.

Yet.

With a sigh, I got out of the shower and pulled on my PJs. The bottoms were a pair of silk shorts from a set of sexy sleepwear some guy had given me. I loved the way they felt, and I'd have loved to wear the matching top, but it was too loose and didn't contain my girls, so instead, I wore a soft, cotton sports bra to keep them in their place.

When I came out of the bathroom, my gaze instantly jumped to the pile of sex toys I'd used earlier that day. They sat on my bed, a reminder of what I was supposed to have been doing and what I'd done, their presence mocking me. *So much for being off men, Ana? Are we not good enough for you?*

"Sorry, but no," I told them. "As good as you are, you just can't compare with the warmth and attention of a real man who knows what he's doing." A shiver rushed down my spine as I remembered Grey's hard, claiming kisses and his deft fingers.

Yeah, vibrating plastic just couldn't compare.

I couldn't stop grinning as I got into bed and snuggled under the warm sheets, imagining it was Grey wrapped around me, warming me. Of course, then my mind took things another step further and added Fen into the mix, both men holding me close and whispering their devotion to me.

I woke feeling rested and energized and my day only got better when Ramsey called mid-morning to say that he and Freyja would stop by at four that afternoon to have a look at Donny.

Thank God! Even Grey's distraction last night and my dirty thoughts in the shower hadn't completely eased my fears and I'd had no idea how long I'd be able to wait for Freyja. It could have only gotten better if she was showing up this morning and not in the afternoon.

The rest of the morning I spent in anticipation of my lunch with Fen, using that to help push my quarter of a billion dollar worry aside, and I was practically giddy as my cab took the 79th Street transverse through the park and dropped me off about ten minutes early.

The alley I was supposed to walk down to get to the side door was clean, not even a hint of litter in the corners, and I easily made my way to a smiling young lady standing at the restaurant's side entrance.

"Miss Baker?" she asked, and I nodded. "This way, please."

She opened the door and led the way through a storeroom and into a long, plain hall. We walked past two open doors, both leading into a long, shiny kitchen where I caught glimpses of cooks and a few waiters hard at work, before coming to a closed door on the other side of the hall.

"In here, Miss Baker," the young woman said as she opened the door to a cozy private dining room.

At the back sat a private booth: a half-circle with dark leather seats around a small table, and a few feet away was a decorative wooden sideboard where servers could set down their trays before bringing food to the table.

The lighting was low, coming from a gold and crystal chandelier, and the room was painted a deep plum purple with gold accents creating a sense of intimacy.

I stepped into the room and shivered with excitement at what was to come.

"Take a seat and Master Fen will be in in a moment. Would you like to see our wine list?"

I was fairly certain I couldn't afford any wine from a place like this. But I was also fairly certain I wasn't paying for this lunch.

"Yes please, do you have any Lambrusco?" I asked.

One of my previous bad boyfriends had been a chef and introduced me to all sorts of wines. I liked to show off my vintage vocabulary whenever I could. I didn't usually drink — especially not out at clubs — but I sometimes had a little wine with dinner. The trouble was, now that I knew what I liked, it turned out I had expensive tastes.

"We do, do you want sweet or dry?" she asked. She knew what she was doing.

I felt like indulging today. "Sweet."

She nodded and left, and I sat on one side of the booth, settling onto the soft leather cushion, and waited patiently.

A moment later, Fen stormed in, all haste and action, but then stopped dead.

"Oh... wow," he breathed as he slowly took off his chef's apron and set it on a hook to the left side of the door. "Wow," he said again, taking me in.

For today, I'd chosen — what I thought was — my sexiest dress. It was a full-length gown, with slits up the front of both legs, high enough that it certainly looked like I was without underwear. Really, I just wore a high-strap thong, which ran up to the top of my hips. The top of the dress had a plunging V-neck that displayed all my wonderful cleavage, and the flowing, baby-blue, silk dress made me feel like some Grecian goddess.

Fen wore black pants and a black dress shirt and his sun-kissed, fair complexion was flushed. I imagined that heat on his cheeks was from seeing me, not from the heat of the kitchens he'd just come from. His wavy, blond hair was just a bit ruffled and messy, but still somehow looked perfect on him. Then there were those aqua-blue jewels of eyes, devouring me.

I rose to meet him, and he scooped up my hand and kissed my fingers lightly, making butterflies take off in my belly. How very knightly of him.

"I think I forgot to breathe for a moment," he whispered as he kept my hand close to his lips. "You completely stole my breath."

Wow, that got my blood flowing. His words made me blush all the way down to my cleavage.

I'm not sure what inspired me. Maybe it was the mention of breath or looking at those full lips of his, but I raised a finger from the hand he held and slowly traced his mouth. He smiled, a flash of heat in his eyes, then captured that finger in his mouth, sucking on it softly, his tongue flicking the end of it.

The heat that had been slowly simmering just under my skin, tingling all over my body, sizzled and rush down to my core. If he had even so much as brushed one of my arms or stroked my hair in that moment, I'd have blown through yet another pair of panties.

Screw the meal, I wanted this buffet of a man on that table. And from the look in his eyes, he wanted the same.

Then the young woman from earlier came in.

"Oh... ah... sorry. I... brought wine?" She set it on the sideboard and scurried out.

Fen gave my finger another savoring sip, then released it.

"Shall we... eat?" he asked, his gaze blazing hot and hungry and never leaving mine.

My breath hitched and my heart skipped a beat.

Something about how he'd said that made it sound like he really wanted to eat *me*!

But I didn't think I was on the menu just yet.

"Yes," I breathed, and he escorted me back to my seat.

He expertly pulled out the cork on the wine and since Lambrescu was often sparkling, the cork popped with a full and satisfying sound. He poured me half a glass, then poured himself the same amount before sitting.

"I've taken the liberty of preparing several dishes, all you need to tell me is whether you prefer: beef, chicken, pork, lamb, fish, or vegetarian?"

As much as I wanted to be a vegetarian and save those cute farm animals, they were just too tasty. Today, however, I decided to be adventurous. Usually, I didn't much like fish or seafood, but I hoped Fen knew how to prepare it well.

"Fish," I said as he took out his phone and sent off a message.

"I've prepared a twist on a traditional Norse meal for you," he said, excited. "Lutefisk is a mild cod, dried and preserved in birch ash, then reintegrated with a salt crust. I'm serving it with a honey-bacon sauce next to curry-mashed peas and boiled baby potatoes. Since you chose the sweet Lambrusco, it should probably pair well. I hope you enjoy it."

I smiled, not really understanding most of that. "Thank you. So, you cook too? You looked like a construction worker when we first met."

He smiled and let out a breath of a laugh. "Yeah, it's not really what most people expect. But these are my two aspects and my two loves. I love to destroy things, so

I went into demolitions so I could help people do it safely. That way, new things can come out of it. I also love to eat." He hesitated then, as if about to say something, but shook it off. "So, I became a chef. With a longer life like mine, it means I've been able to train with many masters and learn styles of cooking from all over the world."

I could believe it. When I'd checked out this restaurant online, I'd discovered it had tons of awards ranging from Michelin Stars to other acclaims I'd never heard of. Everyone raved about this place for the delicate skill and extreme versatility of the chef.

Our meals were brought so quickly, I had to assume he'd actually made all the different meals he'd offered in advance. I hoped the others found a good home.

I'd heard of lutefisk before, in vague comical reference to Scandinavian culture. I didn't know what to expect but found it delicious. The taste was mild, the texture soft and melting in my mouth. The honey-bacon sauce was divine, one of the most moan-inducing foods I'd ever eaten, and the potatoes were soft and slathered in garlic butter.

The portions of each part of the dish were small, but overall, it was sufficiently filling. When I washed the last of it down with my wine, I smiled at Fen.

"That was amazing! I'm not usually a fan of fish, but wow!"

"I'm glad you liked it."

"I can't wait to see what's for dessert," I said with just a hint of sassy innuendo.

"Oh, didn't I mention it?" His smile was almost

wolfish and his voice turned low and heated. "*You're* for dessert."

Aaaand... there goes another pair of panties.

Heat surged through me, crashing into my core so hard I was trembling with the effort to keep my legs tight and restrain my arousal.

Fen shuddered, molten desire in his eyes. The heat in the small room had gone from pleasant to sauna in a heartbeat.

I guessed that was my aspect in action, even though I'd been using some of the breathing and thought-focusing exercises Harmonia had taught me to keep my power in check.

That was all out the window now and I couldn't have cared less.

Then Fen let out an inhuman growl and a wild feralness somehow rolled off him as if he were more beast than human, scaring me and dousing my desire.

What the hell was that?

"Fen?" I whispered.

He jerked back and sucked in long deep breaths to steady himself.

"Your ah... Your power..." The muscles in his throat flexed as he struggled to get the words out.

Shit. I tried to rein it in again, breathing and concentrating on pushing my sexiness back down into my lady parts where it belonged, not floating around the room making others want to fuck like bunnies.

Come on. You can do this, I told myself, straining to get my power back under control, but this was the first time I'd tried to pull it back while I was completely turned on.

Heat billowed from my tingling flesh and another low growl rumbled in Fen's chest.

Just pull it back. Just a little bit.

I squeezed my eyes shut, drawing all my attention inward and dragging that sexiness deep under my skin and into my core.

The room cooled, not much, but enough for Fen to release a heavy breath.

"Thank you," he said and I opened my eyes to see him back to his usual far-too-sexy self. "I see you're starting to get control over your aspect. I hardly noticed it when you arrived, and it seems better again now."

"Yeah, sorry," I said a bit sheepishly. "Your 'I'm for dessert' thing, got me all worked up and I lost control for a moment."

"I'd love for you to lose control again," he said, his aqua-blue eyes no longer seeming cool at all but simmering with intense heat. "Some time when we're both wearing a lot less."

Hell yeah! I could get behind that.

Does this mean we're no longer off men? my horny self asked.

No, we're still off men. But I get a few get-off men, remember? I was off men last night, but Grey still got his hand up my skirt. I wasn't sure what I was trying to prove with that statement, but it definitely confused my horny self. *Maybe I'm just off dicks.*

Something about that rang true and I liked that thought. It had a solid dual meaning: no penises — for now, at least — and no men who were jerks.

"And when would you like to wear less... with me?" I

asked, leaning over the table, squeezing the sides of my arms against my boobs, pushing them together as I drew a deep breath and thrust them out.

"Now," he breathed. "I wasn't really joking about wanting you for dessert."

And the room got a lot warmer once again.

ANAIS

"Does that door lock?" I asked, looking at the entrance to the private dining room.

Finn grimaced. "No."

"Your place or mine?" Though as soon as I said it, I hoped he didn't choose mine. Reia was at school, but Donny would be rambling around.

He pursed his lips. "My place in the city is being renovated, and my castle in Yonkers is a half-hour away in good traffic." Right. Yeah. *Good traffic* in New York was a mythical creature.

Also, did he just say *castle*?

Fine then. "My place is closer, as long as you don't mind my wacky uncle puttering around."

Hopefully my uncle stayed in his room and didn't notice any sounds we might make.

"I don't mind," he said. "And this way we'll be there when Freyja shows up."

Wait. What?

"You know about that?" How did he know about her visit? I doubted Ramsey would have said anything.

"She's my sort-of grandmother, so, yeah," he said, extending a hand to me and leading me out of the private dining room and into the hall.

"Why 'sort-of'?" I'd heard that explanation too many times not to be curious.

"She and Odin raised Loki, my father, but they're not his biological parents."

"Your father is Loki?" Only then did the invitation he'd sent come back to me: *Fenris Lokisen*. "Like, wants to kill the Avengers, that Loki?"

Fen laughed. "Tom Hiddleston is a lot better looking. For that matter, Chris Hemsworth is a lot better looking than the real Thor too. But yeah. It was a complicated childhood. My sister is Hel, and my brother is a serpent the size of Queens. I also have two half-brothers, but... yeah, you get the point."

And here I'd thought I was just starting to get used to this daemon thing, but nope. Not even close.

"Wow," I breathed.

"Yeah, I know."

He quickly led me through the building, instead of heading to the side door, he took me to an underground parking garage, and a parked sleek Porsche 918 Spyder. Having spent most of my life around guys — most of whom loved cars — I'd gotten to know a few, and this one was a beast.

We got in, Fen revved the engine and then we were zipping through the city heading to my place.

"I don't think I said it out loud," Fen said with a side

glance at me, while expertly navigating the traffic. "But you're stunning in that dress. You may only be a daemon, but you look like a goddess."

My face heated and my blush rushed all the way down my chest and arms. "Thank you but I'm sure there are a lot of goddesses who— There has to be some goddess of beauty that looks better than me."

"Nope. And you'll meet one this afternoon. Freyja is a goddess of beauty. But I've met Aphrodite, Hathor, Lakshmi, Oshun, Lada, and Venus. None of them could hold a candle to you," he said, his words ringing with truth.

I didn't know how, but I *knew* he wasn't just being nice or paying lip service. He actually believed what he was saying.

Well, of the three guys who were "protecting" me, Fen had just shot to the top of my list. Grey was amazing and a close second after his ministrations last night, and Ramsey was a distant third despite having the idea to find Freyja. He was too much of a dick, and my new motto was: *no more dicks*.

But dicks made me think of Fen and how he thought I was beautiful and how hot I was for him, and by the time we got to my place, I was starting to fall apart with heated need for Fen.

"You're losing control again, aren't you?" he asked, through clenched teeth. "Talk to me."

I raised a brow at that request. "Talk to you?"

Yet even those words seemed to help soothe him. Curious.

"I'll explain in a moment," he said as we hurried inside and up to my room.

Once safely there with the door closed behind us, he pounced on me like a hunting cat, lips finding mine, hungry and hot.

I opened to him as he pressed himself to me and I felt the rigid length of his cock press against my belly.

Oh yes.

Oh no! No dicks, remember?

He slid the shoulder of my dress down my arm exposing my breast and raked his fingers over my hyper-sensitive flesh right to the already stiffened peak of my nipple, heating up my desire. Then he kissed his way down to that bud and plucked at it with his lips, shooting blissful sensations straight to my core, before dazzling my puckered flesh with some amazing tongue work.

"Yes," I breathed, talking to him like he'd asked because there was no way in hell I was going to remember to control my power. "I want you, Fen. I... we can't... ohhhh!"

He slid his other hand inside my dress and kneaded my other breast, adding fuel to my desire while still sucking and licking my nipple.

Oh God, yes.

I'd been about to say we can't go all the way or some such thing, but I was quickly forgetting all the rules. His touch felt so good and I craved more of it. All of it. Everywhere. Now now now.

To my disappointment, he released my breasts a moment later and nuzzled between my cleavage before straightening and capturing my gaze with his.

"I really want to continue this," he groaned. "But there's something you should know first. Can you restrain your aspect for just a moment?"

My mind stuttered at the sudden change, going from hot and heavy to needing to pull it all back. I wasn't sure if I could do it, but I pushed him away, sat on the edge of my bed, squeezed my eyes shut, and concentrated on my breathing and bringing my aspect back into me.

The heat billowed and shuddered inside me, radiating from my skin in great waves while every part of my body tingled with need.

I sucked in a long slow breath and released it. Then repeated that process.

In.

Out.

Slow and steady.

But it was just so hard to concentrate with my nipples hard and aching, my body on fire, yearning to be filled, and—

I opened my eyes. Closing them wasn't helping, it was just making me hyperaware of how I felt.

But opening my eyes was a mistake and I fell into Fen's aqua-blue gaze, captured by the ravenous need I saw there.

Shit. Focus.

I mentally wrenched at my power, pulling it inside me, pulling everything inside me.

Second by second, more and more power seeped under my skin and sank deep into my core. Except there was so much swirling passion in the room that when I finally felt the air cool around me, I was a squirming, panting, desperate mess. My pussy throbbed with wet need and my clit was so ragingly sensitive that the brush of my panties was nearly making me come.

I clenched my teeth and nodded to him.

He ran his hands through his blond hair then paced my bedroom like a caged animal.

"I'll make this quick. I can see how hard this is for you," he said. "But you should know that I'm a world-ending daemon. I have a beast within me, a terrible, hungry wolf meant to devour the world someday. I—" He swallowed hard and the muscles in his jaw flexed as he struggled to hold himself together. "I need to be careful so I don't lose control and let out the beast."

A shiver of fear raced down my spine. He was so powerful he could end the world if he lost control. And as I'd seen earlier, my power could make him lose control.

Holy fuck!

"I've spent years subduing my wolf, controlling it, but when I'm around you, your power weakens my resolve, makes me want to lose control." He offered me a wry smile. "Admittedly I want to lose control in a different way, and that may be all well and good, or it might not."

Damn. Did this mean we couldn't have sex? Because I *really* needed sex. But I also needed to not end the world.

"I know this much," he added. "Your voice calms my beast. Just hearing you say anything turns the snarling, wild wolf into a playful puppy. So... I want to do this, but you may need to be vocal. Very vocal."

Okay. I could do vocal. I was great at vocal so long as I wasn't trying to keep a thousand pounds of desire locked within my body.

Also... Damn!

I had a real-life wolf-man in my bedroom and I'd read enough shifter romance novels to let my imagination run just a little wild with that.

"Yeah, I'll make sure to say all the words," I said, rising and pushing my dress off. "Also, I'm taking it slow with men these days. So, your cock isn't getting any pussy today."

I pulled off my very wet thong, knowing my actions were not matching my words, but I didn't care.

He whipped off his shirt, revealing a muscular chest, sculpted shoulders, thick arms, and abs for miles. I was sure my eyes bulged out of my head because he flashed me a wicked grin and slid off his pants and boxers. His cock sprang free, standing at attention, more than ready to go and shocking the hell out of me. Both Grey and Ramsey had more bulk than he did but his cock was enormous, bestial.

I knelt before him. "I wanted to do this in the car after you told me no goddess could hold a candle to me, but that wasn't possible with you shifting gears."

I slid a hand down his shaft, seizing it, then licked his tip and slid it into my mouth. With a groan, I pushed him in deep, opening my throat so I could press my lips to his base before withdrawing fully, sucking slightly to pop off his tip.

"If you're going to eat me for dessert, then I'm going to eat you too," I said, my voice husky, desire rolling from my skin like a heatwave.

He growled, but it was different from before. Softer, contented, expectant, not dangerous, but still super sexy.

"As long as you keep talking. Though I don't know how— ohhhh!" He threw his head back, eyes rolling as I latched onto him and sucked hard.

I flicked my tongue over his tip, tasting his pre-cum, before slowly popping off again.

"I love how you taste," I said, needing to keep up my running commentary. Then I plunged back down on him, taking him deep once more, feeling the tight squeeze of his length in my throat.

"Fuck!" he snarled, and I pulled back as fast as I could.

"Are you okay?" I wasn't sure what I'd done wrong, but whatever it was, I'd stop it so he didn't, you know, end the world.

"How did...?" he breathed, his pupils fully blown with lust, his breath short and sharp. "So deep!"

So I didn't do something wrong? Good. Great. Fantastic because I didn't want to stop.

"I'm a sex daemon. I'm made for this." Then I plunged back onto his length, savoring the shudder that rolled up his body and knocked his head back in pleasure.

His hips rocked forward, his body begging for me, so I obliged him, keeping him deep and swallowing, contracting my throat around him, once, twice, three times.

"Ana," he groaned, and he grabbed a fistful of my hair and took control unable to hold back any longer.

He bucked his hips forward, thrusting deeper, then jerked back and thrust again, fucking my mouth with a ferocity that I knew was barely a fraction of his strength. If he wanted, he could have seriously hurt me, but he didn't, staying just on the safe side of wild and driving my own need higher and higher.

Watching him lose control was the sexiest fucking thing I'd ever seen and I couldn't wait to see his face when he came.

With a gasp, I pushed back — which wasn't easy with his grip in my hair and cock as far down my throat as it could be — and pulled away just enough to speak.

"I think we've waited long enough," I said before flicking my tongue over his tip. "I think it's time to suck all the cream filling out of my sweet dessert."

I latched onto him again, pulling a drawn-out "fuck" from his lips.

His rough voice made more moisture leak onto my thighs and I throbbed with anticipation.

I swirled my tongue around his swollen and flared head and brought a hand up to add the pressure I couldn't with my mouth. But the finishing touch was something extra special. I'd had the idea after I'd been able to pull all of my aspect into my core.

If I could send it there, could I send it... anywhere?

I pulled my aspect up from my aching pussy and let it loose through my mouth and focused it all on Fen's cock.

As expected, he couldn't resist that.

He let out a feral roar as he came, heated streams of custard-sweet and salty cum blasting into my mouth. I swallowed but could barely keep up with him and his cum leaked from my mouth and trailed over my chin.

With a groan, he grabbed my hair again and I let my hands fall away giving him complete control to ride out his orgasm. He drove himself deep into my throat again and again in quick thrusts that didn't give me a chance to breathe before finally easing up.

I gasped around him as his release continued, rushing hot and sweet over my tongue, eagerly swallowing it down.

After Grey's near-to-bursting condom last night and Fen's amazing potency today, I was getting the feeling that daemons were extremely virile.

With a final low groan, his breath fast and panting, he finally finished. I cleaned him off with my tongue and swallowed the last of his salty-sweetness, my heart satisfied that I could make him come like that, while the rest of me still ached for release.

"That was delicious," I said, wiping my lips and giving him my sexiest grin.

"Fuck me," he gasped. "That was... That was... Wow. Just wow."

I rose and pressed close to him, letting my heavy breasts press against his chest as I brought my lips to his ear and whispered, "Now, it's your turn for dessert."

I stepped back, leaving him there stunned and I went to my bed where I laid back and opened my legs.

"Devour me, my wolf!" I breathed.

ANAIS

A HUNGRY, FERAL GRIN SPREAD ON FEN'S BEAUTIFUL FACE as he knelt next to my bed. With a low satisfied moan, he pushed his face into my curls and took a long sniff.

Desire shivered through me even though the sniffing was really odd. It was probably a wolf thing. Then his hot, rough tongue lashed out and flicked over my folds, and I cried out.

Oh, yes. No waiting. Which was good because I was more than ready. I was desperate.

His mouth was big, enveloping all of me as he pressed the flat of his tongue to my folds and took another long, drawn-out swipe sending heat and sensation shooting through my core.

My hips arched up, silently begging for more as I pushed my head back into the bed and clutched the sheets, ready for this ride.

But instead of continuing he pulled away... and just stopped.

What the what?

I jerked my head up to see him staring at the tattoo low on my abdomen. Disappointment creeped into my desire at him stopping along with yet another man seeing my tattoo. I really wasn't doing well with my: *the-first-guy-who-sees-this-is-my-true-love* thing.

"It's beautiful," Fen rumbled, his hot breath teasing my clit and making me squirm.

"Less talking. More eating," I demanded.

He smiled up at me, those gorgeous aqua-blue eyes shifting from curious to heated, then he dipped down and latched onto my clit, sucking hard, lapping with his tongue, and yeah... those suction-based sex toys had nothing on him!

I reached down to rake my fingers through his thick blond hair, like he'd done with me when I'd been blowing him, pressing him close as I moaned. And since I was supposed to be talking...

"Suck my clit, you dirty dog!" I whined. "Oh, yeah! You're going to make me come, just a little more!"

He obliged, raking his teeth over me.

Oh! Wow! Yeah, that worked! I felt a spike of bliss, trembling on the edge of a massive orgasm. Then his mouth opened wider still and his tongue was somehow pressing on my clit while also slipping down and flicking into my folds. The naughty boy had a miracle tongue.

And that miracle tongue began a savage licking, back and forth over my clit while darting inside me building my desire higher and higher.

My insides tightened, trembling on the verge of a release, making me gasp and moan and beg for more. I bucked into him, my breath ragged, my head spinning and the need inside me racing like hot lava through my veins.

Then every nerve inside me ignited as I crashed into ecstasy.

"I'm coming!" I screamed as if he'd needed me to tell him. Which was ridiculous since I was pretty sure I was gushing like a fountain, and he was lapping it up.

Then his tongue shifted, leaving off my clit to dive deeper into me, flicking up to dazzle my G-spot, and the fountain became a waterfall.

I tried to find my voice, to keep on talking and tell him just how amazing he was making me feel, but my mind was spinning, my body captured in bliss and my mouth locked in a silent scream.

My hands pulled him closer, nails digging in, and somehow I managed to bundle up all the sexy power bursting from me and shoved it down into my pussy, ratcheting my bliss to earth-shattering levels.

Fen moaned as my orgasm redoubled its intensity.

Oh, God!

It was amazing. I couldn't stop coming into his mouth, my body, my nerves, my everything locked so hard I was sure I'd break.

Then I sensed something else, something savage building around me, filling the room. Fen's teeth raking over me grew sharper and his tongue rougher.

Fuck. My power wasn't just pouring into my clit, it was racing over Fen's tongue and down his throat.

And it was shattering his control.

I looked down in a fog of orgasmic bliss to see him...

shimmering, part man, part wolf, and Holy crap-balls, that wolf looked ravenous.

"Fen!" I gasped, somehow finding enough breath to speak. "Fen, holy fuck. I— I need you, Fen. Fen!" *Please.*

I had no idea how to bring him back to himself and could only pray that saying his name would bring the human Fen back.

"Fen!"

He stared at me, his eyes strange, his expression unreadable in its mutated state. Then the wolf gave a contented growl and faded away, leaving a panting, gasping, stunned Fen.

He sat back, blinking, and his eyes cleared, fully back to himself.

I breathed a sigh of relief and took him in. He looked fine. God, he looked more than fine. He was hot. His mouth was wet, chin dripping with my juices, and his hair was mussed from where I'd dug my fingers in, reminding me that no man had ever made me come that hard from oral sex.

Holy smokes! Fen was the champion, the best of the best.

"Wow!" I gasped, throwing my head back into the mattress as my body slowly untensed and came down from that uber-high. "Fucking. Wow! That was amazing!" I gulped in a bit more air. "If you ever want to give up construction and cooking and take up full-time pussy-eating, I'd hire you in an instant. The pay is crap, but the benefits are... self-evident."

He barked a laugh. "That was the best dessert ever.

Your pussy is so sweet and juicy." He licked his lips as he rose.

His cock was throbbing and hard once again, and standing there, he was the picture of a virile Norse God: all blond, with bunching muscles and that amazing cock.

Sorry, Hemsworth, you've been replaced. And for just an instant, I wanted to feel that god-cock plunging into me like his tongue had been.

From the way he was eyeing my sweat-slicked body and glistening folds, I knew he wanted it too. But somehow I found some measure of resolve and stuck to the rules.

"Shower?" I offered. A sexy shower might help him get off.

He grinned. "Yeah."

"Carry me in," I begged, squirming on the bed. "That orgasm was quite the workout for me. Or should I say, those orgasms? It felt like three all in one, each more powerful than the last."

He gave a contented, *yeah-that-was-me* chuckle and bent to lift me — so very easily — into his arms. He carried me toward the bathroom, stopping just outside the door and shifting slightly.

"Is that a pile of sex toys?" he asked, voice just a little heated.

Fuck! I hadn't hidden those away yet. I'd forgotten about them entirely.

He must have felt me go cold and stiff. "Oh, no, don't get me wrong. I think it's sexy, a woman taking control of her pleasure like that."

"Really?"

"Hel, yeah!"

And that gave me an idea. "Wanna watch me pleasure myself?"

His gaze met mine, an inferno behind those perfect blue eyes. "Hel, yeah," he whispered, low and breathy.

And suddenly I was so very glad I'd left those toys out.

"Put me down," I said, and he did.

I could stand, though I was a little shaky, and I hurried over to the pile, but then stopped, turning back to him. "Did you want to pick what I use?"

His mouth curled into a grin as his cock gave a very noticeable twitch. He came over and knelt, quickly perusing the pile before picking up a purple vibrator. It was an insertion kind, one I hadn't tried yet, looking like a massive dick, but with soft S-curves in it. Once inserted and turned on, it not only vibrated but undulated around and around, pushing against all of you.

He moved it beside his cock, comparing them. His cock wasn't all bent out of shape, but only then did I realize his cock was a match for that massive dildo. They were roughly the same length and girth. Holy fuck.

My pussy was drooling thinking of either of those inside of me.

"It's even waterproof... and it comes with a remote," he said, smiling. It wasn't so much a remote as a controller on a long cord attached to the end of it, but the result was the same, he'd be able to control it. "You pick one too," he whispered. "Use both."

Oh, that would be interesting indeed. I picked up a set of two small vibrators that looked like padded binder clips. I hadn't tried these either and by the look in Fen's eyes, I'd picked the right ones.

"Are those...?" he asked, his voice a delicious rumble.

"Nipple clips, yup." I licked my lips. "And they're also shower friendly and have a remote." This one was wireless with a single button, very easy to use.

We hurried into the bathroom, and I turned on the shower. Luckily, my shower was large and even included a tiled bench. I sat while Fen stood over me, cock in his hands, stroking it softly while I played with the toys. I was very well lubed after that amazing mouth-pounding he'd given me, so I hoped the oddly-shaped toy would slip in easily.

Fen watched me start to insert it, but then hissed, "Let me."

He got to his knees as I handed over the vibrator. He ran a finger around my folds first, making me shiver, then began to slip that silicone wonder into me. I moaned, feeling the curves slip through my channel until it was all the way in.

"Fuck, yeah," I breathed. It felt odd inside me, with all those strange curves, but still very filling and so incredibly deep. And it wasn't even turned on yet!

"Let me put the others on as well," Fen said and I handed over the clips.

He leaned in and pressed his large mouth to each breast first, sucking and licking until my already aroused nipples were hard as diamonds before he carefully clipped on the toys. The padding was soft and gentle on such sensitive areas, but held firm, keeping a constant, exquisite pressure.

Then he stood and smiled down at me. "Ready?"

Hell, yes! "Go."

He flicked the switch on the dildo first, pushing it to max, and it leaped to life inside me, squirming and buzzing so hard, I nearly came. I'd gone from pleasantly post-orgasm aroused to last-stop-before-blissville in an instant. I moan-cried as my body tensed and trembled.

"Holy...ohhhhh... Fuck!" I was screaming. I didn't care.

He dropped the controller and it fell somewhere down between my legs. There would be no turning it off quickly now.

"Fuuuuuuuuuck!" I shouted, not sure whether I was pissed at that or uber-turned-on.

Then he hit the button on the other remote and I was slammed back into the wall with an uber-orgasm as my tits exploded with shockingly wonderful sensations.

He tossed that remote away as well and I moaned, eyes rolling back in my head. This wasn't going to stop.

"You're so fucking sexy," he hissed as he resumed his vigorous cock-rubbing.

I was barely aware, too buzzed — literally — to think, but I wanted to watch him watch me. I needed to see what I was doing to him, see his proud arousal and powerful release.

And wow, was he gorgeous: tall and trembling, those taut muscles twitching as he beat himself like a drum. His half-lidded eyes watched as my toys tweaked me toward yet another orgasm. I twitched and moaned and screamed and writhed, and it wasn't even an act.

He stepped close and — whether intentional or not

— his knee knocked the dildo, tapping it just a bit, making sure it was all the way in. I shuddered and came so hard, I pushed the dildo right out of me. It shot across the shower, bouncing and twisting on the floor.

Apparently, that was just too much for Fen. He grunted and long streams of cum shot out onto my breasts and belly, quickly washed away by the hot waters of the streaming shower.

Most guys I'd known weren't as potent their second time around, but again, it seemed daemons were in a league of their own. Fen had more than enough cum to impregnate a small army.

When he was done, he reached down and grabbed me, pulling me off the seat to hold close, pressing the still vibrating toys on my nipples hard against both of us. His lips were hot on mine, his hunger intense as he pressed me against the wall and devoured my lips. Then he moved to my cheek, neck, shoulder, covering me with steamy, intense kisses.

And yeah, all that hot manliness pressed up against me with those toys going to town? That was soooo very stimulating.

I came again, a quivering mess that wouldn't have been able to stand on my own without him there to keep me up.

When our heat had finally diminished — and I'd carefully removed the clips — he washed me, reverently, cleaning us both up.

"Oh, hey Ana, do you know where I put my... ahh... something?" Uncle Donny's voice came from the other side of my bathroom door.

Fen and I jumped and turned to see the old man opening the door to poke his head in, looking around, luckily ignoring the hot, naked people.

"It's in *your* bathroom!" I shouted, not having any clue what he was looking for, just wanting him out.

"Oh, yeah, probably." He nodded and left.

"Next time you need to remind me to lock my door," I said, playfully slapping Fen.

He kissed me, then whispered. "Done. And next time, if you're ready for it, you can have... all of me." One of his hands slid down my belly to my folds, letting me know exactly where he'd put... all of himself. "And you'll see that that toy is nothing compared to me."

And suddenly... I couldn't wait for next time.

What about being off dicks? my horny self quipped.

Fuck! Right! Oh, screw it. I want Fen's dick.

You want all the dicks. You know you do.

My horny self was right, I did.

Fine! You win!

We'll both win, my horny self purred.

Yup, she was right. I couldn't dispute that.

ANAIS

FEN AND I HAD CLEANED UP AND DRESSED BY THE TIME Freyja, Ramsey, and Grey — which was a surprise — arrived. Fen was back in his black shirt and pants and I was in jeans and a T-shirt, comfortable, and ready to find out what strange and wonderful things were hidden in Uncle Don's brain. I'd also spent a little time working to contain my aspect so Freyja and the others wouldn't be distracted by extreme arousal.

My daughter, Reia, was home from school by then, but she was up in her room doing homework and hope-fully wouldn't interrupt us.

I didn't know why I expected Freyja to be old and wizened. I think because everyone called her "Fen's sort-of grandmother," and grandmothers looked old. Then I recalled Fen saying she was a goddess of beauty and it made sense why Fen's sort-of grandmother looked like a blond bombshell.

She wore a white, button-up blouse and tartan skirt

cut to just below the knee, rocking the catholic schoolgirl look. But she was no *girl*. She was all *woman*.

Imagine Dolly Parton in her twenties, looking completely natural and fresh. The only thing I had on her was height, being half a foot taller. But somehow, being short only made her seem even more buxom and beautiful. We probably had the same cup size, but while mine looked full and round and perky, on her smaller frame, hers looked huge!

Helloooo Grandma!

Wow.

I wasn't into women, but when she smiled at me, even *I* wanted to jump her bones. She was that hot!

And Fen still liked me better. Well, I wasn't related to him, which probably helped though she was only his *sort-of* grandmother. Still...

"Where's the man you want me to read?" she asked sedately, her voice a mellow alto and smooth as silk.

"Ah..." I blinked trying to focus on her words and not how drop-dead gorgeous she was. "Right. Yes. Sorry. One moment." Then I bellowed up the stairs in a very unlady-like fashion, "Donny!"

"Coming!" I heard his distant voice.

I had to call him two more times before he finally came down, probably losing track of where he was going not long after setting out.

"Ah, yes? Ana? Oh, we have guests? Lovely... do I know any of you?"

"No, Donny. These are my friends. They're here to help us with something. Can you come and take a seat in your favorite chair here?" I patted the back of the recliner to remind him it was indeed his favorite chair.

He beamed and nodded, all innocence and bliss. Once he was sitting, I turn to Freyja. "Do you need anything?"

"Just for him to remain still while I work and" — she gave Ramsey some side-eye — "perhaps some knowledge of what exactly I'm looking for. Ramsey was vague. Something about money?"

I nodded. "Yes, twenty years ago, my uncle hid away some money for a mobster named Tommy Two-Toes. It was fifty million at the time, but now it's probably worth five times that. We need to find out where the money is located so we can get it back to said mobster, so he doesn't kill me or my uncle."

Freyja nodded serenely, perfectly poised. "Yes, of course, thank you." She smiled warmly at me. "We'll get this all sorted out for you."

"Chocolate Cosmos!" Donny added, not so helpfully.

Freyja went to stand behind the beat-up old La-Z-Boy chair, putting her hands to either side of Donny's head while I crouched in front of Donny, taking his hands and keeping eye contact with him.

Freyja had asked for him to remain still but that wasn't easy for Donny. He'd forget why he was here in just a moment and try to get up, which meant I had to make sure he stayed where he was. The three guys stood around us, close enough that I felt supported but not crowded.

Freyja began to hum to herself, eyes closed, head tilted slightly. "Oh, yes, there's quite a bit of confusion in here. The dementia has grown deep roots." She blinked her eyes open. "Did you just want the information, or would you like me to remove the dementia as well?"

I stared at her. "You can do that? Just... poof make his mind better?"

She smiled and nodded. "I have many powers. Yes, I can clear his mind again, if that's what you wish."

It was. But it wasn't really my call.

Maybe Donny liked being this way? I didn't think so, but I should ask.

"Uncle?"

"What? Yes?" His eyes were gleaming as he smiled at me.

"Would you like to be able to remember things again?"

"Remember?' He blinked. "I... don't remember... much..."

"Would you like to remember?" I tried again.

"Ah... yes? I think so?"

I nodded to Freyja. "Yes, please."

"This will take a little time, keep him as still as possible. If removing all the fog in here doesn't help him remember where this money is I can do a deeper dive."

I nodded, and Freyja went back to work.

The clock on the wall ticked by the seconds, seeming loud and obnoxious as time passed.

"Mom?" Reia said, coming down around five-thirty for supper. "What's all this?"

I looked at Fen. I didn't know why he was my go-to guy now, but he was sweet and sexy and wonderful. He hadn't professed the depths of his love for me like Grey had, but he'd told me I was prettier than any other goddess. That meant a lot.

He nodded and knelt in my place. Which was good because Donny was getting very fidgety. I didn't know if it was the work Freyja was doing or just sitting for this long, but it was taking more and more work to keep him in the chair.

I rose and went to Reia.

"Sorry, dinner won't be ready for a while. I can give you some money and you can go out and grab something for yourself if you like."

She stared at me with an odd look in her eyes. "You're...?" She looked around me at Donny, Freyja, and the guys. "What's all this?" she whispered, perhaps sensing the reverence of this moment.

At some point, I was going to have to tell her that her mother was a demon and so were all these others, but not now. All I said was, "We're doing something to help Uncle Donny with his memory. I know it looks strange, but please don't interrupt."

Her brow furrowed. "You're being way too serious, Mom," she said in her I'm-worried-for-you tone. But instead of asking more questions, she nodded her acceptance. "I've got lots of money in my allowance account, I'll order a few pizzas and take care of everything. You just do what you're doing and there will be food here for you and your friends when you're done."

And yet again, my daughter was being the parent in this relationship. But I was too preoccupied with Donny to worry about that.

"Thanks, dear." I kissed her forehead, and she pulled

out her phone and went out the front door to leave us in peace.

Twenty minutes passed and Reia came in with three large boxes of pizza and one tiny one. She took the tiny one and went upstairs, leaving the rest in the front room. I nodded my thanks to her then returned to Donny. He had his eyes glued shut, grunting and groaning as if this process was painful for him.

I didn't want to ask Freyja if it actually was painful because she looked to be concentrating intently on her work, to the point of almost being pained herself.

Everyone was tense.

Then Freyja let out a long and heavy sigh and stepped back, hands falling away from Donny. "It's done."

Donny opened his eyes and looked at me. "Anais?" He blinked, looking around as if everything was new. "Ohh-hh," he breathed softly. "I can... remember." He looked down at me with a giddy grin and repeated, "I can remember!"

"Great!" I said, truly happy for him. Except there was also an urgent matter which needed addressing which meant celebrating had to wait. "Can you remember where you hid the fifty million for Tommy Two-Toes? He's come collecting."

"Tommy...? He's not due to get out for another half-dozen years or so. Although..." He looked at me intently. "What year is it?"

I told him.

He blinked in surprise. "Jiminy Cricket! I've lost so much time!" But he quickly regained control of himself, like the Donny I'd known as a kid. "Well then, yes.

Tommy's money is safe. I registered it under a shell company called Chocolate Cosmos."

"Oh!" I breathed, remembering all the times he'd spouted that odd phrase. "So, you *were* trying to help!" Then... "What in hell is a Chocolate Cosmo? Is that some old-timey drink?"

He laughed. "Not Cosmo, Cosmos, it's a type of flower that smells roughly like chocolate."

"Oh."

"The account is set up at the Premier Bank of Commerce," he continued. "Here in town and—"

"Fuck!" Ramsey's curse was so loud we all looked at him. Except from everyone's expression, it was clear Grey and Fen knew the reason the other man was cursing.

"That's not good," Ramsey said, looking from me to Donny.

Donny only then noticed the three large men in the room and frowned. "Who are you?" he asked.

I bit back a sigh. That was going to take a lot of explaining, but then it seemed Ramsey had something to explain as well.

Perhaps it was time we all talked openly.

ANAIS

WE WERE ALL HUNGRY, SO FOOD CAME FIRST. REIA HAD covered all the bases with the three extra-large pizzas she'd ordered: one meat lovers, one vegetarian, and one plain cheese. Donny and I didn't care which we had. Grey and Freyja didn't eat meat though. Ramsey and Fen loved meat. So, the division worked well between us.

After we ate, Freyja left. She wasn't a part of this. I thanked her thoroughly. There was no way to repay her for what she'd done for Donny.

Donny retrieved his little laptop and furiously typed away, while the rest of us waited, sitting or standing around the small kitchen.

Things were just a little too quiet, so I thought I'd start the conversation off with something easy. "Freyja seems nice."

"She was working," Fen said with a grimace and a sigh.

"Working?" I wasn't sure what he meant. "Is she not nice when she's not working?"

Ramsey answered. "Sometimes." He gave a breath of a laugh. "She has a bit of a bad-girl streak in her. It's not that she's not nice, more that she's got absolutely no inhibitions."

"If there was a goddess of infidelity, it would be her," Grey added as he paced the length of the room.

"Heh! Yeah, well put," Ramsey said with a smile that said all too much.

"Wait, you've slept with Fen's grandmother?" I asked Ramsey, a bit disgusted.

"Sort-of grandmother," all three of them said at exactly the same time, in the same tone.

Fuck me! "Have you *all* slept with her?"

Grey stopped pacing, seeming to realize he might be in trouble. "Ah... to be fair, it was hundreds of years before you were born."

And Fen... Fen was actually blushing!

I was about to yell "she's your grandmother" at him, but then remembered, she wasn't, not by blood. "Just... fucking wow. Really?" I mean, she was hot, yeah, but... "Is she that good in bed?"

Fen looked at me earnestly. "Nothing compared with you." His tone was level and honest, even a little heated. That made me shiver all the way down to my toes, heat pulsing with every beat of my heart and dripping down to settle warm and wet in my core.

"Oh," I breathed.

Grey and Ramsey both stopped to stare daggers at Fen.

"Did you fuck her?" Ramsey growled. "No fucking

allowed, no nothing. Those were Harmonia's rules. We couldn't do anything unless—"

"I asked for it," I finished. "And I did."

"Oh..." Ramsey fumed.

Grey's dark eyes were stormy. I figured I should defuse this now.

"First, remember, this was all your plan, not mine. Second, I've got some rules of my own that I'm following, too." Okay, so maybe my "no dicks" policy was on the verge of collapsing, but still! "And finally. I haven't *chosen* anyone yet. Grey got to show me how he felt last night, Fen this afternoon, and you" — I turned my gaze to Ramsey — "you get me tonight. Only once I have all the information will I make a decision, and that's assuming I even *want* to make a decision. You three are supposed to be fighting over me after all. Maybe I'll keep making you fight until I make up my mind."

"If it were a real fight, I'd win," Ramsey muttered.

I sighed. These three daemon princes were filling this small room to overflowing with swaggering bravado and macho ego. It was almost stifling in here.

Perhaps a change of topic was in order.

"So, why is this bank so bad?" I asked.

The suffocating masculinity in the room dropped a notch or two. Though I felt a different sort of aura replace it, something dark and dangerous.

Grey leaned on the table. "Ramsey found out the bank is funding terrorism. When I looked into them, I found several disturbing things. They're behind a good portion of the drugs coming into the city, not to mention weapons, which they sell to anyone anywhere. Initially, we thought the bank was run by a small group of powerful and money-hungry humans. But what we've discovered, is that the chairman of that little cabal is a daemon named Mammon, and he's powerful and dangerous."

I looked at these three men, who I considered to be powerful and dangerous and all of them seemed just a little shaken. "Is Mammon that powerful?"

"He should be a god," Fen said. "He was, long ago, one of the first. His power rivals that of many gods. He's only called a daemon because he still only has two aspects, and gods generally have more."

"Oh." That didn't seem good.

"And," Grey sighed, "he has another daemon working for him. A vicious fucker of a henchwoman named Nemain, who revels in havoc and pain."

"She sounds lovely," I said with a grimace, a new realization hitting me. "This is still a normal bank, isn't it? Do you think there would be any problem with Donny getting his money?"

"Tommy's money, not mine," Donny said, not looking up from his computer.

I'd actually forgotten he was in the room. He had to have heard all this talk of gods and daemons, and he hadn't said anything. He deserved an explanation, but before I could say anything, Ramsey answered the question I'd just asked.

"It's possible. A quarter of a billion dollars is a lot of money and Mammon is a greedy fucker. He may have multiple billions, but I'm guessing he wouldn't want to lose an amount like that. If your uncle went in on his own, Mammon would probably manipulate him into either keeping the money where it was or even possibly signing it over to the bank. He has a way of manipulating the greed in people to make them do stupid things."

I yelped with surprise when Donny's fist slammed down onto the table. None of the guys even twitched.

"Will someone tell me what the hell you're all talking about?" Donny said. When he did look up from his computer, he looked at me.

And here it came. "Ah... well, gods are real, so are demons, but they're not really evil and they're not called demons, they're called daemons. Ramsey, Grey, and Fen here are all daemon princes, and apparently, I'm a daemon, too. *Surprise!* I had no clue until just a few days ago. But my birth parents were celestial beings of some sort and I know it's a lot to take in, but yeah, that's the gist of it."

"Was that so hard to say?" Donny said. "Thank you."

I blinked. "Wait, you're just... accepting everything I said? No questions?" I was thoroughly incredulous. I'd expected a flip-out of epic proportions.

Donny looked up at me. "You may be a handful of a niece, but you've never lied to me. I may not have trusted you with my money, but when it comes to anything else, I trust you. Everything you said is absolutely ridiculous, but if you say it's true, I believe it."

Wow. I'd forgotten how much I'd admired this man. I was so very thankful he was back in my life as his whole self.

Donny turned to the guys. "Do I address you as 'Your Highness' or what?"

"Our names are fine," Grey said evenly. "It's a pleasure to meet you." He strode across the room and shook Donny's hand firmly.

"Yeah, if you helped raise this little hellion, then I'm impressed. Fen's the name," Fen said, also going over to shake Donny's hand. I wasn't sure what I thought about being called a hellion, even if it was an accurate description.

"Ramsey." He stayed where he was, all prideful and prickly.

"Thank you," Donny said and returned to his computer. "Oh... there it is." He gave a low whistle. "Apparently my little account has done better than expected these last twenty years."

I rose, curious, and went to see what he was looking at. "More than two hundred and fifty million?" I asked before I saw the screen. And when I did see the account info my jaw hit the floor. "Three hundred and eighty-seven million? Fuck me."

"Yeah, there's no way Mammon is going to let nearly four hundred million slip out of his control," Ramsey said with a heavy sigh.

"I should have known there was a catch to the high interest rates, and no-questions-asked set-up for these accounts," Donny said. "So, what do we do?"

"If you three come with Donny and me to get the money, would that help?" I suggested. "Mammon may be powerful, but I can't imagine anyone wanting to take on all three of you."

They all beamed at me, even Ramsey.

"Yeah, Mammon wouldn't have a chance going toe-to-toe with me," Ramsey said. "There's no way greed wins over strife in a flat-out fight."

"You're forgetting Nemain," Grey said. "Didn't she once best you in one of those underground fights you're so fond of?"

Ramsey grunted. "Once, in the three times we've fought. Only once."

"And that was in a — mostly — fair fight. I have a feeling she won't be fighting fair if we're on her home turf," Fen added. "Still, Ana has a point, if all three of us go, I can't imagine Mammon would cross us."

"Then it's time to expand your imaginative horizons," Grey said. "He'll double-cross anyone for enough money. Still, I think that's the best plan. We can go tomorrow, first thing. And let's all pray to our respective fathers for a bit of luck."

Fen scoffed. "My dad's luck is usually bad."

Everyone agreed on the plan, though.

The guys left, but not before I'd had a moment with each of them. Grey kissed me passionately and told me not to worry. He also said he was looking forward to taking me to see one of his shelters.

Fen whispered his adoration into my ear as he nibbled on it and said he desperately wanted to see me again. "You're the only woman I've ever met who can both bring out my wolf and tame it. You're amazing, and I'm hooked. I need more."

That made heat simmer in my core, even as a calm contentment settled over me.

"Tonight," Ramsey said. "I'll show you what a real man can do." That sent shivers down my spine and brought the simmering heat to a boil.

"They seem nice," Donny said after they'd left.

I gave my uncle a big hug, squeezing him tight. "It's so good to have you back." I tried not to cry onto his shoulder and failed. I could never thank Freyja enough for this.

He hugged me softly. "I was never gone, just... part of my mind was on vacation. But I've always been here for you."

"I know," I said, sniffing back tears and pulling back to arm's length. "I've got a job now, and I'm working on becoming independent. I'm also a sex demon, but I'm working on controlling that too. I'm off men... well mostly... somewhat... sort of. Being a sex demon makes it hard to go off men entirely. The hope is to take some time to figure out who I am. I still have no clue, but I'm working on it." After that, I spewed everything that had happened in the last ten or so years at him.

We sat and he listened contentedly. At the end of it all, he said, "I always knew you were extraordinary. I wouldn't have put my finger on sex demon specifically, but I suppose that makes sense. I know you're destined for great things. You've just had trouble applying yourself. It sounds like you're doing your best now. I'm happy for you." And I cried again then.

By that time, it was getting on in the evening and my date with Ramsey was coming up. Luckily, I didn't need to do much to prepare. I was already dressed casually and that's what he'd wanted. I just dabbed on a bit of makeup to hide that I'd been crying. When he swung by at eight, I was ready, feeling buoyant and far better than I had in a long, long time.

ANAIS

DINNER WAS CHILI DOGS FROM A STREET VENDOR. I WAS A bit surprised by this, but even more surprised at how amazing those chili dogs were, and I moaned all the way through the foot-long delight.

"You know, if you like swallowing sausages that much, I've got another one you can suck down," Ramsey said, all swagger and lust.

He wasn't in his usual suit, but jeans and a T-shirt, like me. Though on him, they were skintight and stretched to their max and gave definition to all of his many, many muscles. It was the first time I'd seen his bare arms. I'd known they were huge from how they bulged in his shirts, but seeing the mountains of muscle and bunching tendons made me just a little weak in the knees and short of breath.

After dinner, we jumped in his supercar and zipped across town to some underground garage. From there, we took a winding path of underground halls with pipes exposed along the ceiling, leading to brutish guards, standing next to a reinforced door. This was his secret. And apparently, it wasn't an easy place to get to.

Then I heard the sounds of raised voices, cheering. Was this some sort of literal *underground* concert?

Ramsey nodded to the guards at the door, who seemed to know him and let him in. We came out into a large room, and in the middle of it was a boxing ring, surrounded by a heavy cage. Inside, two... *things*... fought it out, bloody and brutal. Definitely not a concert.

"Welcome to the Empyrean fights," Ramsey said with a sweep of his hand.

"This is your secret?" I hissed.

"Yup, you're going to watch me fight."

"Oh." *Let me contain my joy.* This was *not* what I'd hoped the secret would be though it *was* what I should have expected from Ramsey.

I was left — alone, of course — in a seat in the second tier of the arena. Thankfully there weren't many people back here. Most of the spectators were down on the first level, where there were no seats and they jostled and cheered, close to the action and the blood splatter.

And soon enough, Ramsey was stepping into the ring.

I sat forward, suddenly interested, not in the fight, but in the fact that he was only wearing a loin-cloth. And holy fuck did he have a lot to show off.

Fen was tall and lean but still muscled like a Hollywood star. Grey was tall and broad and had a sense of danger about him. Ramsey was massive, with muscles on muscles, rippling over his heavy frame. I'd known from the very first time I'd seen him in that elevator he was dangerous, and I was about to find out just how dangerous he was.

Then his opponent got into the ring, and I gasped. The man — if he could be called that — was announced as Cottus The Hundred-Handed, and he was... impossible.

He was easily twice as tall as Ramsey, so big I couldn't quite fathom his actual height. And he wasn't just tall, but impossibly large as well. Not only was he a mountain of muscle, with smaller mountains of muscle bunched on him, but he had dozens of arms sprouting from all parts of him. They weren't haphazard, but symmetrical along both sides of him.

Except that didn't make him any nicer to look at. He had two arms coming out of the sides of his head and one off the back. Arms protruded off his shoulders, chest, back, down his sides, off his legs. There was even one arm where his dick should have been, which led to all manner of questions my mind didn't want to try to answer.

The beast-man-thing roared and stomped one foot and the entire arena shook.

Ramsey must have been insane because he was grinning like a madman.

Then a whistle sounded and the fight began.

I'd never been much of a boxing fan. It was just too violent for me. And this superhuman version was even worse. There didn't seem to be any rules other than pummel the shit out of your foe and whichever fighter wasn't a bloody carcass at the end was the winner.

I didn't want to watch. I wanted to look away, but some morbid fascination kept me looking — even if it was from my periphery. I winced and twitched with every bone-jarring hit and my stomach heaved with every spray of blood.

Ramsey was surprisingly quick for all that bulk, running up the cage and bouncing all over the place to avoid the many strikes from his foe while landing hits of his own. He was the better fighter by far, hitting far more often, but his hits seemed to do little to the massive hundred-handed man. Whereas every hit the larger man landed sent Ramsey flying, crashing hard into the cage or floor.

And every time, Ramsey got back up and kept bouncing around the ring.

After what felt like hours — but was probably only minutes of watching Ramsey get the shit beaten out of him — he finally lunged in, grabbed, and twisted the hundred-handed's dick arm.

The larger man let out a horrible scream, answering one of the questions I had, namely: was that arm as sensitive as a dick? Then, as the bigger man bent over in pain, Ramsey landed a very solid hit to that massive jaw and the big lug fell back, out cold.

Ramsey was bloody and breathing hard, but he looked up at me and smiled.

I gave a halfhearted wave. I was happy he'd won, but only in so much as I hadn't wanted to watch my date get beaten to a bloody pulp. Still, I wasn't really happy I'd had to witness that.

That said, some primal part of me had responded viscerally to such a display. The part of me that liked bad boys and got all hot and wet at men displaying their brute strength had *loved* it. The savage cavewoman in me had chosen Ramsey as her ideal mate and I blamed her for the heated throbbing between my legs.

Ramsey came to me straight from the ring, he hadn't even dressed. He was all bruised and bloody and manly as fuck with those heaving muscles and that skimpy loin-cloth. And my cavewoman was really hoping he'd throw me over his shoulder, take me back to his cave, and ravage me.

I swallowed hard as he flopped into the seat next to me.

"What did you think?" he asked, seemingly not bothered at all by the blood dripping from his nose, or lips, or above his eye, or any of the cuts on his huge chest and massive arms, or the bruises on his hard abs, or...

...I think my cavewoman must have seized control of me for just a moment, because when I came to myself next, I was straddling his lap, grinding myself against the growing stiffness under his loin-cloth, and my lips were clamped to his, hands fisting his hair. And he wasn't doing anything to dissuade me.

He pulled me close, my chest pressed against his as my rigid nipples did their best to cut their way out of my flimsy T-shirt, and his hard lips opened. He forced his tongue into my mouth, teasing out my tongue as we ferociously kissed.

I lost control of my aspect, wanting all the sex, and heard Ramsey's vicious grunt as the thing I was grinding against surged to oh-my-daemon-lord proportions.

Heat consumed me. Firestorms sizzled out to all parts of me from the blast furnace that was my core and my pussy opened, receptive and ready, dripping with my super-heated juices.

But then Ramsey pushed me back as my grinding reached a fevered pace. I... just... needed... a bit.... more!

"Ana," he breathed through clenched teeth. "Get yourself under control or I'll lose it."

Behind his eyes was a nearly out-of-control tornado of swirling chaos. But still, he seemed to sense my need and his hands slid down from my shoulders to squeeze my breasts, hard and needful. That was all it took.

I came.

I didn't care how loud I screamed, or if everyone in this arena knew I was coming. I hoped some other fight would distract them. My pussy flooded and I soaked through my panties and my jeans as I finished my orgasm rubbing my clit against his cock.

His jaw was tense, every muscle bunching and twitching. I looked down at his loin-cloth and saw the mixed stains of my leaking wetness and his pre-cum where the tip of his cock pressed against the fabric.

God, that had been amazing and primal and hot. But I registered Ramsey's earlier words now and — since I was satisfied — pulled my aspect back within me, as much as I could, given Harmonia's lessons.

I grinned devilishly. A part of me liked the fact that I'd gotten off and he hadn't. And if I drained all the sexy heat from around us, he'd probably go limp. So... I focused a little harder — which was easier now that I'd had a release and my head was clear — and did just that, sucking *all* that steamy sex into me, devouring it.

Ramsey sighed. The storm behind his eyes settled and he let out a shuddering breath.

"Thank you," he breathed, and those two words had a whole world of meaning in that moment. He was grateful I'd saved him from losing control, but also loved that I'd chosen to ride him in the first place.

I sat back a little, more on his legs than his cock, looking down at that huge lump in the loin-cloth. "Really? You're thanking me and you didn't even come?"

That cocky smile returned to his face. "When I come... *you'll* be the one thanking *me*."

I laughed at his confidence, even as my horny self was fully agreeing to those terms.

"Now, I'm going to get dressed and take you back to my place where we can get undressed, and I'll make you come again and again before you... thank me."

And my already hot body tingled with that suggestion. Some part of my mind was trying to remind me that I was off men — off dicks and bad boys like Ramsey — but I was ignoring it. As much as I hadn't been a fan of the fight, all my old instincts had returned. I wanted this powerful man to claim me and make me scream. Again.

"Let's go," I whispered and that was all the motivation he needed.

ANAIS

RAMSEY'S PENTHOUSE WAS LARGE, BUT NOT OPULENT. IT was incredibly clean — which was a surprise — spartan, minimalist. I liked that. No one had commented on the fact that he was topless as we'd come up through the swanky building and rode up the elevator, but then, who would pick a fight with a massive man looking as brutal as he was? Which saved me from answering questions since I was wearing his T-shirt — which was like a dress on me — to hide the rather large and embarrassing wet spot on my jeans.

He closed the door behind us and turned to me. "Do you want me clean or dirty?" he asked. "I could do with a shower, but if you just want to fuck, all sweaty and nasty, I can do that too."

He was blunt. I liked that. Straightforward. No pretense. Also, he was giving me the choice, which disappointed my cavewoman, but was very appealing to modern me.

"What about your injuries?" I asked, stepping in and

running a tentative finger around a massive, nasty black bruise on his chest.

He winced then smiled. "They're nothing."

Okay... so *that* had been a lie. I could tell his wounds hurt. I stepped in and pressed my lips to that large bruise, soft and gentle, as if my kiss could make it better.

I'd been meaning to show him he was wrong and that even such a light touch would be painful. I expected a gasp of pain, but instead, he let out a shaking breath of relief.

Then, we both looked down as the bruise faded away to nothing almost instantly.

What the...?

"Did you just... heal me?" he asked softly, confused and curious.

Had I?

I didn't answer, but I leaned in to kiss a large gash on his right arm, just below the shoulder, tasting the coppery tang of his blood. I'd been thinking about my kiss making it better the last time, so I thought the same thing again.

The heavy gash closed, dried blood flaking and falling away. There was only the jagged line of a faint scar there now.

"Fuck me," I breathed.

"I intend to, but first, I think you've just manifested another aspect." He put a finger under my chin and lifted my face from looking at his shoulder until our gazes met. "That makes you a daemon lady, perhaps even a daemon princess, depending on who your parents were."

"Oh?" And suddenly I really, desperately needed to

know who my birth parents were. Why had my adoption records been lost? Who the fuck was I?

I was lost in thought until Ramsey's hard lips pressed to mine in a heavy kiss. It didn't last long though and he pulled back and whispered, "No thinking about other things when you're with me." He grinned. "Now, kiss the rest of my wounds."

It was a soft demand, but a demand nonetheless and something in that demand suggested we'd be doing the sweaty-dirty sex very soon.

He stripped me, playing and pressing, fondling and rubbing as I sought and soothed all of his many cuts and bruises, kissing all over his upper body. I was naked by the time I undid his jeans, looking for more wounds on his legs, but got distracted by the massive, purple, swollen erection that sprang free from his pants.

"Fuuuuck," I breathed, blinking. I'd thought Grey and Fen had been large. If so, then Ramsey was a monster.

He chuckled. "Yeah, I think the wounds on my legs can wait. I think you've got other things on your mind." He stepped out of his pants.

"Fuuuuck," I whispered again, still mesmerized by that thick, throbbing column of meat.

Ramsey grabbed me and spun me around, pressing my back to his chest. I felt the straining surge of his cock against my ass as his hands slid over me.

He'd already spent time igniting all my many fires and my skin tingled, flushed a deep red. My breasts were heaving, my nipples tight and hard, and my thighs were slick with the lava flow slowly leaking from my core, preparing for the eruption I knew was about to come.

"I think you'll need to be a bit looser before I fuck you," he whispered, his hot breath on my ear.

I shivered at the intimate tone, even as his large hands went to work on me. One clasped a breast, while his other slid down to my messy, drenched folds.

"Gods, you're soaked!" he breathed as his fingers brushed my clit.

I undulated against him, wanting him to feel as good as I did, and he pressed his palm hard to my raging nub while slipping three thick fingers inside me.

"Fuck, you're so open. You really want my cock, don't you?"

"Yeah," I moaned, head lolling back onto his shoulder as he began a rough finger-fucking, rubbing me inside and out, taking my already taut desire higher and higher.

He took me right to the edge and didn't hesitate or tease me, finishing me off by pinching my nipple.

With a cry, the volcano building in my core erupted in a glorious burst of pleasure. I shuddered and mewled and shouted as he viciously continued his finger work until I'd finally stopped spurting. By then my knees were weak, body trembling and mind dazed, and I was in a land of warm contentment, higher than a kite.

Strong arms turned me around, picked me up, and laid me down on something hard. I hadn't been expecting that. I blinked my eyes open to find I was on his dining room table.

Anticipation surged through me even though I was still flying high on my release because it was obvious he wasn't setting me on the table to rest. He'd set me here because it was the perfect height to fuck me.

Oh, yes. I shuddered at that thought, especially when I once again saw his huge cock.

"Condom, purse!" I gasped.

He looked at me, one brow raised. "I don't wear—"

"You do if you want to stick that eggplant in my peach. No exceptions. I've had enough kids. Condom or nothing!"

"That's a fuckin' sexy tattoo you've got there. I—"

"No changing the topic. Condom. Purse. Now!"

He growled, standing there for a long moment. Then, he stepped in and pulled me towards him, laying the throbbing shaft of his massive cock heavily on my oh-so-wet-and-sensitive pussy. He slowly slid himself back and forth in mock thrusting.

"You sure?" he teased.

I reached down and grabbed his tip, and wow, it was so big around I couldn't quite bring my fingers together. Still, I squeezed him hard, perhaps too hard as I glared at him.

"I'm certain," I said. "I'm as rigid and unyielding on this as your cock is."

He released a gasping breath between his teeth, but I didn't let up until he said, "Gah! Fine. Where's your purse!"

I let him go and he left, returning just a moment later with my little handbag. He unceremoniously dumped it out onto the table next to me and then laughed.

"I see," he said, chuckling at my extra pair of panties, my lipstick, and the abundance of various sizes of condoms.

Cocking an eyebrow, he picked up the largest. "We'll see if this fits."

Coming from any other man, that would have been pure bravado. But looking at Ramsey's throbbing monster and that double-X-L Durex, I wasn't entirely sure it would fit either.

He tore into the package and pulled out the large ring, looking at it. I snatched it from him while he hesitated. I wanted to feel his cock as I slid this sucker over him.

He got the point and shifted forward, once again slowly rubbing his shaft through my desire. I pulled the tip of the condom then slid it down over his head, and wow!

At first, I didn't think it would fit, but those things were meant to stretch and I managed to slide that second skin over him, feeling his pulsing veins, twitching strength, and massive length. And still, the condom didn't reach his base, and it was supposed to be over nine inches long!

"Ready now?" he asked me with a hungry grin on his face as he pushed my legs open.

"Ah... well...?"

He looked down at me. "What now?"

I could feel the heat of his cock brushing my pussy. He was ready, I was ready, but...

No dicks. I'd promised myself. And here was a dick of both sorts.

But you know you're curious how that monster cock will feel inside you, my horny self whispered.

And I was.

I *really* was.

I stared at the insane hotness that was Ramsey looming over me. How could I not fuck him?

Fine! Dicks! All the dicks! I give up. I have no willpower at all, apparently.

Yeah, now we're back in the game! my horny self cheered.

Still, I couldn't let Ramsey get off — pun intended — that easily. I grabbed my legs from him, pulling them up beside me, hands behind my knees, tilting my hips just a little, feeling how open and ready I was with my feet up in the air.

"Make me cum with your mouth first, then I'm all yours." That condition seemed reasonable.

He grinned. "Greedy little daemon princess, aren't you?"

"Hell, yeah."

He dove in without hesitation or teasing, licking and sucking and working me into a frenzy. He wasn't as amazing as Fen, but he didn't have to be. I was already primed from his handjob, and when he attacked my clit, mouth sucking hard as his tongue licked and flicked. I didn't need much more than that.

I let go of my legs — even though I was flexible enough to keep them where they were — and reached down to shift his mouth just a little, pressing and sucking just right...

Yes. Right there!

Every nerve in my body lit up with pleasure, making me buck and moan, as I tumbled over the edge with another powerful orgasm.

I quivered on the table, soothed and super-heated all

at once, loose, yet with muscles bunching expectantly at what was to come next.

Ramsey rose, my juices dripping over his chin and glistening on his chest.

"You flood better than the Nile," he said, licking his lips. Then he was leaning over me, my calves on his shoulders and I felt his cock press to my gaping, hungry opening.

"Now it's my turn," he whispered.

ANAIS

He wasn't subtle. There was no soft entrance, no seeking, and no slow push. His massive cock slammed into me, driving to the hilt — and I was very surprised he could go that deep — crashing against my molten core.

I cried out with a mix of pain and pleasure and then he let loose, pounding into me with his savage strength. I moaned and gasped with every hard slap against my folds, quickly rising to the heights of a new and far more powerful orgasm.

But he was only just beginning, confirming this when he leaned down over me, pressing my legs to my shoulders, and whispered — through gasping breaths, "You're going to make me lose control." He licked my ear. "And I want it!"

He drew back and pulled my legs tight to him, hands on top of my thighs as his thrusts became short but somehow even deeper.

I could see it in his eyes, the chaos swirling in those midnight depths, ready to be unleashed. He reached out both hands to seize my tits, not even trying to be gentle, all gripping and squeezing need.

That pain spiked my pleasure to another level, and I cried out as I came, hard, bucking and writhing, spurting my hot juices around his miracle cock.

And that's when I saw the chaos take him.

He roared, and I felt everything around him shift. It was like when Harmonia did her thing. Waves radiated off the massive man and he seemed to grow. Even his cock swelled and suddenly it was very tight inside my more-than-ample canal.

With one hand he smashed through the wood of the table next to me like it was nothing. Then his hands went to my hips, and he picked me up, right off the table, holding me in place as he fucked me like a beast, with a cock so large I felt every savage inch.

He was roaring, and I was screaming, lost in ecstasy.

Then his ferocious cry rose an octave as he planted himself deep within me and I felt it, the powerful, hot rush of his release. And only then did I recall how virile these daemons could be.

But I couldn't hold onto that thought, because he'd rough-fucked me right into another aching orgasm, and I was a shuddering, throbbing mess of spasming, gushing bliss, whirling around and around.

I pulled myself up to his face digging my nails into his jaw as I forced his mouth open and slammed my tongue down his throat. My other hand grasped behind his head, rough-fisting his hair to heave him closer to me. He howled like a primal beast into my mouth as his cock unleashed its torrential flow inside me.

Wild myself, I pushed back from his face and slapped him as hard as I could, then backhanded him on the other cheek. My hand stung, but his eyes sparked with awareness and the roaring finally stopped.

He staggered back a step, his hands on me loosening and sending a spike of fear rushing through me. Was he going to drop me?

But he quickly regained control of himself and tightened his grip around me, holding me securely to him.

"Fuuuuuuuuuck," he breathed, blinking, voice hoarse, body trembling. "Fucking fuck of all the fucks!" he breathed and looked into my eyes, gaze intent and alive. "I think it's safe to say that was a 'Holy Fuck,' wouldn't you? You're a goddess in my books, Silverlocks."

I drank in his words and that possessive, fulfilling look he gave me even as I began to come down and feel parts of me — many parts — start to ache.

I looked down at our joining, where his cock was buried inside me.

"You're still coming!" I breathed, feeling the pulsing of that mega-dick, against my oh-so-sensitive confines.

"Hell yeah, I am," he gasped. "That was one amazing fuck. I've never lost control like that with a woman. It was... terrifying and liberating all at the same time."

I had to agree with those words. This certainly had been the hard fucking my cavewoman had wanted, savage and brutal and wow.

He laid me down on the table again looking at the new hole in the wood. "Did I do that?"

"Yup."

"Fuck. Was I... too rough with you?" he asked, concern clear in his voice.

"A little, yeah. I'm going to have some bruises and aches tomorrow, but apparently, I can heal now, so fuck it."

He looked down at my pussy and his *still* coming cock inside me. "Fuck it indeed."

"Gods, aren't you done yet?" I gasped, laughing a little.

"Nope, you're just too much for me. I'm making a royal mess though."

He began to pull out, and I gasped as every aching inch of him left me.

"Oh... shiiiit... ahh... sorry," he said, sheepish and I looked down as he pulled out. A final spurt of cum shot over my belly... because the condom was torn to shreds.

I dropped my head back onto the table, just a bit too hard. "Ow! And Fuck! If I get pregnant again, you're taking the kid."

"I'm not stay-at-home-dad material, Silverlocks."

"Then you should have thought of that before you fucked your condom into oblivion. Consequences are a bitch, big boy."

He laughed. "Fair enough." Then he surprised me by leaning down and kissing me softly, just a quick brush of his lips. "I'll gladly take any consequences from this. It was worth it. You are worth it. I love you, Ana."

He blinked, as if he couldn't believe he'd said that.

"You barely know me, Ramsey," I whispered. "You're just in love with fucking me. And yeah, I'm just a bit in love with fucking you. But once you've had our kid for eighteen years, then we'll see how you really feel."

He grimaced. "Ah... yeah..." He turned and hurried away. "I'll draw you a bath. I get the feeling you'll want to soak, right?" He didn't wait for an answer and was gone to the bathroom in a flash.

Slowly, I carefully sat up on the table. My pussy must have been full to capacity because his cum wasn't so much dripping as flowing out of me. And yeah, he'd been right, there was a royal mess on the table, on the floor, and all around. Luckily, this was his place, so... not my problem.

I slid off the table gently, leaning heavily on my hands because... yup, my legs were jelly and were barely supporting me.

Yeah, all I wanted was a long bath.

He returned and lifted me easily, carrying me to the bathroom then set me down carefully into the still-filling tub. I gasped as the hot water touched sensitive bits, but quickly got used to it as the tub filled around me.

Then I got a show as I watched Ramsey shower, in a separate, clear-glass stall. When he was done, he came and washed me reverently, and I fell asleep, warm and soothed and tired.

I woke when he finished bathing me, gently urging me to dunk my head and scrub my hair. Still sleepy, I rinsed out the shampoo then he drained the bath and carried me to his massive bed, lying me on his mattress.

He didn't even seem to care that I was naked and wet. He just laid me onto the sheets, covered me up, and snuggled in next to me, warm and hard against my back.

Then he kissed my shoulder softly and stroked my hair as I dozed on the verge of sleep.

"I know I lost control back there, but..." I felt his chest heave with a heavy breath. "I... I've never felt this peaceful and calm before. And I've never met anyone, woman or man, who could bring me back from my chaos before either. You're truly special, Ana Baker. I... I need you," he murmured.

I wasn't sure if I'd heard that last bit or dreamed it, but either way, my heart swelled, and I slept so very well that night.

I woke, however, to an empty bed.

The massive windows in his bedroom overlooking the New York skyline showed that it was still dark outside but with a faint haze of light on the eastern horizon.

I rolled over as Ramsey came in dressed in a suit, looking immaculate and sexy and dangerous.

"Come on, Silverlocks, it's time to go. Let's get you home and cleaned up so we can be at the bank first thing."

Right.

Donny's money... for the mobsters...

At the bank...

... with the scary-ass daemon, Mammon.

Fuck.

ANAIS

AT THE BANK, THE FIVE OF US WERE USHERED INTO A PLUSH backroom that looked like a "high rollers" suite in Vegas. Not that I'd ever been to Vegas, but I'd seen lots of movies.

I looked as much like a businesswoman as I could get, in a respectable blush-pink blouse and burgundy, calf-length, flared A-line skirt which I kept smoothing down over my legs.

I may have been just a touch nervous, though I found my trepidation fading whenever my mind wandered back to last night with Ramsey, something I wasn't ever going to forget.

My parts were still sore from that punishing caveman sex. But mostly I kept thinking of how tender and gentle and caring he'd been afterward. He'd carried me and bathed me and stroked my hair until I'd fallen asleep. Those weren't bad boy things. Bad boys fucked you then went to watch the game or rolled over and fell asleep. There was a hidden tenderness to Ramsey that I'd never suspected and I was a bit disappointed that I'd been so sex-dazed and tired last night to appreciate it.

"Just wait here, and Mister Kinz will be in in a moment," our guide said. She was attractive and young and acted more like a hostess than a banker. "If there's anything I can get you, just ring that bell." She pointed to a heavy cord with tassels on it. "I'll make sure you have *everything* you need." And the way she said it, eyeing the guys, suggest that *anything*, including her, was on the table. She winked and left.

I wanted to slap her.

They're mine, bitch!

I blinked. Where had that come from? Why was I suddenly so possessive, and vicious about it?

These guys weren't mine at all. I hadn't even known them for a full week!

But I couldn't deny that a part of me wanted to claim them.

All of them.

That might be a problem, given how contentious they were with each other, especially when it came to me. Still, right now, I didn't think I could choose. Fen was kind and fun and sexy. Grey had the tall, dark, and handsome thing and was a billionaire to boot, while Ramsey was all dangerous energy, chaotic and carnal.

They appealed to different sides of me and all of them had shown me they knew what they were doing when it came to pleasing a woman.

That's right, and they're all mine! This time I identified my horny self as the source of my hostility.

You just want them for the sex, I chided myself.

You bet I do! I AM a sex daemon after all. Those hunks are mine, and I'll scratch out the eyes of any bitch that even looks at them the wrong way!

Whoa. Okay. So *that* was good to know.

I tried to quell my raging libido and think about these guys honestly for a moment. Since it seemed we were waiting, I sat in one of the comfortable chairs and looked around at the three men who I barely knew and yet already felt close to.

Fen wore comfortable black dress pants and a black button-up shirt, and I was beginning to wonder if all his dress clothes were black. His aqua-blue eyes looked around the room, noting the door we'd come in and two others. He was an odd one, a paradox, so courteous and thoughtful, but with a world-ending beast lurking deep within him.

The way he looked at me and spoke to me, the things he said and did... all of that told me he saw me as more than just a sex daemon. He saw *me*.

I didn't even know who *me* was and yet he seemed to have accepted *me* already. He hadn't said the *three words* yet, but I could see in his pale blue eyes that what he felt for me was deeper than just attraction.

And that terrified me as much as it thrilled me.

Grey wore a gray, three-piece suit and tie, tailor-made for his tall, broad form. He looked immaculate and deliciously gorgeous, and I just wanted to lick him. He'd been very vocal about how he felt, and though he'd also not used the *three words*, he'd pretty much vowed his undying devotion.

Which was still crazy to think about.

The intensity of his devotion was too much at times, and I wasn't prepared for that because I knew I couldn't return it. Not yet. Not until I had a better grip on who I was and what I really wanted in life.

Ramsey was in a midnight blue suit that matched his eyes, with a light blue dress shirt and no tie. He looked good in a suit, but far better without one.

My body tingled with warmth as I remembered last night, but now wasn't the time for that.

Ramsey glared around the room, clearly ready for a fight, and the flick of a grin I saw twitch his mouth made me think he wanted one.

Which was the trouble with Ramsey. He was just a bit too erratic.

He'd actually said he loved me last night. He'd seemed shocked, and I'd immediately dismissed it, but given how gentle and soft he had been after our rough sex, I was beginning to think maybe those words had been real. Except here he was the next day, looking a little too much like he wanted to break some bones.

What was a woman supposed to do with a man like that? He wanted to protect me, and I knew he wouldn't hurt me, not intentionally. But what if he lost control again and I couldn't bring him back the next time?

I sighed, shaking my head. I wanted these three sexy men but was terrified of actually having them in my life. Yeah, that pretty much summed up how messed up I was right now.

So, I looked over at the other man in the room. Donny was in a subdued brown suit, carrying a small metal briefcase. I'd asked about that, pretty sure that four hundred million wouldn't fit in there.

He'd laughed, saying that the amount we were going to withdraw, if stacked in hundred-dollar bills, would weigh almost eight thousand pounds. Luckily, this bank also dealt in diamonds, which was how he planned to withdraw the money.

When I asked how many diamonds that would be, he shrugged and said it depended on the size, but that a few thousand diamonds most likely wouldn't weigh more than six or eight pounds or so.

I tried to imagine *thousands* of diamonds or eight *pounds* of diamonds and couldn't.

Donny I could trust. I was so happy he was back to himself.

Perhaps I could talk to him about the guys?

No. That would just be odd.

Maybe Harmonia would be willing to listen?

I'd have to go in early before my next shift and have another chat with her, but just having someone listen would be helpful.

One of the other doors opened and two people entered. The first was a man who exuded opulence.

He was average height, but heavyset and it was clear he loved to indulge in probably everything. His cream-colored suit hid many faults though, tailored to perfection, and he wore more gold than most rappers: chains, earrings, rings, bracelets, even his shoes were half gold. And most of the gold sparkled with gems studded or set within it.

He had a flabby face with drooping lips and a bald

head, and his complexion was dark, a bit darker than Ramsey's bronzed-god look.

The woman with him moved like a hunting cat and her green eyes were hard and cruel. She wasn't tall, but she made up for it with a sure and strong build. Fiery red hair was cut short and stood spiky on her head, like flames. She wore a black tank top, black cargo pants, two long knives at her belt, and tattoos on her arms, neck, and face. She looked like the token female in some commando-team movie.

"Gentlemen!" the man said, arms outstretched. "How may I help you today?"

"Cut the schmoozing Mammon. We're here for business and hopefully a quick transaction," Grey said, rising.

The others followed suit and I got up too, feeling the tension escalate in the room.

The woman — Nemain — glared at each of the guys, though she cocked a smile when she saw Ramsey. It wasn't a nice smile though. It was a challenge-to-fight sort of smile.

"Yes, I heard mention of a withdrawal," Mammon said, glancing about before he laid eyes on Donny. "Ah, Mister Baker. It's so good to see you again after such a long time. Your investment has been well tended, I assure you."

"I'd like to close the account and take the funds as diamonds," Uncle Don said smoothly. He didn't seem intimidated by Mammon or Nemain, though it did seem like he was trying hard not to look at Nemain. I guessed that was because she wasn't wearing a bra and her tight tank top left little to the imagination.

"All of it? Such a pity, but yes, this way and we'll oversee your withdrawal," Mammon said, motioning to the third door in the room.

We all moved and Nemain put her hands on those knives. "Only the account holder," she hissed.

"Ah yes, I'm sorry, rules are rules. Only the account holder is allowed into the diamond room," Mammon said with a smug grin. "Unless any of you are family? Then you may also enter."

"I'm family," I said, then instantly regretted it. All eyes were on me. My guy's gazes varied from concerned to furious to proud. Mammon looked a bit stunned while Nemain licked her lips like I was lunch.

"Oh, I see. Well, then yes, the pretty lady may also come in." Mammon looked me over, but oddly, not in the way most men do. There was a hint of the lustful undressing look, but most of it was a sense of appraising my value.

He raised his brows after he did. I didn't know what that meant, but I didn't like it.

"Rules are made to be broken," Ramsey growled, coming to me and wrapping me in those huge arms. "We're all going in."

Mammon laughed. "My bank, my rules, my way, or the highway. If you want your money, follow my rules. If you want a fight, Nemain will be more than happy to oblige."

"She wouldn't have a chance against the three of us," Ramsey scoffed.

"Oh, did I forget to mention our little pet?" Mammon was grinning ear to ear as he withdrew a small device and clicked a button. The entire wall on one side of the room lifted away with only the barest whisper of machinery, revealing a massive cage with a monstrosity inside.

"A chimaera?" Fen hissed.

"Gods, Mammon, what are you doing?" Grey asked aghast.

"Fuck me," Ramsey whispered.

The beast was royally messed up. It looked like someone had taken a lion, an oversized goat, and a massive snake and mushed them together. It had three heads, one for each animal: roaring, bleating, and hissing. The front part of its body looked to be that of a lion. The hindquarters were that of a goat, and the tail, was long and all snake.

Then the goat head breathed fire, and I yelped. The gout of fire didn't make it out of the cage but left the room smelling of ash.

"Disobey my rules and I'll open that cage," Mammon said with a sneer.

"You wouldn't!" Grey breathed, horrified. "Can you even stop that thing? Chimaeras are impossible to control!"

Mammon laughed. "I had Ogun craft three collars for the beast, and I control each of them. I'm the first in history to have tamed a chimaera. Care to take it for a test run? Or shall we all be civil and stick to my rules?"

And I could see the three thick iron bands — with strange markings that glowed as if heated by fire — around each of the three necks.

The guys hesitated.

I turned to Ramsey, feeling safe in his arms for the moment.

"I'm a daemon too. I'll look after Donny," I whispered. "Don't worry."

I forced a smile. I was terrified of being alone with Mammon, but I didn't want that beast let loose on my guys either.

"Too late, I'm fuckin' worried!" Ramsey hissed, clearly not happy. "Your aspects are sex and healing, what are you going to do?"

A valid point, but I still felt like this was the only way. "I'll be fine, I promise."

Ramsey stared at me for a long moment, then looked up and glared at that beast for equally as long.

"Fuck," he hissed. "Just be very careful in there. Mammon is tricky and powerful. Be on guard."

I nodded.

As soon as Ramsey released me, Grey was there in an instant.

"You sure, Ana?" he asked softly. "Mammon has ways of playing with your emotions and mind. I—"

"I'll be okay," I assured him. "I've been handling bad boys all my life." I was fairly certain this would be far different, but that seemed to ease Grey enough. He kissed me softly. When he let go, I found myself in Fen's arms.

"If you need us, scream or bang on the door or something. We'll be there in an instant. There's nothing in this world that can stop my beast or Ramsey's chaos or a determined Grey. Don't worry, we're here."

That was the best news I'd heard all morning.

"Thanks," I said, then brushed his lips with a kiss. He smiled as he released me.

"This way then, Mister Baker, Miss Baker." Mammon went to the other door and proceeded through a song and dance to unlock it which included an eye scan, a palm scan, a voice print verification, and a passcode punched into a keypad, which was longer than I'd ever be able to remember.

The door — and yeah, it was a vault door, more than a foot thick — clicked open and Mammon ushered Donny and me inside.

My eyes went wide as I took in the aptly named Diamond Room. Two big bruisers of guards stood next to each of the two doors and with four more guards, one in each corner, that made eight tough-looking men stationed in here.

Another door stood directly across from where we entered while every other surface in the room was cabinets all crammed full of gems, most of which were diamonds. The wealth in this room could probably feed, house, and clothe every underprivileged family in America, if not the world.

"Amazing, isn't it?" Mammon said, his voice silky and superior. He clicked the vault door closed behind us. "Now..." He drew out the word. "Let's discuss your transaction." And the way he said it suggested there was indeed something to discuss as opposed to a straightforward withdrawal.

"I wish to close my account and take what's mine," Donny said, not intimidated.

"Do you?" Mammon asked. "Or do you want... *more*?"

My pulse picked up. There was something in that last word, something both soothing and thrilling.

His voice seemed to ripple around me, like when Harmonia did her thing, and suddenly I was on board. Who wouldn't want more? If fifty million had turned into almost four hundred million in twenty years, imagine what just another five or ten years might do? A billion? More?

Images of the life we could live flashed through my mind. There would be so much I could have: dresses galore filling an entire house full of closets and my daughters would never want for anything. I could leave my job and Donny could...

Donny...

I blinked, returning to myself. No, we needed this money so Donny could pay off Tommy. If we didn't, we were dead.

"What are you doing?" I said, stepping between Mammon and Donny. "Stop it. We're here for our money. We don't want trouble, but if you don't give us what we want—"

"Then what, my dear?" Mammon breathed. "You'll sic your men out there on me? Trust me, they're about to have their hands full."

"What do you mean?" But then I remembered that horrific beast. "You wouldn't?"

"I would, and I will. *I* need to keep *my* money safe after all."

"Yes," Donny said behind me. "That would be a sound investment. If we reinvest for another twenty years, I estimate we'd have almost three billion."

I spun on Donny, trying to talk some sense into him. "Not if Tommy Two-Toes kills you first. We need that money."

"Tommy will see the benefit in reinvesting. Why wouldn't he want more?" Donny said with easy justification.

"Indeed," Mammon purred. Then he laughed. "The minds of humans are so easy to manipulate. They all want more!" He stepped in close to me. "But you, my dear, you're special, aren't you?" He was just a bit shorter than me and had to raise his hand to stroke my chin with his fingers, though I suspected he would rather have stroked elsewhere. "Why don't you stay here with me and let me shower you with more wealth than you could ever imagine?"

I tried not to puke on him.

"Fuck no, you bastard."

All the guards tensed, and I realized suddenly how outnumbered I was. Ramsey was right. What was I going to do against eight armed guards and a beefy businessman? I couldn't fight them.

Mammon grabbed my wrist, possessive and tight. "I *will* have you, woman. I take what I want, and I want you. It will be your choice whether you are discarded with nothing once I'm done with you, or whether you live with wealth beyond your imaginings!"

I looked back at Donny, but he was standing there, head cocked. I could almost see the dollar signs in his eyes. He was fully in Mammon's thrall, dreaming of riches.

I turned back to Mammon. "There's no fucking way

I'd ever be with you," I hissed. "Now release me or feel my wrath." There was one thing I had going for me. Mammon probably knew I was a daemon since he hadn't affected me earlier, but he didn't know what my aspects were. So, I could threaten him and see what he did.

Mammon grinned, and there was nothing nice about it. "Oh, you'll *be with me*, one way or another. It doesn't much matter to me whether you enjoy it or not."

Ick! This guy was a creep-and-a-half!

"You asked for it," I said, though I wasn't sure what my next move would be.

Then Mammon lifted his other hand, holding that strange remote thing from earlier, and clicked a button. I heard a loud clanking coming from the next room.

"No, *you've* asked for it, my dear. I've released the chimaera, but I can still control it. Submit to me and I'll let those men out there live. You care for them, yes?"

Shit. He'd called my bluff and I was screwed.

Something crashed and someone screamed, making my heart race.

No. Please no.

Except there was no way in hell I'd submit to Mammon, either.

I had to think of something quick.

FEN

THERE WAS A LOUD CREAKING AND CLANKING NOISE AS THE cage door slid aside, and the slavering and savage chimaera leaped out at us.

I didn't even have time to curse before the beast split in three: a giant venomous snake, an oversized, fire-breathing goat, and a massive, savage lion, one coming for each of us.

Not to mention Nemain, who dove at Ramsey.

I'd suspected things might go this way but hadn't really thought Mammon was crazy enough to unleash a chimaera at us.

Off all of the Great Beasts, chimaeras were the most dangerous, since there was no known way to kill one. They were thought to be invincible. But then I'd never fought one, so perhaps the tales were wrong?

I hoped so.

The goat charged at me, breathing a gout of flame, and I threw myself to the side, feeling the heat far too close to my back, burning away my shirt. I came up with long claws on my hands and a howl. I could control my wolf enough to let just a bit of him out to fight, but it was a tenuous thing. If I lost consciousness while like this, that might just release my beast on the world.

But I wouldn't let that happen. I'd never put Ana in danger like that.

I leaped with the strength of a world-ending beast and tackled the goat, tearing at it with my claws, taking chunks of its tough hide with me.

The goat let out a horrid sound and twisted its head around to breathe more fire at me despite its body being in the crosshairs. I assumed it was immune to its own fire, so I tried to leap over it as the flames erupted, but I wasn't quite fast enough.

Flames incinerated my pants and burned my calves. My thicker shoes had protected my feet, but the leather disintegrated when I hit the floor.

Howling, my wolf took just a bit too much control and I laid into the beast with claws and my mouth, which was now a snout full of fangs. I tasted the bitter, rancid flesh, laced with the snake's venom, and immediately spit it out.

The beast turned its head to burn me again and this time I headed straight for that massive horned head. I swatted its face with my claws as it breathed, knocking its head — and the flames — to one side.

The fire incinerated the drywall and studs of the wall nearby, revealing the reinforced steel of the vault, and I prayed Ana was safe, even as I vowed to tear out Mammon's throat for this betrayal.

Except I had other things to worry about now. Mammon would have to wait.

I wrestled with the beast's head, keeping it from turning toward me, but I forgot that goats had hooves, and one of its front legs lashed out and caught me in the leg.

Pain screamed through me as my bones snapped and shattered.

Roaring, my wolf dug its claws deeper into the goat as I stumbled back, digging deep trenches into the beast's hide. But I had to let go or it would kick me again. So, I threw myself to one side and fell next to a long table. I immediately grabbed the table and threw it at the goat as it breathed fire. The table took the brunt of the flames but was incinerated too quickly, and fire licked over me, searing flesh.

I screamed — no howled — again with my wolf struggling to break free.

Damn it. I could easily swallow this massive goat in my wolf form, I could swallow this whole building... and I would, without thought or care for anyone, even Ana, if my beast was released.

I had to keep it contained. But the pain from my broken leg and my burns were nearly too much as I strained to remain in control and still win this fight.

I rolled away from another blast of fire, feeling burns blister my one arm and leg, then roared, blocking out the pain as best I could as I came to my good leg and launched myself at the goat once again.

I dug my claws deep into both sides of its neck and

ripped away gore and flesh, hoping to decapitate the thing. But even with all the damage I'd done to it, it didn't seem affected.

With a smoky snort, it slammed its horns into my head and threw me back, sending me crashing through a wall.

My mind swam, disoriented, and black spots threatened to take my vision as my wolf growled with pleasure, knowing it would soon be released.

Fuck. No.

I strained to regain the control that was quickly slipping away from me. I was barely aware, barely able to move, but I rose and charged back to where I thought the goat was — my vision was so blurred I couldn't see anything — and felt its fire even as I connected with it.

I turned my head to one side as heat consumed me while I slammed my claws through the beast's neck at the base of the skull. I ripped and tore and... the fires ended abruptly. I couldn't see a thing. One of my eyes was burned and blind, the other still watery and blurry, but I heard the crash of the head hitting the floor.

I staggered back, charred and broken, falling against a wall as I tried to keep control of my wolf for a moment longer.

Somehow my vision cleared in my good eye and... my heart fell.

I'd hoped removing the goat's head would kill it, but the creature's body was still going, flailing around wildly with its hooves.

The last of my strength was ebbing out of me. I

couldn't get up. I couldn't fight. It was everything I could do to contain my wolf, which thrashed and raged within me, desperate to be released.

If the others didn't finish this fight quickly, I would. Permanently.

GREY

MY ASPECTS OF CONQUEST AND ACQUISITION GAVE ME SOME significant ability to fight. I was used to hunting, where I could trap or snare prey, where I had time to plan and strategize, that was my true strength, but sometimes you just had to wrestle your prey to the ground and that's what I was doing now.

The lion had come for me, a beast easily twice the size of any normal lion and blessed with supernatural savagery and strength. I'd done well enough avoiding its yellowed fangs and tearing claws so far, but I knew it was only a matter of time before it hit me. Its strength far exceeded mine and I was only just a match for it in speed, but I was starting to tire and slow down.

It leaped again and I punched the side of its head, redirecting it to crash into a wall. Pain blossomed across my hand. Something had broken. My knuckles were already bleeding from hitting that beast's rock-hard hide, but I knew I couldn't wait for it to recover, so I dove at it, picking up a broken table leg, hoping the jagged wood would be enough of a weapon.

I slammed the makeshift spear into the lion's side and felt it sink in... but only a little and the rest of the sort-of weapon shattered to splinters.

Fuck.

The lion was still trying to rise, and I leaned heavily on it, reaching out to dig my fingers into one large eye. I felt the ichor and mucus burn my fingers as I crushed the soft eyeball and the lion roared and bucked, throwing me off it.

Staggering back, I hit a chair and fell into it, but quickly rolled back off it as the lion came at me again, its massive jaws tearing the chair nearly in half, spitting out the wood and fabric.

I surged my conquest to try to find some way of dominating this beast and felt my muscles strengthen and harden. Then, when it came for me next, I captured its jaw in both hands, keeping it from closing over me as the lion knocked me back to the floor and loomed over me.

With a roar, I poured every ounce of strength I had into my arms to keep the beast's mouth from closing on me. Rancid, hot breath blew on me as its tongue lashed out, striking my arms and almost knocking them away. Its claws pawed at the floor, tearing up the wood, and then one found my leg, rending my flesh and scoring to the bone as it tore at my calf and foot.

I used the pain to augment my strength as I pushed hard, opening the beast's jaws wider and winning the struggle for a moment. Its jaw broke, as the bottom went slack and fell away.

The lion went mad, crazed, backing off from me, its jaw hanging uselessly as it danced in a rage around the room. I'd hoped that would finish it, but I'd only turned it into a frenzied beast. And I'd spent nearly all my power in that one act of strength.

Slowly, I rose, the pain of my torn-up leg screaming through my body, forcing me to fall back, gasping. On my second attempt to stand, using a chair to help myself, I managed to get up on my good leg.

But then, one of the lion's wild and flailing legs caught me solidly in the chest, the claws raking through muscle. The impact threw me across the room and slammed me through a wall, shattering drywall and wooden studs, and tossing me into the hall beyond where the slightly too-flirty hostess was cowering. Seeing me, she screamed and ran and I was sure she wasn't going to get help.

I lay there for just a moment with one arm dislocated, searing pain in my shoulder, and the other torn up and scraped. My suit was shredded, my body broken and bloody. Determination, a raw and unbridled thing, clawed its way up from my belly and gave me the strength to stand. I couldn't let that thing run wild and I sure as Hades wasn't going to lose to it.

Hissing against the pain, I staggered to the broken wall, found a still-standing stud, and slammed my dislocated shoulder into it. The pain of putting the joint back in nearly made me black out, but then it subsided to a dull roar and I limped forward into the room.

I had to finish the lion. Fen was down, struggling. I could see his body shift and contort, his wolf trying to escape and I prayed he could contain it. The goat he'd been fighting was beheaded, but the body flailed about as much as the lion did. Ramsey was fighting both Nemain and the giant snake and somehow managing to fend off both, but not seeming able to attack either. I had to help him.

But that meant finishing my beast first.

My foot nudged something and I looked down to see a long knife. One of Nemain's. I picked it up with a savage grin, then let out a roar. The lion stopped its flailing, its semi-knowing, one-eyed gaze landing on me.

"Come at me, you big fucker."

The lion charged me and I stood my ground for a moment until it leaped. Then, I threw myself on my back and thrusted up with the knife as the lion passed over me. The blade sunk deep and tore open the beast's belly. The lion let out a shriek of pain, then slammed into and through a wall like I'd done moments before.

I rose slowly and went to its still-flailing body. Kneeling next to it, I pushed it over, reached into the bloody gash in its chest, and yanked out its heart.

The creature finally stilled, dead, and I huffed a relieved breath then tossed away the massive organ.

I staggered to my feet yet again. I could feel the last of my strength ebbing away, but lying down wasn't an option. I had to help Ramsey. Then *we* had to help Ana. Who knew what was happening to her?

That solidified my resolve, even as I felt the last of my physical strength leaking out of me.

RAMSEY

NEMAIN WAS QUICK BUT NOT AS FAST AS ME. SHE WAS A daemon of war and chaos, but I was a daemon of conflict itself. She knew battle and strategy, but I knew how to land a punch *and* I was stronger. The issue was the damned massive snake trying to take chunks out of me with its huge fangs dripping with sickly green venom.

I'd researched the chimaera once. I'd been challenged to fight one, but eventually declined. Any one of its beasts I could take, but altogether it would be too much for even me.

But my in-depth research had given me a unique knowledge of these creatures. And when it came to the snake, I knew I couldn't get bit, not even once. Just a scrape of that venom would knock me on my ass and kill me within a few minutes. A full-on bite and my life would be measured in mere heartbeats. So, getting away from it was my main objective.

My research had also told me chimaera's were not invincible as most people thought and could be defeated.

It was just incredibly hard to do so since each of the three separate beasts had to be killed. If any remained alive, the others would heal and remerge, and it would live.

Luckily, the snake didn't see Nemain as an ally. So as long as I kept her between me and it, she was the one who'd have to worry about it. But she knew that too and was trying her best not to get into that position.

Which meant I couldn't spare a thought or a look for my two companions. I had to hope they could handle themselves since I had my hands full. My other significant issue was the Celestial Laws which forbade Empyreans from killing each other. I could hurt her as much as I wanted, but killing would get me a very nasty punishment in one of the lowest of the low underworlds for a few centuries, if not millennia.

Yet, I didn't think Nemain cared, given how she was fighting. She was out for blood.

Nemain slashed with her one remaining knife — I'd disarmed her of the other one at the start of the fight.

I dodged the slash and caught her hand, twisting it behind her back. I had her now! I shifted, forcing her toward the snake as it struck. She launched herself up, kicking the beast's jaw — knocking it away from her — even as she flipped over me. The motion tore her arm from my grasp and now she was behind me.

"You're mine," she whispered as I felt the knife slide into my back.

I spun instantly, tearing the knife from her grip, but it also hurt like the bite of Ammit as the move twisted the blade, tearing my flesh.

I reached around and yanked out the knife, which

was both a good and bad thing. Bad because the large wound was now free to bleed. Good because now I had the knife.

But before I could bring it to bear on Nemain, she'd kicked my legs out from under me. I fell, landing hard, my head hitting something, jarring it and making me see stars for just a moment, but that moment was enough.

I regained my feet as the snake launched itself at me. I reacted with all my razor-edged, battle-honed instinct and shoved the long knife up through its bottom jaw. I hit it so hard the jaws snapped shut, pinned closed by the knife.

But drops of venom sprayed down on me, burning my skin where it landed and I had no clue what effect that would have. My research hadn't said how effective the venom was if it just dropped on your skin. It might do nothing, or it might still kill me, just slower. Also, I no longer had the knife since I really liked it where it was, keeping that beast's mouth closed.

I spun and blocked a punch from Nemain, managing to counterstrike and land a solid blow on her shoulder. She staggered back. I could have followed up, but instead, I took that moment to get a sense for how the other two guys were doing.

Not well it seemed. A headless goat was tearing up one side of the room. Fen was down, his body shifting between man and wolf.

Fuck me, if he lost control, we were all screwed.

Grey was limping toward me. He looked rough, but there was a grim and determined smile on his face.

I met his glance just for a moment, long enough for recognition to pass between us, then I shifted slightly so Nemain wouldn't see Grey's approach, ensuring that her back was fully to him.

She came at me again and I tried to push-kick her. She dodged with a quick hop back. Right in the direction I wanted.

Grey caught her and landed a crushing punch to her neck, and she staggered back toward me, stunned.

"I can't kill you, but the laws say nothing about standing here and watching you get trampled." I picked her up and threw her toward that thrashing goat. She landed exactly where I'd hoped, right next to its flailing hooves. The next wild kick of those steely feet hit her solidly in the head, killing her.

"Fuck yeah," I hissed.

Grey handed me Nemain's other knife even as he stumbled to lean heavily on a wall, clearly not doing well. I went to the snake first, carving it into bits until I found its heart, then I moved to the goat.

Getting close to the goat's body was hard, but I managed to cut it down, one leg at a time, then carve out its heart. Something in the room shifted then as the unmoving parts of the goat, lion, and snake all hissed and shriveled a little. That was it. The chimaera was dead.

Thank the gods.

I turned to Grey. "Help Fen or we're all doomed. I'll go after Ana." He didn't argue, limping toward the other man as I went to that vault door.

I'd lost a lot of blood and it was still pouring out of my.

back, still, I managed to punch two holes through the outer layer of the vault's steel door to see the inner workings of the lock. With a groan, I put one hand in each hole and, with every ounce of super-strength I had, I tore that door completely off its massive hinges.

Hang on Ana, I'm coming!

ANAIS

WE'D WATCHED ON A MONITOR AS THE BATTLE HAD progressed in the other room. Mammon had laughed with delight until Grey had killed the lion. Not long after that, the snake's tail had taken out the camera and all we'd had to go on were the crashes and noises from the other room.

Then things began to quiet.

My heart pounded with fear and I strained to hear anything that indicated that my guys were still alive.

"Your men have lost!" Mammon crowed, gripping my arm tighter. "Submit to me now. If you don't, I'll make this human sign over his account to me and lose everything. Do you want that?"

No. I didn't want that and I didn't want to accept that Fin, Grey, and Ramsey were dead. My chest squeezed tighter and I couldn't catch my breath even as a small, desperate voice inside me screamed that I had to stay calm. I had to get both me and Donny out of there.

If the guys were dead— I swallowed hard not wanting

to accept that thought. *If* they were dead then it was up to me.

And really, getting out of a vault room wasn't as difficult as getting in. I just needed to get to a door. If I could somehow subdue everyone in here, I might be able to get both of us out.

But how could I get all these big men to—

Men!

Perhaps I did have a weapon in my arsenal after all. My horny self giggled with glee and I gave Mammon my wickedest smile.

"You want me? You want this body? You want me to be your willing sex slave and pleasure you over and over again? Is that what you want?" I let my heated words sink in as I began to let my aspect leak from my control. "You want me to suck your cock until you come down my throat? Or let you bury your dick in my pussy? Perhaps you'd like to fuck my ass. Inject your cream filling between my buns?"

My words alone had the men all teased up.

Praying it would work, I surged my aspect out to everyone in the room, except Donny. I pushed as hard as I could, surprised at the immediate reaction.

My aspect hit Mammon first, his lusty smile turned to a look of shocked bliss as his little pecker solidified, then unloaded in his pants. With a groan, he released my arms as he doubled over. A wet spot spread over his crotch while the other guards were similarly bending or shifting, trembling with their release as I pushed power into each of them.

"Yeah, I didn't think you'd last that long," I said. Then

I slapped that greedy fucker as hard as I could, knocking him to the floor. I grabbed Donny's arm and pulled him toward a door.

No.

Wait.

We'd come for money, and by my sexy daemon ass we were going to leave with it!

I pushed my lust harder into all the men, then returned to where Mammon writhed on the floor and searched him for a set of keys. Finding them, I returned to the jewel cases and began to unlock them.

"What's... happening?" Donny asked and I glanced at him, seeing him blinking and coming out of his greed haze.

"We're stealing our gems," I said with a grin, opening one of the cases. "Take everything, we'll return any extra funds later if we feel like it."

Donny reacted to my command and opened his brief-case, starting to fill it.

That's when I heard two heavy, resounding smashes on the door behind me. The impacts reverberated through the floor into me. My heart pounded with fear. If that was the monster, we were dead since I was pretty sure my aspect wouldn't work on it.

Then, with the screeching groan of tearing metal, the door began to move. Steel ruptured and split, and the door was ripped away entirely, thrown behind a savage-looking Ramsey as he loomed in the doorway.

Relief swept through me and I released the breath I'd been holding as he looked into the Diamond Room and blinked.

"What...?"

Most of the guards were on the floor, grabbing their crotches. A couple of men had managed to keep standing, but only because they'd liberated their dicks and were pumping them hard, making a mess around them.

"Did you—?" Ramsey looked at me.

I smiled. "We lust daemons have a few weapons we can use. I talked dirty to them and surged my aspect. Now we're stealing gems. Wanna help?" I said with a tilt of my head.

"Ah... no, you need to get out here and heal us guys before we die or Fen's beast is released," he said, and all playfulness was drained out of me.

"Take everything you can carry!" I shouted at Donny as I fled the room.

I reached Ramsey as he turned, showing me the gushing wound in his back. Even as he did, he collapsed to his knees and had to lean heavily on the wall.

I'd healed him with kisses last night, but there was no way I was going to put my lips to that large and bloody gash so I covered it with my hands, his blood pouring out between my fingers. I had no clue how Ramsey had managed to rip a bank vault door open with this massive wound, but then again, he wasn't human, was he?

I imagined focusing my healing energies — since I had no idea where it was focused and what it really felt like — and sent the thought of "kissing it better" through my hand. Thankfully the blood slowed its surge over my fingers, then stop altogether without me having to figure out anything else. The hole closed and I pulled my hands away, wiping off blood to see a puckered scar.

Last night, I'd been too swept up in my desire for Ramsey to fully register the fact that I'd healed him. I'd done it and seen its effects, but some part of me had still thought it was a fantasy.

But now... I'd done it again, and I was just a bit shocked.

"I'm good. Help Grey and Fen. Fen needs it," Ramsey hissed, breathing heavily.

At the mention of them, my gaze leaped to Grey and Fen. Grey was trying to bandage the other man up as best he could, but Fen was...

Bile rose in my throat and burned over my tongue. I bent over and made a mess on the floor, losing my breakfast. Fen was barely recognizable. His beautiful blond hair was mostly gone, and half of his face and scalp were seared away. The rest of his body wasn't much better. And to make matters worse, a half-burned wolf seemed to be shimmering over him, chomping and raving.

I forced myself to stand and found the energy to run over to the two men.

"I can heal," I said dropping down next to Grey and Fen.

"You can?" Grey was shocked. Then he shook his head. "Whatever, great, help him!"

I hesitated. I didn't want to touch Fen anywhere. Those burns looked horrible and touching him would be painful. Still, I forced myself to put one hand on his chest and the other on his leg, closing my eyes to block out the horrid sight.

Then I prayed.

I hadn't prayed in years. Though... I didn't seek out

the God I'd known from my childhood. I was aware of so many more now. *Dear gods and goddesses, please help me. I don't even know my full power yet. Apparently, I can heal, and this man desperately needs healing. Maybe I can do this on my own, but if anyone out there is willing to help, I'd really appreciate it!*

I thought I heard a distant mocking laugh, but it vanished before I could concentrate on it. And besides. I *needed* to save Fen.

I focused all the power I could, imagining that "kissing it better" feeling then added all my love and caring as well, pushing it as hard as I could through both hands into him.

For a moment, I wasn't sure if anything was happening. Under my palms, Fen was far too still.

Then he suddenly howled, like nothing I'd ever heard before, pained and desperate, the sound tearing through the room. It tried to shred my soul and spirit. Agony shot through my very essence and I screamed too.

Then, as abruptly as it started, it stopped.

It took me a moment to recover, my ears still ringing from that savage noise, and I blinked, focusing on Fen. The wolf was no longer shimmering over him, and his body had started to heal.

He smiled at me, eyes glazed with pain, then slumped over and passed out, reminding me that not all of his injuries were healed.

I put my hands on him again and pushed hard once more. This time, I dared to watch and saw the burned skin reform and mend. The bones of his shattered leg fused, and the muscles knit over them once again.

After another moment of extreme effort from me, he looked normal. His face was healed and his hair returned.

Gasping, I sat back feeling both exhausted and nauseated at the same time.

I turned to Grey. "Your turn."

But instead of standing and walking to him, I got to my feet and promptly crumpled.

Grey caught me before I hit the floor and pulled me into his lap, cradling my head.

"I'll survive for now," he said, a hint of mischief tugging at his lips. "You can do me later."

With my head in his lap, I smiled up at him, my vision swimming. I'd used up too much of my abilities or something and I'd never felt this drained before.

"Healing first," I said, my words slurred. "Then *doing*."

Then I passed out.

ANAIS

I woke in a plush, soft bed that wasn't mine and dragged my gaze over the unfamiliar room.

It was huge and opulent, colored in rich reds and golds. I lay in a decadent four-poster bed complete with a gauzy curtain. Next to it stood a large nightstand with an ornate lamp. Beyond that, was a small table with two chairs sitting in front of a large bank of windows. The sheers were drawn with daylight pouring into the room, but it was close to fading, and I could see the brilliant hues of sunset in the sky beyond the translucent curtains.

Across from the bed were three doors. Two were open, one leading to a massive walk-in closet and the other to an ensuite bathroom. The third door stood opposite the windows and probably led to the rest of the house.

Much to my surprise, Ramsey sat against the wall beside it, looking weary with his knees pulled up, arms folded across them, and his head turned and resting on his forearms.

"I'm awake," I said softly, and the man perked up instantly.

Raising his head, he smiled at me. There were still a lot of cuts and bruises on him and his suit had been shredded in that fight, but there was something else wrong with him. His eyes looked a little glassy and were red and swollen while strange spots dotted his skin with black tendrils snaking out from those points.

"Hey," he said weakly. "How are you feeling?"

Good question... how *was* I feeling?

Tired still, but no longer exhausted. Depending on how long it had been, I was doing quite well actually. Ramsey however...

"I'm fine," I said, "but you look like shit. Let me heal you some more."

"I was hoping you'd say that," he said and rose. Even just how he got up, so tentative and slow, showed how much he was suffering. "I got some poison on me from that Wadjet-blasted snake. I'm feeling a little... rough." The last word came out in a huff as he fell onto the bed and passed out.

"Fuck," I hissed and shifted over the covers to him. I was still fully dressed, but I had blood on me, lots and lots of blood. This outfit was definitely ruined.

I touched Ramsey, but before I just dumped my healing power into him, I paused.

There was no doubt, no hesitation this time. Apparently, I'd accepted that I could heal him. This second aspect, though a surprise, hadn't been as big of a shock as finding out I was a sex daemon. And having accepted it, I wondered if I shouldn't explore this aspect a little instead of just dumping power into Ramsey. I think it had been pushing raw energy into Fen which had exhausted and nauseated me last time.

So, I touched a finger to Ramsey's skin near one of the spots that looked like strange burns. Not really sure what I was doing, I tried to *feel* the wound. For a moment there was nothing, then... I felt a faint sense of... wrongness.

Frowning, I closed my eyes and concentrated, sensing that the black spots were dying tissue and that it was spreading now that it had filtered into his blood.

Sighing, I then went to work trying to heal that. The trouble was, I still had no clue how to moderate my power. So—

I woke with a gasp.

It was dark out. Ramsey was still lying, passed out on the bed and I'd been lying on top of him.

I scooched over to the bedside table and the lamp there, turning it on, then went back to Ramsey. The spots I'd been trying to heal were indeed cured, the skin looking smooth and healthy.

It then took me a while to manhandle that massive form of his to roll him over so I could take a look at the rest of him. He still had a few cuts and bruises, but there were no more of those nasty acid-burn spots. Except he'd mentioned something about poison, and I wasn't sure if it was completely out of his system. I needed to know how he was feeling.

So, I slapped him.

He groaned, seemingly semi-awake when he mumbled, "Yeah... I like it rough... hit me again."

Just for fun, I did, though not as hard.

"Wha—?" he gasped coming fully awake.

"So, you like it rough, do you? Want me to slap you around next time?"

I was leaning over him, upside down from his perspective and he smiled up at me.

"You bet." Then he blinked and cocked his head. He rose slowly and looked himself over. "I feel a lot better. You healed the poison?"

I shrugged. Apparently I had. "Guess so."

He nodded to himself. "Everything else is minor, I'll be fine. But if you're feeling up to it Grey could probably use some help."

I sighed. No rest for the weary.

My sigh must have sounded really bad, because he shifted, coming to kneel on the bed with me. "Grey can wait a little, he's not that bad off. Just a torn-up leg and lots of bumps and bruises. If you needed... *anything* to help you recover, I could...?"

Yeah, I knew what he wanted to give me to help me recover. "No, I'll be fine. If you make me orgasm, I'll probably just feel all warm and contented and want to sleep again. I'll heal Grey first. You can give me all the orgasms you want... later."

He grinned. "Promise?"

"Promise." I kissed his hard lips, teasing him — and me— before sliding off the large bed. "So ah... where am I going? Where are we?"

He stood. "I'll show you. We're at Grey's place. It was closest." He opened the door and led me out into a hall.

"Is Donny here?"

"Yeah, and according to him, the gems he took are

worth between five hundred and seven hundred million, depending on the buyers and other factors. You've got what you need."

"Great," I replied. That was one less thing to worry about. "But we're returning the rest. I don't want to give Mammon any reason to come after me. He may be a creepy-ass, back-stabbing shithead, but we're not. We deal fair."

Ramsey frowned at me. "The bastard's not worth it, just keep the extra."

"No, worth it or not, I won't steal from anyone. We take what's ours and return the rest."

Ramsey raised his hands. "Fine, your call."

We passed several other doors before exiting the hall into a massive living area. The large bank of windows covering two walls revealed a massive deck which included an infinity pool.

Beyond that, the many lights of New York were blossoming to life below us as evening darkened the sky. Given how high above the city we were, I guessed this was a penthouse, though with things growing dark, I couldn't quite make out where in the city we were.

To my left and ahead was a long living room divided into two areas. The closest was a TV "nook" with three massive couches and several large padded chairs facing the wall where a TV larger than my dining room table was mounted.

The area beyond that was slightly sunken to define the separate space and in the middle was a large open fireplace with a round base and large round uptake and chimney hanging from the ceiling. There were many couches and chairs, most of them positioned to get a view of the fire and the windows. Grey was lying on one of those, his eyes closed while Fen puttered around in the kitchen which was on the other side of the large open area.

I went to Grey but stopped as I rounded the couch and saw... the most massive dog ever, lying there beside Grey on the floor.

The beast was the size of a pony and built for strength, with massive shifting muscles under a tan fur coat. The dog's ginormous head lifted and turned to look at me. As he moved, there seemed to be strange, shifting after-images, which made it look like he had several heads for a moment, sending a wave of primal fear whispering through me.

But as soon as I saw his face, my fear of the creature fled and my heart melted. Large, brown, literal puppy-dog eyes looked at me, so full of fear and sorrow. It was like he could feel his master's pain.

"Don't mind Kerberos," Ramsey said. Again, I grinned a little at the name. It sounded too much like Care-bear-oos. "He's a big softy unless your intent is deceptive or evil. Then he'd eat you."

How... comforting?

I sidled around the dog — who shifted and let me get close to Grey as if he knew I was trying to help his master — and knelt next to the couch.

I woke Grey with a soft caress of his cheek, his gaze unfocused as he blinked to clear the sleep away.

"You're the toughest of them all, aren't you?" I whispered to him. "You made it all the way back here without any healing."

"Hades, yeah, I am," he croaked, voice rough and hoarse. He smiled, then winced, clearly still in a lot of pain.

"Let me help you," I whispered, leaning down to kiss him, as if my kiss would somehow soothe his pain. Perhaps it did, because his smile softened and he seemed to relax after that.

Ramsey helped me carefully undress him to find all his wounds. The major ones seemed to be a shredded lower leg, and heavy bruising under claw marks on his chest. His hands were torn up and bloodied, but that didn't seem quite as bad. All his other wounds — and there were a lot — were only minor cuts and scrapes.

I healed his leg first, then his chest. After that, I grew faint and woozy and needed a break. Fen brought water, and I drank heavily. I even munched on a few tasteless crackers, but given my uncertain stomach, I didn't eat anything else.

Once I felt strong enough, I tended to Grey's hands and other wounds. When I was done, Ramsey and Fen laid me on another couch, insisting I rest.

"Where's Donny?" I asked, my mind hazy as sleep slowly took me again.

"He's in one of the guest rooms. He's fine," Fen said. He sat at my feet, picking up one of my legs to massage my foot in the most achingly wonderful way.

Ramsey knelt on the floor next to the couch. "Shall I keep my promise?" he asked, voice low. His hand came up to rub my belly in a way which was currently comforting but could turn steamy quickly if he shifted the location of his hand, just a little.

I grinned sloppily up at him. "Why don't we save that for later?"

He leaned down, kissed me, and whispered, "As you wish, divine one."

Yeah, that sent a tingling warmth all through me and I was fast asleep soon enough, dreaming of all my guys pleasuring me: Fen massaging my feet and legs, Grey kissing me wonderfully, and Ramsey slamming that amazing cock of his deep into my core.

I woke squirming and warm and just a bit sad when I realized that had all been a dream and reality was... less fantastic.

I sat up on the couch. Fen was asleep at the far end, sitting up, which couldn't have been comfortable. Ramsey had moved to another couch, lying down.

It was still dark out, but there was light on the horizon.

Donny came charging into the room. "I called Tommy and let him know we have the money. We're going to meet him— oh..." He trailed off realizing I was the only one awake and listening. "I suppose it's still early. I'll get breakfast ready."

ANAIS

Our trip to meet Tommy Two-Toes involved several stops.

The first was Ramsey's place where he changed and picked up a long case of some sort and stashed it in the trunk of Grey's Bentley Mulsanne Grand Limousine. The second was to Mammon's bank, where Fen went in and returned roughly two hundred million in gems. He didn't stick around or wait for Mammon, just deposited them at the counter saying there had been a slight error on his last withdrawal, then left.

After that, we stopped at Fen's place for some clothes, then back at my place so Donny and I could change. Then we drove out to a container yard in Jersey.

Donny, being back to his old genius self, had chosen a spot that was out of the way but had easy access from both directions since we didn't want to be boxed in. On top of that, we arrived early, so we could prepare.

While we were getting ourselves into position,

Ramsey took his case and walked away and when I asked what he was doing, Grey answered, "He's a crack shot."

It took me a moment to realize that case was large enough for a big gun and he was setting himself up as a sniper. "Oh."

Tommy and his goons arrived just before eleven that morning. I recognized the two who had been harassing me, but Tommy was new. He was a heavyset man, but the type where there was still a lot of muscle under his bulk. He had gray in his hair and a lined face and his suit was immaculate.

"G'day Donny, m'boy, you have my money?" he asked.

I stayed back, leaning on the car while Grey and Fen flanked Donny as he walked forward and brought up the briefcase, opening it.

"I think you'll find this more than adequate," he said as Tommy practically drooled over the jewels in the case.

Tommy waved over another man, a new guy, rail-thin with a haughty look. This one put in one of those gem-appraising eyepieces and surveyed what was in the case. Donny had told them the exchange would be in gems and to bring their own way of verifying the value.

The tall, thin man nodded. "These are all real. I'd esti-mate their value at somewhere between three hundred, and four hundred million."

"I think you'll agree that should be more than adequate interest," Donny said.

Tommy nodded. "And what if I wished to reinvest some of this?" he asked, his face becoming a mirror to Mammon's from yesterday: greedy as hell.

"Then you'll do it with someone else. I'm done with you after this, agreed?"

"Oh, of course, Donny-boy, of course," Tommy chuckled, his voice dripping with sarcasm.

Swell. Donny had done such a good job, the gangster wanted to keep him.

He closed the case and took it from Donny, flashing him a wicked grin. "A pleasure doing business with you."

He turned to go, but Grey stepped forward and put a large hand on Tommy's shoulder.

The guards bristled, reaching for weapons and Tommy spun, his expression dangerous, his voice low. "Take your hand off me."

But Grey wasn't intimidated by the man who barely came up to his shoulder. He loomed over Tommy and glared down at him.

"Just wanted to make it clear that you're never to come anywhere near Donny and his family ever again. And just in case you need a bit more incentive." He raised a hand, one finger out, then tipped it forward.

Several cracks, in rapid sequence, rang out from behind us, making me jump. They pinged into the metal of Tommy's car door, and we all looked to see a happy face of bullet holes.

"Do we understand each other?" Grey growled.

"Ah... yeah, I wasn't intending to, and who the fuck are you anyway, buddy?"

"Just a messenger."

Tommy looked at Donny, who shrugged, then hurried away. But since I was just a bit pissed at all the trouble and anxiety they'd caused me, I sent a heavy gust of lust their way. Tommy and his men would have a *very* uncomfortable ride home.

And that was it.

We were free.

I was practically giddy as their car sped away and Ramsey sauntered back to us with his rifle case in hand.

"Nice work," Fen complimented him.

"Don't make his ego any bigger than it already is," Grey warned.

"Thank you," Donny said, shaking each of their hands before getting back into the car. There was only room for four in the back, so he was sitting up front with the driver.

I smiled at my three guys. *My guys! All mine!* my horny self asserted.

"I'd like to thank you in a different way," I said my voice husky. "Later."

Except I didn't realize the consequences of those words until we got home and all three guys came in, and began glaring at each other, no one willing to leave.

"I have something for you, for your trouble," Donny said as he went to a drawer in the front room. He took out a small pouch and brought it to the guys. Opening it, he reached inside and handed the guys several *large* diamonds each.

"I thought we returned all the extra gems?" Fen asked.

Donny laughed. "We did. We just didn't give all of them to Tommy. He'll never miss them. He got more than he was expecting. And this allows me to thank you for all your trouble."

"What are those worth?" I asked, looking over

Donny's shoulder into the pouch, which sparkled with more diamonds.

"We gave Tommy roughly three hundred and fifty million. A hundred million more than he was expecting. That left about thirty-five million. Since these fine gentlemen almost died for us, I've given them ten million each. That leaves five million for us.

"Fuck me," I whispered.

"Speaking of... ah... *that*, I'll leave you four alone," Donny said, tying up the pouch and taking it upstairs with him.

And that left me with three guys, all with hungry looks in their eyes. Fen's aqua-blue pools were heated and hooded. Grey's dark orbs sucked me in, taking my breath away. Ramsey's midnight stare simmered with savage masculinity and brutish appetite.

A shiver rolled down my spine and I was suddenly hot. *Very* hot.

Sweat pooled between my breasts as a different moist heat sweltered in my core, whipped into a whirlpool of expectant lust.

"What do you want, Silverlocks?" Ramsey asked, voice growling with desire. I should have known he'd speak up first. "You also owe me what you promised last night."

Which was actually more orgasms for me. I could live with keeping that promise, but what would I do with all three of them?

"Jewels are nice," Fen added. "But nothing sparkles like you do, Ana."

It was Grey who saved me from having to figure this

out, though I didn't know if he made things better or worse. "I think we all know our charade is up. We aren't just claiming Ana for show anymore. I for one won't let her go. I'll fight for her, if I have to."

Ramsey was instantly in his face. "As would I. And we know who'd win between us, don't we?"

"And what if my wolf wished to claim her," Fen said softly. "Would you both like to fight it?"

Grey and Ramsey turned to look at him. His tone had been conversational, but his look was deathly serious.

"You wouldn't unleash Armageddon just to claim her. She'd be destroyed with everything else!" Grey stated.

"I won't have to start the end times if you two back off and let me be with her."

Wow, these three powerful and sexy guys fighting over me was super-hot, but I was really hoping they wouldn't fight at all. "And what about what I want?" I piped up.

They all turned to me.

"Good point," Ramsey said, arrogant and sure. "Which one of us do you want?"

"What if I wanted... all of you to share me. Equally?" I asked.

Fen grinned. "I wouldn't mind. One-third of you would still be preferable to all of anyone else." Trust him to find the right words and make me feel amazing. Also, I was glad he was so willing to share.

It was Grey and Ramsey who were the problems. They glared at each other. I didn't think they'd share well.

"Oh, for fuck's sake!" This new voice caused the guys to turn. I flinched. I knew that voice and was suddenly super-heated with embarrassment instead of desire.

"Reia?" I peeked around the guys and saw her at the bottom of the stairs. "What are you doing home, it's the middle of the day?"

"It's Saturday, Mom."

"Oh." I'd completely lost track of time.

Reia, the small and intruding powerhouse that she was, walked right into the middle of this tense standoff and looked at each of the guys.

"I don't know what you did to have three hot guys fighting over you, Mom," she said to me, even though she hadn't looked at me yet. "But there's no reason in this day and age, they can't all share. It's called polyamory. Look it up. As long as you all know the rules, then there shouldn't be any issue with all of you dating my mom. If you have any problems with that, take it up with me."

She'd laid down the law and all three men looked a little dumbfounded.

Then she turned and shot me a hard look. "And these three seem like they might *actually* be keepers, so don't fuck it up, got that? Now, I'm hungry and I'm getting something to eat." She marched off into the kitchen.

"Did we just get told off by a pre-teen?" Ramsey asked.

"She's sixteen actually," I corrected him.

"I'm over three thousand years old, pardon me if they all look like babies to me."

That was fair.

I took up where Reia had left off. "Well, I guess that's it, isn't it? Either you all figure out a way to share, or...

none of you gets me, which is it?" I was desperately hoping for the sharing option and not the all-leaving-me option.

Ramsey growled, shooting a look at Grey.

"I'll share," Grey said, getting there first, infuriating Ramsey even more. "Like Fen said, even part of Ana is better than all of someone else." Turning to me he added, "I have to be near you, and if this is the only way, so be it." The desperate, aching need in those dark, all-consuming eyes not only made my pussy drool but made my heart warm and my breath hitch.

"Yeah, fuck. Sure, I'll share," Ramsey spat the words.

I felt like pushing his buttons. "Say it nicely."

He turned that glare on me, then it softened. He sighed heavily. "How can I say no to the woman I love... fucking," he said with a grin. "My cock can't get enough, and my heart isn't far behind. Yeah, I'll share," he said, then sniffed with smug superiority. "Let's ruin another condom again sometime soon."

Oh... that cunning bastard, telling the others he'd had his dick in me while professing his sort-of love. He'd one-upped them and swayed me all at the same time. The other two bristled but settled after a moment. Especially after I locked eyes with each of them. I hoped that look said, *you'll all get lots of turns with me.*

And that was that. Suddenly, I had three demon princes — sorry, *daemon* princes — as my own little harem.

I told them I was tired after everything that had happened these last few days and wanted a day off. They accepted that and left.

I went into the kitchen and sat at the small kitch-enette table as Reia put together a salad.

"Did you work it all out?" she asked.

"Yup," I said, then I caught her gaze and held it for a moment. "How did I get so lucky with you? You're so smart and wise, and assertive, and... everything I'm not. Half the time I feel like you're the parent in this relation-ship. I'm so sorry if I've put more on you than I should, if I've been relying on you to mother me. I probably don't say it enough, but you're an amazing young woman and I love you, Reia."

She blinked, stunned for a long moment.

"I know we don't often see eye-to-eye, but—" Then she was in my arms, squeezing me in a tight hug. "—I love you too, Mom." Her voice was muffled in my shoulder and when she pulled back there were tears in her eyes. "Most of the time you seem so distant and I don't understand you, but then you say stuff like this and... I remember all those times when I was little and you were there for me, playing District Attorney Barbie with me when Caia and Eva wouldn't. I'm sure you had no clue what I was doing, but you sat there and smiled and played along." She sniffed. "I know I'm an odd child. Even the kids at school think I'm strange. I'm more inter-ested in sneaking off to the library to read law books than running off behind the bleachers to stick my tongue down some jock's throat."

I pulled her into another hug. "You don't have to understand another person to love them," I whispered, and she clung to me tightly once again.

"Thank you," she said, then pulled back and wiped

her cheeks. "So, how did you meet those three hot guys?" she asked changing the topic.

And thus began a very long afternoon of telling my daughter about daemons. How I was one and that — I hadn't even realized this until *she* mentioned it — as my daughter she was probably one too. Though, she didn't show any signs of having either a sex or healing aspect. She took it all in stride, a bit stunned but trusting me, like Donny had. I shouldn't have been surprised. Reia had always been so adaptable and quick to pick up new things.

"You're going to need to tell Caia and Eva," she said before she left to go to her room.

I nodded. "There you go again, being all responsible."

But there was no way I was going to give news like this over the phone and Caia wasn't due back from college until the winter break.

As for Eva? Who knew when she'd be back? It would all depend on how long her current fling lasted. Either way, I'd wait for my girls to come home to tell them in person.

Reia paused at the archway to the front room. "I promise I'll never change, if you promise the same."

"Deal," I said, and I felt like I'd gotten the better part of that bargain.

She smiled and left.

ANAIS

THE NEXT COUPLE OF WEEKS WERE A LEARNING PERIOD. Learning more about myself and my aspects. Learning how to be in a three-way relationship, which was a scheduling nightmare. And learning about my guys and how different they were.

Grey was a bit rigid in his affections. He was exacting in everything he did. He saw the world in black and white: not good and evil, but more order and chaos. And he was going to maintain order if it was the last thing he did.

The only place he seemed to relax was at one of his animal shelters. I went with him and was astonished to see all his rigidity and austerity melt away, replaced by a broad, innocent smile. He was a kid, rolling on the floor and playing with all the kittens and puppies and other animals. The difference was almost unbelievable, and I smiled and laughed with him and enjoyed every moment of it.

Ramsey was all hot and lusty, which made him the easiest for me to understand of my three men. Passion and sex were things I knew well, and the two of us burned brightly when we were together. Also, I didn't have to worry so much after the custom-made super-condoms we ordered arrived.

He never said he loved me after that first time and I convinced myself that it had been as I'd said: that he loved *fucking* me, not the other thing. Still, after a while, that relationship began to feel like many of my other bad boy relationships: a bit stale. Don't get me wrong, the orgasms were amazing, but I just felt like there could be... more.

It was Fen who showed me what that *more* could be.

Fen was kind and considerate and the easiest to just be around, even if he had a world-ending beast lurking within him — something I tried not to think about too much.

We hung out and just talked and I learned about him and his odd extended family — all those sexy Norse Gods — and he learned all about my sordid past.

What was amazing was that he never asked anything of me, giving of himself instead. He especially loved giving me orgasms, his miracle tongue always sure to please. Yet, other times, we'd just kiss, making out for hours like teenagers.

But then things started to get complicated.

He was the first of the guys to say he wanted to be more than lovers and I didn't know what to do with that. It was yet another thing I learned about myself: I'd never really loved a man, and *real* love scared the fuck out of me.

Sex was fun and made me feel good, but anything deeper than that and I began to resist, push back. I was terrified of a real, loving relationship, scared I'd screw it up somehow.

So, I went to talk to Harmonia.

She sat behind her desk and nodded with a heavy sigh. "It's a challenge for a lot of sex- aspected daemons. Other female daemons with the aspect of sex or fertility or passion, but not love itself, like Hedone, Lada, Tlazolteotl, and Zamani, all have a really good time but have had trouble settling down. There's something about their aspect that wants to be with many people, not just one. It's the same with men, Freyr, Jarilo, and Pothos, even Eros, have all had trouble finding just one mate. Not that they need to, but true affection seems hard for them to achieve."

"That doesn't really help me," I grumbled, a little dejected. Then anger bubbled up within me and I rose, throwing my hands up in the air as I paced. "I don't even know if I want love like that. But still! I feel like it should be possible at least. Shouldn't it? Why am I so scared to love someone?"

"Do you love your daughters, your uncle?" Harmonia asked.

I stopped pacing. "Yeah, but they're family, that's different."

"It is and it isn't. The only real thing that separates romantic love from familial love is sexual desire. But then, there are a lot of people out there who love someone romantically, even when sex isn't an option. Love is love. If you can love your family, you can love others. I think the main difference is choice. Love 'em or hate 'em, we didn't get a choice in our families. When it comes to others we *can* choose to love them but that's a distinct choice. And for some, that can be hard and scary."

I nodded. That made sense. "You're so wise."

"It comes from thousands of years of living."

"Yeah, right, sometimes I forget that." I sighed and sat, a bit worn out. "So, what you're saying is that I'm afraid to *choose* love?"

"Because if you do and it doesn't work out, then you've made a mistake. And mistakes where our heart is involved are painful. With family, if they don't love you, well, it wasn't your choice to be their family so it's not your fault." She smiled softly. "In some ways, that's what makes adoptions so much more meaningful than birth. They're parents who *chose* you, *chose* to love you."

And that made me break down and cry because I knew my adoptive parents had loved me so much and I'd always been a wild child and a terror for them. I regretted so much of that now.

Harmonia came out and rubbed my back, using some of her power to soothe my pain until my tears dried up.

"Thank you," I whispered, still sniffling, then I drew in a big breath and got up. "Thank you," I repeated. "I think that helps. I have a lot to think about now."

She smiled and embraced me gently. "I don't think any of your men will rush you. Take your time to figure this out, to figure yourself out."

I gave a halfhearted laugh. "Just another addition to the long list of things I need to figure out about myself."

"It's a lifelong journey, you'll get there," Harmonia said, as wise as ever.

That night, after my shift, Grey walked me out.

"What would you say..." He was a bit hesitant and tentative, which was *very* unlike him. "What would you say, if I wanted to move in with you?"

I stared at him, stunned.

"I'm not saying I want to share your bed every night and take you away from the others. I'd be happy to stay in a spare room. My intention is only to be closer to you." He took both my hands in his and his dark eyes were filled with steadfast affection, not his usual soul-sucking avarice. "The closer I am to you, the less my void consumes me. When I'm near you, I feel... fulfilled."

I blinked. "Fulfilled?"

Oh.

Wow.

He'd said stuff like this before, but this time, with him asking to move in, I knew it was serious. Heartfelt. True.

He smiled. "Yes. I've been searching all my life for something that fills my void and... and I've finally found it. It's you, Anais. So... I want to be as near to you as possible. I'll... I'll do anything. I can help out around the house. I'll cook. I'll clean. I've never done laundry, but I can learn. How hard can it be? Please Ana, whatever you need, let me be that, as long as I'm near you."

I stepped away from him, looking him up and down. "Who are you and what have you done with Grey? You want to *clean* for me?"

He smiled tenderly. "Yeah... I actually do. I'll do anything to be closer to you. Screw all my businesses. I don't care about them." He grimaced. "Well, except for the shelters, I care about them, but you get the point. I care about you *more*. So, I want to put as much energy into you as I have into my businesses. I'll become your domestic god. Doesn't every woman want that?"

Well... yeah... but I'd never have expected this from a hard-edged, rigid, mega-billionaire.

"What do you say?" he asked softly. He even got down on one knee as if proposing, my heart fluttering just a little at that.

What could I say?

"Yes?" I hadn't meant for it to sound like a question so I tried again. "Yes."

He leaped up and hugged me. "Thank you, Ana. You won't regret this!"

And just like that, a daemon prince became my live-in house servant. He lived up to his word, cooking and cleaning and doing laundry. Everything really. Reia and Donny were a bit taken aback by his presence and domestic fervor, but they adapted quickly enough. Fen and Ramsey were jealous, but only until they realized everything Grey was doing, then I think they were just as confused as I was.

And finding out I was a daemon, then having Grey move in with me... that was only the beginning of the strange things that happened that October.

Eva returned home, but that was more awkward than strange.

Then Grey's sister moved in with us, and that's when things started to get really weird.

Then there were the zompires.

Had I mentioned the zompires yet?

No?

Oh... well... that's a whole *other* story.

EPILOGUE: FEN

A GRAVEYARD AT MIDNIGHT WASN'T MY FIRST CHOICE OF places to be. But then, the man I was meeting had always been eccentric and dark of mood, not to mention, he actually lived here... in the ramshackle caretaker's hut, hidden behind a few trees off to one side of the cemetery.

Well, technically my half-brother, Nari, didn't actually live in the hut. He lived in a whole complex built underground, dark and secret, just the way he liked it.

I knocked on the creaky wooden door and waited. Several hidden cameras would be checking me out, but I didn't wave. I didn't want to be here, except his letter had made it sound urgent.

And yes, it was a letter. In the age of smartphones and email, he'd still sent a letter.

The door creaked open and there he was, gray-as-death skin drawn over a skeletal frame with dark sunken yellow eyes and a mop of messy black hair.

"Brother," he whined, but not because he didn't want

to see me, that was just his tone, he always whined. "So glad you could make it."

He didn't ask me to come in, but that didn't surprise me. I'd only seen his subterranean lair once, when it was being finished. Since then, he was all sneaky secrets. Instead, he stepped out of the caretaker's hut and joined me in the brisk fall evening.

"What's this all about?" I asked, a bit annoyed.

He was my brother — well, half-brother — and I should have respected him, but I found that exceptionally hard. The trouble was, Nari was the daemon of corpses, not death or the underworld... just... corpses. And ever since I'd known him, he'd hated that aspect. He whined and complained and always made a fuss, and part of me couldn't blame him, but still... it was annoying, and I generally tried to avoid him.

"The bodies are restless," he said, voice sibilant and lacking strength.

He looked out over the sea of tombstones. He lived in Calvary Cemetery in Queens, the largest graveyard in America. More than three million had been buried here, and Nari had been around since the founding of this place, so most of them were... well preserved since Nari tended to them, making sure they didn't decompose too much. Because if they did, they wouldn't be corpses anymore.

"Restless?" I asked, sighing heavily. "But, not like the last time they were... restless, right?" I had to hope.

"Yes, like that. Like last time."

"Fuck," I muttered.

This sort of *restlessness* usually meant the dead got up

and went for a walk. And, as you might expect, people generally reacted poorly to that. Like when the corpses had been restless under Nari's supervision in the late 1700s up in Salem.

That hadn't turned out well for a lot of people, mostly women. Then it had happened again in the early 1900s in Sleepy Hollow. Someone had written a story about that one, though they'd gotten the details all wrong.

But those had been just a few dozen dead from local graveyards. This time, with all of Calvary Cemetery, I couldn't imagine what three million walking corpses would do to this modern world.

Nari claimed it was a natural thing and he couldn't stop it.

"You sure you can't keep them contained?" I asked. I had a suspicion he *could* stop it, but didn't want to.

"No, they'll rise on Samhain. I can't stop them. That is unless..." He paused with a mischievous smile. "Unless you can elevate my divine status?"

And there it was. This was the reason I suspected Nari was actually in control, because every time it happened, he claimed that if I or others could promote him more, make him a known and respected daemon, then perhaps, with that extra energy, he could stop all of this.

"Nari, you know I can't do that. It's not something I have any control over. It's not like anyone can give you a second aspect and make you a daemon prince. You know that as well as I do. And even if I tried to get your name out there, that wouldn't do anything for your level of ability with your aspect." I sighed heavily. "And frankly, Nari, I'm guessing you *can* control whether the dead rise or not, and if that's the case... you can't do this! Having a little fun in Salem or Sleepy Hollow was one thing, but they were smaller towns and back when people didn't have smartphones. If you do this in today's world, with millions of corpses and millions of people around... All that's going to do is put a spotlight on us daemon. We're trying to keep a low profile. Well most of us anyway. If you do this—"

"I'm telling you, *I'm* not making them rise, brother!" Nari hissed. "I'm the one who keeps them down, keeps them still, but if no one will respect what I do, then why should I do it!" Which meant he *was* the one in control.

"Because it's your duty," I said. "You think I like that I'm going to end this world? No, but it's my duty and I will, whenever that time comes."

"Easy for you to say. That may be several millennia away and until then, people know your name, they respect you."

"They fear me because I'm a world-ender. That's not quite the same."

Nari hissed at me and slunk back to his hut. "Fine! Ignore me if you will, but there'll be consequences!" The whine was back in his voice. "Consequences!" he repeated with more fervor, but his warning was undercut by a rasping coughing fit.

Swell.

I left the cemetery and hoped to any god who would listen that Nari would be able to do his part and keep the corpses quiet. Because if the dead did rise on Halloween this year, it was going to be one Hel of a shit show.

Don't miss the next book in the series!

Chaos Demons
The Secret Gods Keep: Book Two

My name is Ana Baker... and I really am a demon.

I also still don't know much more about who I am and I've completely broken my "no men" rule.

Like shattered it and toss away all the pieces, because I now have three incredibly sexy, bad boy, demon princes who are all madly in love with me.

There's Ramsey, The Lord of Strife, who's all gorgeous bulky muscle and barely-contained chaos, Fen, The Lord of Destruction, a silver-tongued sweetheart with a world-ending wolf inside him, and Grey, The Lord of Conquest, who was my stunning billionaire boss and is now my live-in butler.

Yep, you read that right. My billionaire boss is now my live-in butler because he wants to be near me all the time.

Life couldn't get much better so, of course, my second daughter returns home and all she wants to do is fight. Then Grey's sister (who's the demon of madness and nightmares) forcibly moves in and things get completely out of hand.

Add in a zombie apocalypse... and you have the makings of just another messed up week at the Baker house.

OTHER BOOKS BY TESSA COLE

NEPHILIM'S DESTINY

ANGEL'S FATE

ENSNARED BY THE PACK

Wolf Decided, book 5

Wolf Devoted, book 6

THE GRECIAN GODDESS TRILOGY

Co-written with Clara Wils

Kiss of the Goddess, book 1

Power of the Goddess, book 2

Bonds of the Goddess, book 3

THE SECRETS GODS KEEP

Co-written with Clara Wils

Craving Demons, book 1

Chaos Demons, book 2

Claiming Demons, book 3

OTHER BOOKS BY CLARA WILS

THE GRECIAN GODDESS TRILOGY

Co-written with Clara Wils

Kiss of the Goddess, book 1

Power of the Goddess, book 2

Bonds of the Goddess, book 3

THE MISTS OF ELISTA TRILOGY

Bonds and Blood, book 1

Shape and Shadows, book 2

Form and Fury, book 3

SISTER SPIRITS

Double Discover, book 1

Double Danger, book 2

Double Disaster, book 3

Double Doom, book 4

Double Destiny, book 5

THE SECRETS GODS KEEP

Co-written with Clara Wils

Craving Demons, book 1

Chaos Demons, book 2

Claiming Demons, book 3